The Moonstorm Series

Special Thanks:

Peter Gawtry
Stephanie Gawtry
Ren Johnson
Chris Mayer
Pat Sullivan
Jack Svenningsen
Ricki Terry
Tracy van der Leeuw
Christopher West

BOOK OF DREAMS

A. P. Malloy
The Moonstorm Series

Ardilla Blanca

Cover design and artwork: Mari Fridley Larsen
marilarsen.com

Learn more about the series
and order promotional copies:
moonstormseries.com

The author welcomes correspondence:
apmalloy1@gmail.com

CONTENTS

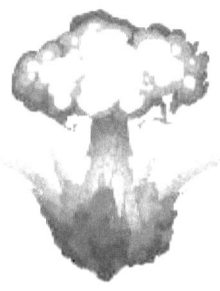

CHAPTER ONE
Home

DARKNESS AND SILENCE give way by slow degrees to dim flashes of red and a faint rat-tat-tat. In the distance, a bomba cries out, and a hint of old blood rides the air.

Ami-kan! someone thinks.

But a deep lethargy has settled in Lightning's bones, urging her to disregard the thought, to imagine it is meant for someone else. So she lets it go, along with the snapping of teeth and the harsh smell of bile. Seething white blobs? Malfunctioning throwers? These are concerns for another kezel. Sleep! That's the thing for her.

But the thought refuses to be ignored.

Ami-kan! it repeats, and it is joined by a jabbing sensation on her shoulder; someone is poking her.

She wills her eyelids open.

A knotted strip of talihew floats before her.

You fell asleep again, the talihew seems to think, but Lightning knows it is Joy, camouflaged and invisible. She vaguely recalls wrapping the talihew in place, as if the memory belongs to someone else. Whatever poison has deadened her legs also makes her vision blurry, although the dizzying sensation of movement in the room has long ago ceased. She blinks and shakes her head, trying to clear the fog from her mind.

How long? she asks.

A hand caresses her spikes, and a gentle, buzzing

melody fills her ears, its tone solemn.

A while, thinks Joy. *What happened to us?*

I don't know. Lightning grimaces. *Don't touch anything—and don't* think *to anything.*

She attempts to stand, but her rear limbs remain unresponsive, pocked by circular wounds. Settling to the floor, she examines the room through eyes half closed. The moving images have disappeared, but in other ways, the space is unchanged. Lights twinkle in the same location and style, and where her gloved hands touch the floor, it is as smooth and cold as when they first entered. By almost every measure, they haven't moved a stride. But her nose—and silence at the door—say otherwise.

What do we do? asks Joy.

Nothing, until I can stand.

What were those things?

Good question. Never seen anything like them.

We must go back!

Lightning pins her ears.

Like I said. One thing at a time.

She retrieves the cutter from the floor and uses her vest to clean white stains from its blade. Then she removes two spongy leaves from her pack. The rich brown of the corpuses has faded since their harvest near the Eye Tower, but they remain intact, their scent loamy as ever. She cuts them into squares and peels them as the bombas had taught her, exposing their gelatinous hearts. Pressing these against the worst of the bites, she waits until they have adhered before collapsing with a sigh.

Gami-kan's whiskers, she thinks. *I'm thirsty!*

I'll find you water, thinks Joy.

Not alone, you won't. Lightning takes Joy's hand in hers. *Just give me a few breaths.* She closes her eyes and bows her head. Many more than a few breaths pass.

+ + +

Lightning wakes to the sound of Joy whistling an aimless tune. She sits up slowly. Each corpus section has changed from tan to bright green; two have fallen to the floor. The others peel away easily, having done all they can to extract the poison from her body.

I can feel my tail again, she thinks, and she takes a deep breath, exhaling as she grits her teeth. Though it requires prodigious effort, she rises to four limbs. What she keeps sheltered is that the return of sensation brings with it searing pain. It starts as a tingle in her toes but is soon a fire spreading to her hips.

Could've used twice as many, she thinks of the corpuses, almost preferring the numbness to this.

I don't hear bombas, thinks Joy.

No. Lightning flexes her fingers. *We've moved.*

But moved to where?

I don't know; I think the accrete.

The room's the same, Joy objects.

Similar, but not the same.

How is that possible?

Lightning growls.

You sound like Ilda. How has anything been possible in the past few moons? Someone told us to select a destination, we saw a picture of the accrete, and now we're here—and close to the Sugarfoot range, too, or I have the nose of a kish. She hobbles to the door, jaws clenched. As she sniffs at the threshold, her brow furrows. *We're alone, but I don't know for how long.*

The images haven't returned.

No. Maybe they only appear when you enter.

What do we do? Joy wonders again.

But for the moment, Lightning has no answer. Her mind is sluggish like a muddy river. Home. As clearly as she feels the bitter complaint of her legs, she can smell signs of the Sugarfoot range. Conflicting emotions make decisions that should be easy seem tiresome and difficult. Home. She imagines Submission and Thunder close by, within howling distance in a favorable wind, and Gami-kan too, safe in her nest and missing her.

But these are idle fantasies.

The kind that might get us killed, she thinks to herself. To Joy, she thinks, *We'll go out and come back in, see if the images return. But I'm not ready for a fight yet. I need water first.* She adjusts her pack, tightening its straps and handing the cutter to Joy. *Just in case.*

Joy buzzes to show her understanding. The cutter and the knotted talihew float to the door.

OK. Are you ready? she asks.

As I'll ever be, Lightning replies wearily. And so:

Open, thinks Joy, more in hope than command.

The door obeys, sliding from right to left. Its clamorous, screeching objection echoes in the distance before at last fading to silence.

They stand ready, staring out into darkness.

+ + + + + +

The door's noisy grievance ricochets down a stony passage, quickly leaving Lightning and Joy behind. Some part of it finds a way through fissures and holes to the sunlit surface, where it discovers a new audience.

A bushy, green virble leaps out of the snow in surprise, blinking its lone eye at the metallic screech and squeaking angrily. What was that? How can it be expected to dig for sneers when so badly startled? Its tail lashes indignantly, and its tiny heart races.

Nearby yits, clustering against the wind and always in the mood for panic, break formation and flutter for safety. They follow a hundred different routes, crazed and random, like an exploding rainbow.

At this disturbance, a cremlin, using suction cups to cling to the scales of a fanning, yellow accrete, gathers its many tentacles and leaps to the forks of a nearby red. It hoots an alarm that spreads through the canopy. Fast as sound the message travels:

Something foreign! Something loud!

Virbles, yits, and cremlins all listen to discover if the screech will be repeated.

They are not the only creatures who do.

+ + + + + +

A crystal for light? asks Joy.

Lightning hesitates. She has few of the precious items remaining, and if the sound of the door hasn't already betrayed their presence, a glowing crystal surely will. And yet, considering the condition of her legs, she can see no way around it. Stumbling into a hole or a pit of tar would be a fine ending indeed. She stands silent for a time, ears bent forward. When satisfied they remain alone, she cracks a yellow crystal into halves, holding them between her teeth and coaxing her aching limbs out of the room and into a hard, dry passage. Joy stays close, clutching the cutter and a handful of spikes.

Still air greets them, stale and dusty, along with the distant voice of running water. This is soon overwhelmed by the screeching of the door as it slides closed behind them. They stand in a wavering sphere of yellow light, waiting for the last echo to fade.

Tell me you can open that, thinks Lightning.

Joy gives the order, but the door remains fixed.

Open! she thinks again, to no use.

Lightning curls her lip as Joy pounds on the door and repeats her command. Pain and worry shorten the jabi kezel's patience, and thirst has turned her tongue to parchment. If this tunnel is now a dead end, they mustn't remain. She rubs her tormented legs.

I'm sorry, thinks Joy as she gives up on the door.

You didn't make this happen.

Maybe. But who did?

I wish I knew! I'd give 'em a good biting. Come on. We need to move.

But Ami-kan! The bombas...

Are in a place we can't get to at the moment. Please! I need water.

They proceed cautiously, glad to encounter no holes, tarry or otherwise, and had Lightning's legs not trembled at the exertion, they would have made good time. The passage is neither as symmetrical nor polished as those in the maison, but its dimensions are similar, as if it is an unfinished version, carved from rock. It travels a true line, gentle and downward, until at last, the sound of water growing louder, a pinpoint of blue appears before them. It twinkles from a gap in a pile of small boulders and slabs of rock that rises suddenly before them, reaching to the ceiling and blocking their way. Lightning sniffs at the gap, no larger than her finger.

All that time, she thinks, *and I never knew.*

What? I don't understand.

You will. Help me move these.

Using great care, they remove rocks and dirt from around the opening. The blue light grows until they've created a hole large enough to squeeze through. This they do, Lightning in the lead. As if they have fallen backwards in time, they find themselves standing in the moon cave.

+ + + + + +

The listeners outside don't need to wait long.

The peculiar, metallic screech does repeat, although with less effect, as it is not the surprise it was at first. When no harm comes from it, and after many breaths it does not return, most residents of the neighboring accrete lose interest and return to their business. Many forget the sound altogether.

But their initial, noisy response has been noticed.

Two ears angle forward, the left well-formed and brindled, the right ripped to shreds long ago. The bibija kezel to whom they belong is brindled himself, from his massive snout to the tip of his spiky tail.

What color is his vest? He doesn't wear one.

Gloves or boots? Not for this kezel.

He is a Redtooth, lean but not rangy, his hands and feet like plates of stone, his claws and teeth sharp and white. Around his left eye he has smeared bomba essence, but his right is missing, replaced by an ugly scar. He compensates for his impaired vision with exquisite hearing, and he promptly identifies the direction and distance of the cremlin's first warning. The second time it happens, he is able to pinpoint its source. He turns his nose to the south, where, far away, a ridge of stone rises at the head of the sulphur trail.

His growl is low and resonant. Investigating the disturbance will mean a long and smelly hike, and at first, he considers ignoring it. But curiosity and an empty stomach prevail. Striding into the wind and the rotten breath of sulphur, he seeks an answer to the riddle.

+ + + + + +

Just like I remember, thinks Joy, and she gazes about the moon cave, taking in the familiar sights, her eyes glittering. Dust motes dance in a shaft of sunlight, crystalline walls reflect boundless shades of blue, and the water curtain scatters tiny droplets like a fountain of sapphires. Along with sunlight comes the faint voice of wind, carrying signs of life in the accrete.

A proper cave, thinks Lightning, and in spite of her thirst, she takes a moment to caress the wall, breathing deeply. Ari had not overstated. Her caches are indeed ruthlessly dug up, her hiding rocks broken and strewn. Desiccated feces litters the floor, and the nest of grass, most of which is scattered, reeks of old urine. But the cave itself is beautiful to her, its most appealing feature the rushing stream that passes under the curtain before diving out of sight. She strides eagerly into its flow, gulping as if extinguishing a fire. The taste of clean, cold water washes away the murk in her head, and her vision at last becomes clear.

I remember falling in, thinks Joy as she looks at the stream. *I was so scared.* She wades in, the current lapping at her calves. *But it's small, shallow.*

You were tiny back then. Lightning wipes her eyes with the back of a gloved hand. *When it happened, I was scared too—very.*

She steps to the water curtain, holding one rear limb at a time under the tumbling sheet. She gasps at the initial pain, but the frigid water soon kills this, bringing a blessed, if short-lived, relief. After another drink from the stream, she feels able to go on.

OK, she thinks. *Let's see what we can learn.*

+ + +

The entrance to the cave, its clever design once making it nearly impossible to see, now stands exposed, the stone door shattered in malice. Sensing no danger, Lightning leads the way through this small, square opening to the tunnel beyond. Before them, by light of crystal and cave, appears the tar-filled crevice in which Cliff had received sticky, putrid compensation for his betrayal. A finger of accrete spans the gap, layered in dust. Lightning uses this to cross, and Joy is close behind.

When they emerge from under the lone accrete, they are met on the small, snowy island by filtered sunlight and the strident call of those yits strong enough to endure the wind. A family of dow, surprised by the sudden appearance of a kezel, waddle from the rocks they had been napping on and dive into the safety of the lake, honking in terror. Slow and silly though they are, Lightning is in no condition to catch one.

What do you smell? she thinks, and she winces as she rises to two legs, bracing herself against the accrete. Joy sniffs the gusting wind, and her skin changes from blue to snowy white.

No bombas, she replies sadly. *No maison.*

No kezel either, thinks Lightning. *And no kish.*

But there is something. She reads the wind, confused by the mix of information. Strange smells travel from the south, an undercurrent of ash and an indescribable scent she's never encountered.

What's that? asks Joy. *Something bad?*

Lightning narrows her eyes.

Not sure, she thinks. *We need higher ground.* She stretches her legs, testing their strength and disliking what she learns. *I guess it's swim for us. There's no way*

I'm jumping across these stones. She secures her vest pockets and tightens her mask.

Maybe you should rest, Joy worries, but Lightning has already waded in. With awkward paddling and considerable pain, she makes her slow, splashy way across the lake. Joy reaches shore first, adept at swimming as always, whether four-limbed or six, and unfazed by the cold. Lightning pulls herself out of the water, panting from the effort, and together they address the north face of the canyon, daunted by its height.

Another thing I can't do. Lightning turns away, limping to the west. *The wedge trail is longer,* she thinks, *but it's not so steep.*

Joy rubs her palms together, slow and raspy. Memories of that deadly river inspire a tickle in her gut made worse when she learns she must walk, not ride.

Sorry, thinks Lightning. *Can't be helped.*

And so, she begins scaling the narrow switchbacks, pain jabbing her rear limbs and the wedge roaring threats from deep in its cleft. Joy follows close behind, and all the while she hugs the sheer wall. When the path finally opens to the east, they step gratefully onto a clearing in the highlands above the moon cave, where wind sweeps away much of the snow.

I can see it, Joy whistles and points to the north. *There's the Eye Tower!*

There indeed, alone on its narrow promontory and hazy in the sulphur fumes—fumes that conceal the distant Redtooth and his smell—a needle of light gleams at them like a taunt, recalling endangered friends beyond help. Joy clicks a mournful cadence.

Lightning turns away.

What she sees to the southeast only worsens her mood. The rainbow canopy stretches out below them for five thousand strides. But at that point, a broad expanse of charred black appears, itself several hundred strides across, surrounding the rocky foothills of the Sugarfoot caves. It is as if a giant ball of tar has been dropped from the heavens into the middle of the world's largest heap of bomba feathers. Lightning stares, unable to understand. She has never heard of a storm causing damage like this. If a fire, why hadn't her clan extinguished it? She can't imagine them allowing it to burn so far or so close to the family caves. Look at all the ruined accrete!

I should stop expecting normal, she thinks.

What happened? asks Joy.

But Lightning has no answer; exertion has taken its toll. At the moment, she is useless for solving mysteries. She bows her head, and her tail hangs low.

Can't stay awake much longer, she thinks.

Joy's mind returns to the bombas.

Is the fight over?

Probably.

Will they be OK?

The whole maison would have joined, thinks Lightning, but her reply is for herself as much as Joy. *Their crewels were better than this thrower.* She tries to muster certainty. *They'll be more than OK.*

But as she thinks this, she recalls the awful cry from her dream. At least one of the bombas had been injured—or killed—fighting in their defense. Who would seal the door they opened? Who would explain their sudden disappearance?

They'll think we're dead, Joy guesses.

They won't be far from wrong. Lightning bares her teeth and limps back to the trail. *I've seen enough.*

+ + +

By the time they have returned to the moon cave, pulled the accrete to their side of the crevice, and made their best attempt at refitting the door, Lightning's eyelids are low and heavy. The tattered hide she had once used to block out the light is gone, but she is too tired to care. She takes a last drink from the stream, sweeps away the stained grass, and flops to the stony floor, oblivious to ceremony or comfort.

Stand guard, she thinks. *Poke me with that cutter*

when it's my turn. Like Ancian always says...
But she is unconscious before she can finish.

+ + +

Her dreams roll like a turbid river, one flowing into the next. At first, she envisions herself standing in the maison, flipping the cutter end over end into the air and catching it by its handle. Higher and higher she tosses the weapon, round and round it flashes. Each time, her clawed fingers close around the handle—each time but one. At the last moment, she pulls her hand away, and the cutter sinks, blade first, into the floor...

...and the floor becomes water, and Lightning is swimming, with Joy on her back, toward a shore that eludes them, until the desperate pair is lifted from the water by a bomba and away to a warming fire...

...and its smoke fills her lungs and becomes the scent of the accrete tortured in flames.

Can't breathe, she thinks and is startled awake.

Her eyes blink open, but she lies still for a time, waiting for her heartbeat to settle. Joy sleeps beside her, her sleek body invisible but twitching and grasping in dreams of her own.

Or are we sharing dreams again? Lightning wonders. She stretches her legs and rolls over, trying to find a comfortable spot on the unforgiving floor. She lies, eyes open, gazing at the play of water and blue light. Had Joy tried to wake her? Guilt prods her to fight sleep and stand her turn, but it fails utterly.

+ + + + + +

Outside, standing at the lip of the northern precipice overlooking the canyon, the brindled kezel with one good eye looks down at the lone, lavender accrete on its island of stone. He sniffs and wrinkles his snout. A jabi ah-lah, more adult than wabi, is easy to identify. But what is the other thing? He's hunted every edible creature

Book of Dreams

in the accrete and never encountered tracks like the ones he followed here—or their eerie, clinging scent.

What's the play? he thinks. *What's the move?*

Wait and watch, he answers himself.

And so decided, he settles into a naked berry thicket, eating snow to soothe his empty stomach.

Show yourselves, he thinks, peering down to the island accrete. But for a long time, no one does.

+ + + + + +

Upon waking, Lightning and Joy share a modest breakfast: thin strips of awl and cold water. The meal is finished too soon for either of them.

Wasn't planning on a long trip, thinks Lightning. *Come on. We have work to do.*

They exit the cave quietly, but no dow are caught unaware this time. They, along with other creatures in the vicinity, have moved to safer locales. Lightning faces south, nose to the rising wind.

There haven't been any kezel here for a long time, she thinks, rubbing her legs. *Or anywhere near.*

Joy's eyes sparkle.

That is good, yes?

I don't know. Maybe.

She yearns for answers, but hunger calls louder than curiosity. Their meager supplies won't last long, and Joy eats only one thing.

We need awl, thinks Lightning, recognizing a moment later a possible way to satisfy their need for food *and* information. *There's a river near the home caves—the Sweet. My api-kan awled there. My amolis and apotis too. If we hurry, we might eat before the next storm.*

She moves as quickly as her legs allow, leading Joy to the wedge trail, this time following it south until they reach the base of the Stifle. From here, they move east, with the sun to their right. The trail remains ungroomed every labored step of the way, and they make slow progress. As she wills her aching limbs to cooperate, a dread unrelated to her injuries grows in her mind.

They angle south with the wind in their faces, and they never smell the brindled kezel who trails them, stealthy but sure.

+ + +

The first dead accrete they encounter has been reduced to a blackened stump, like a dirty icicle melted over a thermal pool. Its remaining scales, their original color impossible to guess, curl up at their edges, made thin and brittle by some tremendous heat. One such stump is soon followed by others, until, by the time they draw near the Sugarfoot caves and descend the jagged ridge outside the main entrance, the foothills have been transformed to a wasteland. No creatures move or make sound, and despite the wind's bluster, the smell of ash and suffering hangs in the air. As they tread through deep, untracked snow, Lightning struggles to count the charred trunks, desolate fingers pointing to the sky.

I remember these accrete, she thinks. *That was a scarlet fan; that was a yellow fork. I used to play there...*

Her thought trails off. Joy shelters hers.

All signs indicate the caves are lifeless, but they take cautious steps, avoiding the main entrance and making their way to the rear of the stony bank. At the mouth of a small fissure, the singed remains of a biting cyrilis stand mute guard, toothless yet somehow threatening. Terrified at what she will find, Lightning feels drawn inside, unable to resist learning the truth. She hands Joy the cutter and steps up to the fissure, sniffing at the blackness within.

Stay and watch, she thinks. *Mind, not mouth.*

+ + + + + +

From his sheltered position above the caves, the brindled kezel can make no sense of what he has seen— or not seen, in this case. The Sugarfoot ah-lah is her own mystery. By her appearance, he judges her to be the murderer chased from Redtooth territory moons ago. How had she managed to return without being noticed? And why now, with her home cursed and desolate?

But it is her invisible companion and its unfamiliar scent that keeps him from simply leaping down and overpowering her. What in Aranae is it? And wielding a Moondweller cutter of all things, seeming to float with a life of its own. More sobering still is what he had seen when the Sugarfoot had drawn the weapon from her belt—he had scarcely been able to believe his one good eye. Though he had caught just a glimpse of the thrower riding in its holster, a glimpse was enough.

A jabi armed with a thrower.

An invisible biped and a cutter.

Moondweller devilry!

Combined, the mysteries are too much. There isn't a Redtooth alive who would blame him. He backs away from the caves, and as is his practice when faced with the unknown or overwhelming, he turns for home, loping through the snow.

His chief will know what to do.

+ + + + + +

Joy takes a position near the entrance, the cutter held before her as Lightning swallows her dread and steps inside. She doesn't need a crystal but pulls one of the broken halves from her vest anyway. It has lost much of its power, but its feeble glow soothes her nerves.

Kezel scents are stale and faint, made foul by the lingering remnant of toxic fumes. With each intersecting passage she crosses, a quick sniff is all she needs to tell her she is alone. She doesn't bother to send a thought; it seems the entire moon family has come and gone since the last kezel passed this way.

She walks on, though more slowly now, as her feet have grown heavy with foreboding. Something terrible lies ahead, she is sure of it, and it draws her forward like water over a fall. She doesn't realize she has a target in mind until she reaches the feast cave. The crystal light wavers off its ribboning walls, and long shadows loom and shift as if alive. She steps toward Gami-kan's nest. The gigika kezel's faded vest lies under a thick coat of dust and several bones that have been gnawed and broken.

The bones are kezel, bowed with age.

Lightning stares, unable to look away, and it isn't grief she feels, but guilt.

Ancian, she thinks. *No...* Her ears sag, and she closes her eyes. *I should have been here. I'm so sorry.*

But she is given little time to mourn. Just as she is leaning forward to touch her nose to one of the bones, a sudden thought reaches her, its alarmed tone sensible even at this distance.

Ami-kan! I see something!

Muttering angry curses, Lightning turns to leave. She glances one final time at the faded garment and bones, lonely and futile, much as she feels herself.

I'll be back, she thinks.

CHAPTER TWO
Reunion

OUTSIDE THE CAVE, Joy peers to the south, clicking quiet but fast.

What is it? Lightning wonders. Blackened accrete puncture the mantle of snow as far as she can see, raising skeletal arms to the sky like an appeal. She senses no threat, but the wind is unfavorable.

I'm sorry; it's nothing, thinks Joy. Her gaze sweeps in vain from left to right. *I was so sure...*

Lightning turns away.

Keep watching, she thinks. Unwanted images of bones and Gami-kan's tattered vest push their way into her mind. What other horrors will she discover if she dares another trip inside?

Did you find food? Joy asks.

No.

What do we do?

I don't know. I feel sick.

Where are the others?

Joy! I know as much as you do.

When the wind shifts, coming again from the south, Lightning growls, eyes narrowing. She crouches low to the hill, pulling Joy down beside her. As they hug the snow, she points down the slope to the northern bank of the River Sweet, three hundred strides away.

You were right, she thinks.

But I see nothing.

It's lying still. Wait; it'll move again. There!

Joy's eyes sparkle when she catches sight of a figure weaving between the ruined accrete. Its ashen coat is an ideal match for its surroundings, and at first, they can't identify the form. A moment later, it pauses and turns, rising on two legs, and when it does, they exchange equally surprised glances.

Cliff! they think in unison.

The lame kezel drops to four legs and limps through an open space, lit by the sun. He has grown, it's true, but is more gaunt than ever, a fact easy to see as he wears no vest. The various grays in his coat camouflage him well, and he disappears as he passes into the shadows cast by blackened stumps. Not bothering to explain, Lightning moves down the rocky hill toward this new arrival, a grim purpose smoldering in her eyes.

Ami-kan! You are injured. Joy whistles a quiet warning as she hurries to follow.

Yes, and he has one bad leg, thinks Lightning, *and only half a heart. Plus, he's downhill and upwind. There won't be a better time.* She pauses to take the cutter from Joy and remove the talihew from around her arm.

He may be dangerous, thinks Joy.

He is. Lightning returns the cutter to her belt. *Like a kish, only not so brave. Pay attention: this is the plan...*

+ + + + + +

Cliff pauses, his nose to the wind. The rising gusts are from the south, but that's apt to change. He has little time to make this kill before his prey becomes aware of him. At the base of an accrete, seared and lowly, something burrows silently beneath the snow. Cliff crouches, quivering in anticipation, gray ears angled forward.

A blind, tubular creature with a hundred wriggling legs emerges from the snow, dirt staining its expressive snout: a middling sneer, half a stride long. Cliff's pounce is awkward but accurate, and a wild, reflexive spasm of surprising vigor can't free the sneer once his jaws have locked. The sneer screams once, pink fluid spattering the snow, then is broken and screams no more. Cliff wastes no time, tearing into his meal. As he does, swirling flakes of snow appear, just as an unexpected thought enters his mind.

It's polite to share, it thinks.

Cliff jumps as if burned by a crystal. He wheels around, his eyes wild and darting, but he sees nothing—unless maybe a hint of movement, like heat ripples. And yet his nose tells him something stands before him, a few strides away, visible or not. He snarls and bares his teeth, the spikes rising along his spine. Whatever it is, the invisible creature has an evocative scent, unique and compelling. It calls to mind images of a blue cave and tar.

Could it be? From so long ago?

As these thoughts flash through his mind, Cliff realizes in a heartbeat their implication. He spins to his downwind side just in time to see Lightning deliver a blow to the side of his head.

+ + +

Consciousness comes slowly, bringing with it a fierce headache. As his eyes blink open, Cliff finds he is bound and muzzled, his front limbs tied to each other and his snout wrapped shut by strips of talihew. He is tethered to an accrete's ashen bole at the edge of the Sweet, a noisy channel a dozen strides across and overhung by a rock shelf three kezel-lengths above.

Lightning and her strange companion sit nearby, or so Cliff assumes, for he is unable to see the one. He determines its location by smell, two faint sparkles, and a floating piece of awl it appears to be chewing. Lightning unapologetically downs the remainder of his sneer. They are thinking sheltered thoughts to one another, but Cliff's sore head can penetrate none of their defenses.

Seeing he is awake, Lightning turns to face him, a scowl crinkling her snout.

Took you long enough, she thinks.

You were stupid to come back, he replies. *If any other kezel see you, you're dead.*

There are no other kezel. Why is that, Cliff? Why is the biggest coward I know skulking around where no one else has set foot in moons?

Maybe he ate them, thinks the invisible creature.

You're the reason there are no other kezel, thinks Cliff, and his tone is harsh. *Whatever you are!*

Lightning glares as she puts the finishing touches on his sneer, and to her right, the twin sparkles brighten to a glittery flash—but only for a moment.

Cliff strains against his bonds.

I'll kill it and eat it in front of you!

No, Lightning replies. *What you'll do is tell us what happened here, and why you're the only one left.*

Cliff would have snapped his jaws if not muzzled.

Why should I?

If you don't, you won't outlive your hunger.

Oh, you're a good one with threats. How do I know you're not going to kill me anyway?

You don't.

Then you can find your own answers!

Fine. Lightning rises to her feet. *Come on. We've wasted enough time on this one.*

And she closes her mind, limping away up the bank. Her invisible companion follows close behind, its footprints marking the snow, not six as Cliff had expected, but two. He has no time to consider this mystery, for he is busy casting anxious glances at the water.

There are awl in that river, he thinks. *Big ones!*

Yes, thinks Lightning. *I hope they like your smell.*

You can't leave me here!

But Lightning is soon out of sight.

Certain that he has been abandoned, and panic tickling his innards, Cliff scrapes his bindings against the ashen accrete, hoping to cut himself free but having little success. He is scrambling to devise a better plan, when—

He glances up, gray eyes squinting.

Book of Dreams

Something approaches him in the river.

A long, green stalk the width of his wrist protrudes from the water, rising above the flow by a full stride. Atop the stalk rides a single green eyeball, large and unblinking. It peers at him, holding its position five strides from where he continues his futile scraping. He knows an awl is connected to the other end of that eye stalk, an awl strong enough to resist the current, with a mouth full of teeth designed to drag him underwater—if he wasn't tied to an accrete.

He works at a furious pace, scrape and scratch, the eye stalk moving closer, parting the current in a frothy V. It passes beneath the rock shelf and draws within striking range. A blunt head breaks the surface, knobby and blotched in green. The awl makes no sound as its gaping mouth opens to expose double rows of serrated teeth and ropy saliva.

Its breath is warm and smells of rotting meat.

As Cliff steels himself for the worst, Lightning appears on the rock shelf overhead. She holds a long fork of charred accrete like a spear, its tip bound to her cutter. She hurls the weapon downward, driving it into the rubbery flesh of the awl, piercing it behind its eye stalk. Her throw is ferocious and accurate. The cutter sinks into the awl's giant head, staining the water green.

+ + + + + +

The awl's bellow is terrible, and it thrashes about so violently that Lightning fears her shot missed its mark. Soon, however, both thrashing and bellowing cease, and the beast is still except for the bobbing of the current.

Hugging the rock face behind her, Joy buzzes.

Oh! You did it!

Lightning re-shoulders her pack.

First time, she admits. *Not counting the thrower, I mean.* She watches as the awl floats away, trailing a slick of green. *But I watched my api-kan do a lot of spearing on this ledge. He was good at it.*

A.P. Malloy

It is getting away. Joy's antennae bend forward.

No, thinks Lightning. *There's a fall to the south; it's too big to pass over. It'll get caught on the rocks and be waiting for us when we get there.* She looks down at Cliff, who has recovered from his surprise and returned to scraping at his bonds. *We'd better get down there,* she thinks. *The silly fool's going ruin my rope.*

+ + +

When Lightning untethers Cliff, leaving his muzzle in place and his front limbs hobbled, she orders him to march. At first, he refuses, but the sight of the thrower changes his mind. For a thousand strides he limps due south, Lightning and Joy close behind. Once arrived at the fall, where the Sweet grows fat and lazy and the awl lies beached in the stony shallows, Lightning lashes him to a boulder. He watches as she retrieves her cutter and begins the messy business of reducing the awl to food. Her first target is the fatty layer that once insulated it, and she and Joy indulge eagerly.

The smell is too much for Cliff.

You win! he thinks. *I'll tell you what you want to know. Just give me some!*

Prove it, thinks Lightning. *Tell me where my family is. Tell me why you're alive when the others aren't.*

Most of them are. Cliff shakes his head. *Or they were the last time I saw.* He closes his eyes as if hiding from the awl. *They were taken.*

Taken! Lightning scoffs. *By who? Who takes an entire clan of kezel against their will?*

Cliff groans and goes limp.

Feed me!

But Lightning only curls her lip.

Who took them? she repeats. *Where?*

South, onto the plains. Cliff paws at his muzzle, his futility pathetic. *I don't know where after that. I wasn't going to follow them.*

Follow who?

But at this question, Cliff squints his eyes and stops struggling. He looks in Joy's direction.

Ones like that, he thinks. *Or like it used to be, with six legs, not two. Camouflaged sometimes, blue others. More than I could count.* He returns to staring at the awl, and his thoughts end in a hacking cough.

Like me? thinks Joy.

Disgusting like you, yes. But they didn't think kezel—not that I could sense.

You'd better tell us from the beginning, thinks Lightning. *Be quick and honest; I'll know if you're lying.*

Cliff hunches his shoulders.

I guess it takes a liar to know one.

I'm waiting.

We are both waiting, thinks Joy.

Cliff growls; the muzzle allows him that much.

What do you consider "the beginning?" When you left me to drown in that tar?

Lightning returns to her work with the awl.

You can't drown in tar that isn't over your head.

Maybe not. But you ruined my only vest. That's not very honorable, is it?

You're a fine one to judge honor. Something tells me you're only going without a vest to keep the Redteeth happy. Tell your story and spare us your opinions.

Yes, tell your story, Joy insists.

Cliff grumbles and glares.

I don't suppose you want to hear how many times I had to soak in the most horrible smelling baths your gami-kan could make to get the tar out of my spikes.

No.

Or how my skin is still stained.

Cliff! Lightning brandishes the cutter. *A full belly makes me a little more patient, not a lot.*

Cliff's ears pin back.

Fine, he thinks. *From the beginning.*

+ + +

It was your oti-kan Crag who pulled me out of the tar, he thinks. *His hands got covered in it, and he cursed me like it was my fault. But that was nothing compared to what the other kezel were thinking about you. You should have sensed the names they used when they learned what you'd done. Submission tried to keep the peace, but you stole weapons and poisoned Rock's food.* Cliff shakes his head at the sacrilege. *His food, Lightning!*

I didn't poison it, she clarifies. *He woke up, yes?*

He woke up all right—howling mad. When Crag and I told him what we'd seen, he couldn't wait to track you. You wouldn't have liked it if he had caught you.

No, thinks Lightning. *I don't suppose. But I bet they treated you like a hero.*

I got invited back to the feasts, Cliff thinks. *If that's what you mean.*

I hope you were happy.

I was! For a little while. His eyes track the snow that has begun to fall. *Gully and Pounce saw you on the Redtooth side,* he thinks, *but they weren't allowed to cross. Everybody thought you'd gone crazy and would end up in the belly of a kish. No one—outside of Ancian, Submission, and maybe Thunder—seemed too upset about it. Everyone else said it was a good riddance.*

He pauses as if hoping to make the news sting, but Lightning concentrates on the awl. The rising wind speaks of trouble; they'll need shelter soon enough.

Of course, thinks Cliff, *nobody knew what to make of the blue thing. In the beginning, I didn't share with anyone that I'd sensed it thinking. I knew they'd figure I had the same sickness you did and send me packing. When Crag said he'd seen it, I admitted I had too, but the rest I kept to myself.* Cliff strains uselessly against his bindings. *I had a feeling they were wrong about you being eaten. I figured you were in hiding. I think Thunder did too. He knew something about that one...*

He glares at Joy.

When I convinced him to tell Submission about the Thing, they found it burned to a heap, a stinky, black pile.

We didn't know how at the time, but we figured it out later. Your api-kan posted sentries in case you or more of those blue things showed up. That's how we learned the Redtooth clan was on the move—against us. He glances sidelong at Lightning, and a strange tone enters his thoughts. *Turns out a Redtooth was killed near the northern crossing. Their chief's oti-mu! Stabbed with a cutter. Know anything about that?*

Will you finish your story faster if I say yes?

Well, they weren't happy. There was a big fight at the northern crossing, and the southern crossing got pitched into the wedge. That made folks even more mad at you. Submission and Thunder kept searching, but no one helped. Anyway, with the Redtooth troubles, and then the new wabis being born...

Cliff's thought trails away.

We should've paid closer attention, he thinks. *We didn't know... There was no way... We couldn't have...*

You're not finishing your sentences, thinks Lightning. *I get it. The blue things caught us by surprise.*

No! They caught us *by surprise. You were off with one of them having a fine time.*

We got by.

I guess you did. Doesn't look like you missed any meals. Your legs have looked better, though.

Where is my api-kan, Cliff?

Cliff ducks his head as if dodging the question.

I don't know, he thinks. *They were like a swarm, camouflaged. We could smell 'em but they were quick— hard to catch. It took a lot of 'em to bring down a single kezel, but that's what they were: a lot.* He puckers his lips as if remembering a bad taste. *The ones they bit fell asleep. They were bound up and dragged off.*

Dragged off where?

I told you. The way they came in. He shudders. *Out onto the plains, where the Thing was.*

And you ran. Lightning rests from her labor; this news is sapping her energy.

You don't know what it was like! thinks Cliff. *This*

wasn't about honor and following the Way. They burned the accrete, like I've never seen accrete burn. He shakes his head. *When I came back later, I found some who had hidden in the caves suffocated—but there was no smoke, just fumes.* He pauses. *Your gami-kan...*

For a moment, all three contemplate sheltered thoughts. Then, as if to himself, Cliff thinks:

I liked Ancian. She was nice to me.

Lightning scowls.

How many moons since they were taken?

Too many, Cliff thinks, and he grumbles. *I've been alone a long time. Gapi-kan the Red had passed...* He pauses, calculating. *It wasn't long after that.*

Lightning groans, hanging her head.

The trail will be ice cold!

The trail leads out to the plains. What difference does it make whether it's cold, or hot, or paved with tali-hew? You're not going to follow it.

When Lightning doesn't reply, Cliff presses.

Are you?

What would you like me to do, Cliff? Stay here skulking with you? Cliff fidgets, nibbled by shame, but Lightning doesn't relent. *One moon after another passed over your cowardly hide while my clan—while kezel!— were taken captive. You make me sick. You've done nothing to rescue, nothing to avenge.*

I would have been taken too. Cliff's ears lay flat to his head. *Or eaten by a derka.*

Better than being eaten by guilt!

Um, thinks Joy. *What about the bombas?*

What bombas? Cliff's eyes dart to the sky as if hoping to see a meal, but Lightning sighs.

I haven't forgotten, she thinks, *but we can't go north and south at the same time.* She tries to stretch the ache from her legs. *Who do we turn our backs on?*

Joy makes prints in the snow as she paces a slow circle, casting a faint shadow.

Not on the bombas, she thinks.

But the kezel are my family, thinks Lightning. She

knows this is the wrong idea to share the moment the thought escapes her mind. Joy clicks low and fast.

Bombas are family too, she thinks. *Nicer than kezel were.* A moment later she adds, *To you and me.*

Lightning suppresses the desire to bare her teeth, and she returns to the last of her work, taking particular care to extract the small, orange glands at the base of the awl's brain. These she places in the small dowskin pouch that once contained her reed of bomba essence.

What are you going to do with those? asks Cliff.

But Lightning ignores his question. As he looks on, she stuffs Gami-kan's pack and her empty pockets with the choicest cuts of awl. Then she cleans and dries the cutter, handing it to Joy.

I'm caching the rest, she thinks. *Watch him; if he tries to get free, poke him a couple times.*

+ + +

Joy stands gripping the cutter in both hands as Lightning wades from the shallows, dragging her prize away from the fall. The moment she is out of sight, Cliff begins to scrape his bindings against the rough edges of the boulder. As he is having little success, Joy supposes no poking is expected of her. Still, imagining Lightning's response to his attempt, she points the cutter and buzzes in what she hopes is a threatening tone.

He squints his eyes, scraping harder.

You don't scare me, he thinks.

Yes, actually, I do, she replies. *I read your mind.*

Good! Then read this: The first chance I get, I'm going to kill you and eat you.

No, you are not, thinks Joy. The cutter waves side to side. *You fancy my ami-kan.*

Your what?

Yes. You fancy her.

Cliff stops his scraping and looks up.

That's the most stupid thing I've ever sensed. "Ami-kan?" You think as bad as you smell. I'd turn her in to the

A.P. Malloy

to the Redteeth in a heartbeat—*if I thought they'd feed me.*
You lie.
Cliff returns to scraping.
The very first chance.

+ + +

When she returns, Lightning hoists the pack to her shoulders and unties Cliff, leaving his front limbs bound. She coils the rope and hands it to Joy, retrieving the cutter as she glares at Cliff.

March, she thinks.

He rises slowly to uncertain feet, his defective leg cramped and even less cooperative than usual.

Where are we going?

Back to the caves.

Cliff grimaces.

What if I say no?

I can muzzle your mind, too. Lightning pats the thrower. Cliff shrinks back, his eyes rolling white.

Fine, he thinks. *But they're cursed, you know. Nothing but bad luck to go inside.*

That explains us finding you. Lightning points to the north. *Get moving.*

+ + +

The return trek to the caves is not long, but their pace is slow, and the thickening storm clouds blot out the sun as they labor through falling snow. Lightning's injured legs ache the entire way, and while she travels fully loaded without complaint, she is also glad for Cliff's awkward, sluggish gait. Upon reaching the caves, he refuses to go more than a few steps inside. No threats or taunting can change his mind, so convinced is he of the curse. Distant thunder echoes.

Nothing but bad luck, he repeats. *I went in once; I'm not going back.*

And so, Lightning binds him to a stalagmite near

the entrance, leaving him on the naked cave floor with hunger as his lone companion.

Come with me, she thinks to Joy.

They walk together in darkness, returning to the feast cave. There, they take out a fading crystal and begin the somber business of locating the rest of Gami-kan's bones. These they find scattered, victims of terrible disrespect and covered in dust. After wiping them clean, they make a neat pile on the gigika's nest, covering them with rocks and her raggedy vest's faded remains. In its last serviceable pockets, Lightning finds a mending needle and the folded square of yellow bearing the alleged Moondweller markings. She keeps both, though only the needle promises any use.

Ancian taught me to mend, she thinks.

She wouldn't... Joy hesitates. *Try to eat me?*

Not once she got to know you. Lightning bows her head. *She was like my ami-kan, you know. After mine...* She frowns at the cairn. *Sometimes her stories went on too long, that's true, but I didn't mind. There was a lot to learn. I should have paid better attention.*

Joy clicks a slow rhythm, placing another stone on the pile and gazing into the dark recesses of the cave.

Are there other ones? she asks. *Dead ones?*

Lightning removes her mask and wipes her eyes.

I don't know. But I'm going to find out.

They make their way to the story cave next and the cooking cave soon after, shadows waving in the crystal light. Silence weighs heavy, broken by the shuffling of their feet across floors that haven't been cleaned in moons. The smell of fumes worsens as they proceed into the deeper passages, and when they reach the guarded place, the cave of treasures, no treasure do they find, nor any guard. All the throwers, large and small, are gone, as are the projectiles, cutters, and crystals.

Killers and *thieves,* thinks Lightning.

They continue on, their dread growing. Not long after, they find more bones, most likely strewn about by scavenging vermin. But worse by far is what they find in the most secluded caves: complete corpses, not disturbed at all. They find an ibiwa and two wabis this way, as if they had been sharing a pleasant nap. It is Stone's fancy, Flake, the Sugarfoot sentry, his body wrapped around the two wabis whose names Lightning had never gotten to learn. So short, their lives! The sight of their tiny bodies pierces her heart, and she turns away.

By the time every cave has been explored, they have found the remains of ten different kezel, some they can identify, like the gapis Prowl and Bluff, others blessedly anonymous.

Can we go back? thinks Joy, buzzing distress.

Lightning's ears droop.

Nothing would make me happier.

+ + +

When they return, stark shadows jitter across the walls as electricity leaps between the clouds and strikes the planet like a hurled spear. Wind howls across the entrance, and Cliff lies curled in a miserable ball, snow frosting his spikes. He looks up when Lightning removes her pack and tosses a portion of awl in his direction. His muzzle keeps him from getting teeth on the food, but he extends his tongue, licking at the awl and mashing it to a pulp, a shameless, slurpy mess.

Joy falls asleep soon after a meal of her own, though her bed is nothing more than a cobbled floor and her pillow Lightning's spiky flank. Cliff follows close behind, slouching in fitful dreams against the base of the stalagmite. Though weary from head to toe, Lightning remains awake, tormented by doubt, grief, and pain—and Cliff's snoring, almost as noisy as the thunder.

Dunk it! she curses. *Dunk it and stunk it!*

Curling her lip, she rises, careful not to wake Joy, and steps to the cave's entrance, looking out through the narrow fissure. Sparkling flakes, tinted orange to match the Big Brother, whip and drift as they please, with nothing to block the wind. But much worse are split seconds of crackling electrical discharges, for they reveal tableaux of tortured accrete, black and forsaken.

Someone will pay for this, she thinks. *I don't know who or how, but someone will pay.*

She lifts her gaze to the rolling, coral clouds, and her mind returns to the looming question: bombas or kezel? She sits massaging her legs as she weighs her options. The thought of doing nothing, of laying low and staying safe, enters her mind but does not remain. She imagines life on a range devoid of kezel, a life within sight of the Eye Tower, and it sickens her. She winces at the memory of a bomba's desperate cry.

So, she thinks. *What's it going to be?*

But as icy flakes pepper her nose and ears, and the wind threatens to drive her from the entrance, still she sits wondering. When Joy wakes to summon her inside, the answer has refused to reveal itself. It wiggles around in her mind, jeering like a virble, maddening, close, and impossible to catch.

Lightning returns to the darkness of the cave, kicking Cliff as she passes. He remains asleep, but his snoring does grow quiet—for a time. Lying next to Joy, she attempts to find sleep of her own. If only it were so easy! But while her companion soon drifts away, she is snatched again and again from the brink of slumber by the call of friends and family in need or the twitchy ache of her legs. At last, she does what she had promised she would never do again, does what she hasn't done since Joy's metamorphosis.

Don't see how it could hurt, she thinks. *Just to relax, so I can think properly...*

She removes one of the fresh awl glands from her vest and holds it up to Oti-kan the orange. Why? Seeking his blessing? Guidance? She can't say. Then she tosses the gland into her mouth, biting down. Pop! Her nose and mouth go instantly dry, and she squints as she inhales the bitter gas. Soon, however, the harshness passes. She swallows the gland, and a sweet langour spreads through her limbs. Powerless to resist, she settles her weary frame to the floor, exhaling audibly.

Sleep consumes her, but still the dilemma burns.

+ + +

What are you doing here, Little Spark? Gami-kan asks her. Lightning looks up, surprised. She is in the feast cave, though she can't recall how she got there, standing before Ancian's newly-built cairn. The gigika kezel sits casually in front of it, filing her claws. Her spikes are as wilted and patchy as ever, but a luminous aura surrounds her like a vest of light, driving away the dark in this part of the cave.

I...well, I'm not sure, Lightning admits. *We were in the maison, you know, where the bombas live, way up north of kish country, beyond the Shattered Plains. I think it was the Moondweller fortress, Gami-kan. You would have liked it. But there was some trouble, and we went into this little room, and—poof! Just like that!—we were sent back to the accrete.*

Hmm, yes, thinks Gami-kan, nodding, and she blows the tiny shavings from her claws. *Wondrous Moondweller magic, that. But that's not what I was asking. I mean, what are you doing here?* And she gestures broadly at the cairn and the shadowy cave.

Oh. I don't know.

Of course you do.

Lightning pauses to reflect. Does she know? She looks down and counts her toes and fingers, wiggling them. Is she dreaming? But her dreams have never felt like choice, never exercises in free will. They have always seemed like action observed from a distance, over which she has no control. This is different.

I...I miss you, Ancian, she thinks simply.

Oh, goodness. You didn't come down here to tell me that, did you? Come now, Little Spark, you're getting yourself all wound up for no reason.

But...you're gone. You're...dead.

So it would seem. But look at this nice light.

Yes. It is nice.

And see how we can think to one another. Just like old times. Remember the babelrack feast?

I do. Can I touch you, do you think?

Oh, I shouldn't think so. You can try, though.

Lightning reaches out a clawed hand, moving it as if gently stroking Gami-kan's spikes. They make no contact with the image, passing through it like smoke, but she feels a tingle along the tips of her fingers, and the aura of light ripples like water.

I love you, Ancian. I'm real sorry about all of this.

I know you do, and I know you are. But you still haven't answered my question: why did you come here?

Lightning takes a deep breath.

I need help. I don't know what to do.

Don't you?

No. Do I?

Of course you do.

Then what? I can't just leave the bombas.

Can you get back to them?

Lightning pauses to consider this. She imagines attempting a trek to the maison. How would she cross the wedge? And what chance would she have of ever making it through Redtooth territory a second time? Then there are the kish to consider. Only Oracio's assistance had saved them the first time, and she feels certain that was a grace not to be repeated. Short of the Moondweller device suddenly coming back to life and allowing them to return, she sees no road back.

So? Gami-kan presses.

No, Ancian, we can't get back to them.

Then why fuss about it? Is that what I taught you?

No, Ancian.

So. What can you do?

I suppose I could stay here...

Gami-kan rises slowly to four legs and stretches, her aura shimmering.

But... she prompts.

But I would feel sick, thinks Lightning. *All the time.*

Like physically ill, you know? I would want to...vomit my guilt, if that makes sense.

It does. So, what else?

Only one thing. Follow the kezel that were captured and see if there's anything I can do to help.

Well! There you have it. Gami-kan sits again. *That wasn't so difficult, was it?*

But... Lightning reaches out a second time and runs her hand through the light. *I'm scared.*

You'd be a fool not to be.

Was it...does it hurt? Being dead? What is it like?

Can't say, thinks Gami-kan. *Against the rules.*

Oh.

Gami-kan's glowing form leans forward and Lightning's nose tingles where the image seems to touch her. They sit like this for a time, and even when Lightning closes her eyes, she can see the light in her mind.

You've been through a lot, thinks Gami-kan.

I'm so tired...

Then you should get some sleep. Both of you.

Lightning opens her eyes. Gami-kan is looking past her at something—or someone—behind her. Coming uncertainly out of the shadows, a small figure gradually takes the form of Joy, her eyes lit and her antennae leaning forward.

What are you doing? she asks.

Talking to Ancian, thinks Lightning, and she turns to indicate the glowing figure. But the image is gone, the light nothing more than her depleted crystal.

You were sleepwalking, Ami-kan. Joy steps close, wrapping an arm around her and gazing up.

No, I... Lightning looks at the cairn. Was that all? Sleepwalking? Then why does her nose still tingle?

Come back to bed, thinks Joy.

But...

Please. You're scaring me.

Lightning blinks and gives herself a shake.

Sorry, she thinks. *Yes, let's go back.* She runs her claws through Joy's curling locks. *You're very brave.*

I am?
You are. I'm...proud of you.
I'm proud of you.
Then it's settled, thinks Lightning, and she rises to her feet. *Let's go get some sleep.*

+ + +

When Lightning wakes, her muscles protest in memory of each pebble and knob, but she is refreshed in spirit, energized by certainty. Joy is no longer beside her, but Cliff snores nearby, chewing dream food. Grimacing as she stretches, Lightning moves outside, where she finds Joy standing in new sunlight. Against the backdrop of a snowy boulder, her skin has turned a clean white.

She buzzes a cryptic melody.

You have decided, yes?

She asks it as a question, but Lightning reads it as a statement and is gratified to realize that she has indeed. For good or bad, her choice has become clear. She nods, flexing her legs and rubbing the welts.

I have, she thinks. *I guess I knew it all along, but I was afraid. Debating it was me putting off the inevitable.*

Joy's eyes glitter as she considers this.

The kezel, she thinks.

Yes, thinks Lightning. *But Cliff is right. It's probably a terrible idea.*

Joy turns to the south, antennae bending to the sun. She switches from buzzing to a patterned whistle.

I dreamed about Ari, she thinks.

Lightning nods.

So did I. Whose dream was it, do you suppose? Yours or mine? Or both?

But Joy has no answer.

He seemed very happy, she thinks. *Eating rixli.*

Yes. In mine, too.

Was it really...real?

Lightning ponders this. Before her, an army of black spikes in loosely ordered ranks stands at attention, dimpling the snow as far as she can see. She imagines they await her orders or are judging her somehow. Gami-kan had believed dreams could predict the future, but they hadn't predicted this.

I don't know, she thinks. *I sure hope so.*

+ + +

Inside the cave, they find Cliff awake, making an awkward attempt to reach an itch on his tail.

Here are your options, Lightning thinks. *You can come with us and redeem yourself or go free as an outcast and an enemy. Either way, we're following the kezel—to rescue or avenge.*

Cliff blinks in the shadows, his mouth open and his head foggy with sleep; he offers no reply.

Maybe you'll understand this, thinks Lightning, and she unties Cliff's bonds. He rises to four cramped legs and tears away the muzzle, eyes darting from the exit to Lightning and back again as if expecting a trick, frozen, it seems, by the ultimatum.

It's not difficult, Lightning snarls. *In or out?*

Sharing no thoughts—and never looking back—Cliff limps out of the cave and into the sun, soon disappearing amid the scorched accrete.

Joy clicks sharp disapproval.

No surprise, thinks Lightning, *and no loss.* She pulls some awl from her pack. *Eat first, then one last search of the caves: anything useful we can carry.*

Their effort reveals very little. Aside from one light crystal, a string of talihew gut, and two buttons, the caves have been scavenged moons ago.

Wait here, thinks Lightning.

And she leaves Joy to stand guard at the entrance as she makes a final visit to the absolute darkness of the feast cave and Gami-kan's cairn. The echo of her shuffling stride whispers from wall to stony wall, and she approaches the monument slowly, her heart heavy and her tail hanging low. Menacing smells linger nearby, and thoughts of the curse send shivers down her spine. Trying not to think about the bodies hidden in the lower levels, she offers a final apology as she removes Gamikan's tattered vest from the cairn.

I'll put it to good use, she thinks. *I promise.*

She bows before turning away.

Why? asks Joy when she sees the faded garment. But her answer is soon in coming, as Lightning uses nimble fingers and her mending kit to transform the raggedy vest, useless for its original purpose, into a sling for Joy to carry over her shoulder. In this she places several slabs of the awl from her pack.

No eating until I say, she thinks. *No telling where we'll end up, or how long we'll be gone.* The salvaged crystal and other items she tucks in her vest. *Outside,* she thinks. *I can't be here anymore.*

+ + +

They exit the caves, their moods dismal. Stepping into the sun fails to lift their spirits. Joy's mind turns again to the bombas, while Lightning listens to the wind sing a woeful dirge. As they stand, waiting for some signal to begin their journey, Joy points to the south, where a limping kezel can be seen in the distance.

He is coming back.

Lightning scowls.

I can't believe it. She curls her lip at Cliff's filthy spikes and haggard frame. Even at this distance she can count his ribs. *What do you think?* she wonders. *Is it his honor or his stomach making this decision?*

Probably his ah-tah parts, thinks Joy.

But when Cliff reaches the cave, it seems all their guesses are wrong. His mood is easy to read—fearful—and his ears are perked high and alert.

I smelled someone, he thinks, peering over his shoulder. *Might've been a Redtooth.*

Why do you care? thinks Lightning. *That's your side of the wedge, isn't it?*

That depends on which Redtooth you ask. Cliff reads the wind, his nose anxious and twitching. *I'll go with you to the plains,* he thinks. *But no farther.*

Lightning hands him the pack.

Good. Carry this, she thinks. *And don't open it.*

Cliff shoulders the laden pack, grumbling as he straps it into place. It is heavy and does not fit well.

If he threatens you, Lightning turns to Joy, *or does you any harm, you will tell me, yes?*

Of course.

And you, she thinks to Cliff. *Cross the line once, and it will be the last time. Understood?*

You don't have to bully. But her gaze wears him down. *Fine, I swear it. Can we go, please?*

Lightning turns again to Joy.

Are you ready?

If I must be, thinks Joy.

We all must. Lightning tugs at her boots and gloves. *We can't let a Redtooth catch our scent. It's east across the Spine, then south to the plains.*

Then I am ready, thinks Joy, though her tone says otherwise. She twists her hair into nervous curls.

I can carry you for a while, thinks Lightning. *But ride backward and keep an eye on that one.* She hands the cutter to Joy, who straddles the jabi kezel's back, her eyes glittering at Cliff. Lightning downs quick bites of snow. *Maintain the pace,* she thinks.

And so situated, the small party sets out from the Sugarfoot caves. Lightning never looks back, but as Cliff limps through the snow behind her, he continues to peer over his shoulder as if expecting trouble. As they march, Lightning does something she has never done before. She feels neither foolish nor nostalgic. Her motivation is simple, and until the moment the thoughts leave her mind, she isn't aware they exist.

Weaver, she thinks, and she faces the sun in its southern sky, *if you are real, please forgive all my, you know, all the bad things I've done. Please weave for us a good ending. Deliver us victory or honorable death.*

Book of Dreams

Joy buzzes agreement, but Cliff shakes his head. *The second one's most likely,* he thinks.

But then Lightning turns and begins marching to the east, and he must still his thoughts and concentrate on keeping up.

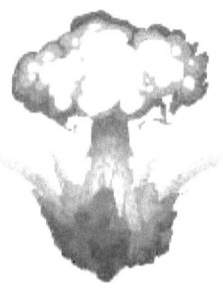

CHAPTER THREE
Book

THEIR JOURNEY'S BEGINNING reminds Lightning of when she and Thunder had first seen the Thing. Then, while the trek had been long, the siblings had been able to follow a relatively direct route, some of whose trails had been groomed. Now, those same trails hide beneath layers of deep snow, and the scorched accrete offers no protection from passing derkas. They must travel out of their way, first heading northeast between the Sour and Sweet, picking their way under cover of icy bluffs and ledges where travel is rocky and slow. They catch no sign of pursuit, but that doesn't prevent Cliff's fretful ears from angling back at every shift in the wind.

Did you hear that? he asks.

No, Lightning replies. *I sure didn't. Because there wasn't anything to hear.*

What was that? he asks a while later.

The same thing it was before, thinks Lightning.

Nothing, adds Joy.

But Cliff is not convinced; he marches faster.

Several thousand strides later, they ford the River Sweet and reach the Spine, a place untouched by fire. From that point, the canopy has blocked much of the snow, and they scale the stony vertebrae and descend the eastern side without mishap.

The eventual appearance of the River Tongue tells

them is time to move south. It is talkative as always, and it speaks to Lightning of happier times visiting the Bristle range. Now, as much as she would love the help and companionship, meeting a Bristle might also spell disaster for Joy. So, they keep the Tongue to their left and march as quickly and quietly as possible.

When Lightning's legs begin to nag, Joy dismounts and walks behind, holding the end of the jabi kezel's tail, lost in thought, her mind filled with an assortment of concerns. Measured though the pace is, Cliff labors to stay close. He glares at the shimmer of light trailing behind Lightning and scowls at the taunting smell from inside its laden sling, which seems to float along unsupported.

What do you see in it? he thinks to Lightning.

Her name is Joy.

Cliff makes a sound like a coughing bark.

You're not the kezel I thought you were, he thinks, and he struggles to adjust the straps over his shoulders.

I'll take that as a compliment, thinks Lightning.

Take it however you like. At least I can see why you didn't eat it. It's obviously poisonous. But it would've made good sport.

That is not nice, thinks Joy, but Cliff presses on.

It'll be the death of you, he prophesies. *Thunder was right to want to kill it.*

Quick as a blink, the sling moves to the side, footprints appear off the trail, and two small stones levitate from the ground. Snip! Snap! They fly forward. The first misses its target, but the second strikes Cliff on the tip of his nose. He yelps more in surprise than pain, and he makes a fine show of flaring his spikes.

But he doesn't retaliate.

If you let him irritate you, thinks Lightning, *all you do is make him feel important.*

Cliff rubs his nose, and his tone is sulky.

How is it able to understand me?

Ask her yourself.

I am an anom...anomaly, thinks Joy, buzzing. *Or-*

acio told me so.

What does that mean? And who is Oracio?

Joy ignores the first question.

Our friend, she replies. *Bombas are good thinkers.*

Thinkers? Cliff puzzles. *All bombas do is squawk a lot and poop on the accrete. They taste good, though, if you can catch one without getting scorched.*

Joy's eyes sparkle.

Shows what you know.

+ + +

For the remainder of the journey, Cliff plods along with his thoughts to himself, eating mouthfuls of snow and peering over his shoulder, his nerves on edge. Upon finally reaching the southern fringe of the accrete, he drops the pack in the snow and falls to the ground.

Promise kept. Don't expect another one.

I didn't expect the first one, Lightning replies. She looks out at the plains, awash in sunlight and scoured by wind. A slight mound beneath the snow is all that remains to mark where the Thing once stood, near the bank of the River Tongue, thin but chatty. *What did they do when they left the accrete?* she asks.

Who?

The six-legged ones! Who do you think?

Cliff sits up.

You won't believe it if I tell you.

Try me.

OK. They met up with some babelracks—big ones. They pulled three other Things, like the first one, from the way Thunder described it. They moved across the snow on round legs. That's where they put the kezel: inside.

So that's what it was, thinks Lightning, glad for a mystery solved. *A Thing to be pulled by babelracks. A Thing to put other things inside and move them.*

Fast and far, thinks Cliff. *They went south until they were out of sight. After a while, I lost their scent.* His ears grow droopy at the thought.

Lightning reflects on this information as she contemplates the plains. Tufted yellow grass and flat, snowy ground march together all the way to the horizon.

It goes on forever, thinks Joy.

All the more reason not to go out there, thinks Cliff. *Regret your decision now?*

Lightning curls her lip.

We'll find a way. Other creatures live out there with the wind and the derkas—and whatever else—and they do it without all your sniveling, I'm pretty sure. She stretches her legs as Joy seeks to improve her view by climbing into the low reaches of a fanning accrete, where her skin changes to match its scaly pink. *Anyway, why do you care? I thought you weren't going with us.*

I'm not, Cliff is quick to assert. *But I'll feel guilty if I don't try to talk you out of it.*

He casts a meaningful glance at the pack, but Lightning ignores this. Troubling thoughts occupy her mind. Gami-kan hadn't ever shared much about the plains, as few kezel with any sense travelled there. Of course, teams of hunting adults might pursue a babelrack for a thousand strides or so, and harvesting grass is common—the long, yellow blades make fine wraps for cached meat when woven together. But that task only occurs on the edge of the plains, where accrete still provide some cover. As for creatures other than babelracks, Gami-kan had mentioned derkas, of course, and had alluded to others. *A "panoply"* she had said, but Lightning hadn't sought details at the time, preoccupied with other concerns. She regrets that now.

I heard if you travel far enough, thinks Cliff, *the world ends. You could fall off the edge.*

Lightning shakes her head.

Something tells me we'll run into trouble before that. Gami-kan says storms out there are a lot worse. No breaks to the wind, no landmarks, and no cover from the snow. She pauses. *Said, I mean.* Her tail hangs low.

Assuming you don't get plucked up by a derka before the next storm, thinks Cliff.

Disheartened, and trying not to second-guess her decision, Lightning looks up to where Joy perches in the accrete, hidden from sight, and her eyes grow wide. A sudden idea has formed in her mind, so obvious she wonders why it had taken her so long.

Grass! she exclaims.

What about it? thinks Cliff.

We weave it! Like a cache wrap, only bigger. We cover ourselves! From above, we'll look like part of the plains—just a bunch of yellow grass.

Oh, sure. That won't look suspicious at all. Just a bunch of grass walking along like grass does. Even a stupid derka would look twice.

Think about it, Cliff. Lightning's tone is fit for a thick-headed wabi. *Why are babelracks white and yellow? You think that's an accident?*

I understand the concept, thinks Cliff, *but it's a rotten idea. It'll never work.*

Do you have a better plan?

Yes. Like I've been telling you: don't go.

Lightning dismisses this, snarling.

Cowards live the longest, she thinks. *If you're not going to help, keep your discouraging thoughts sheltered.*

She calls to Joy, energized by her plan, and they venture to the plain's snowy fringe, often glancing at the sky. Joy's antennae bend in the wind as she keeps a tight grip on the grass that Lightning hands to her, their fibrous strands no match for the cutter. Each blade is as long as Joy is tall, wide as her wrist, and yellow as the sun. She soon has all she can carry, and when Lightning has cut her own share, they return to where Cliff stands on two legs, waiting. He takes in news from the wind and casts darting glances into the shadows.

What is it now? thinks Lightning.

Nothing. But I have a bad feeling.

That makes three of us. Why are you still here?

Joy tosses her burden to the ground.

Because he is hungry, she thinks.

Too bad. Lightning adds her grass to Joy's, care-

fully placing rocks on top to prevent the blades from being scattered. *The food's going with us out onto the plains.
He's welcome to change his mind and join us.*

Cliff drops to four legs.

*No way. I'm going north. I don't want to hear your
screams when a derka gets you.*

Lightning bites down on the inclination to chase
Cliff from her sight. Gathering and weaving will take time
and focus, and she desires his presence as a sentry until
the job is complete. More than that, in the face of the re-
lentless plains, she realizes a second kezel, even a three-
legged coward, could be useful.

*Before you begin your heroic journey running away
from kezel in need,* she thinks, *stand guard. It hurts me to
make this promise, but I'll feed you if you do.*

How much?

A little less each time you ask a stupid question.

Fine, he thinks. *But hurry. I don't trust this wind.*

+ + + + + +

The brindled kezel, whose name is Spike, hastens
back to his home range. He is determined to share what
he has learned with his chief before the arrival of the next
storm. But Lightning, Joy, and Cliff have taken shelter in
the Sugarfoot caves and the Oti-kan moon has come to
call before Spike reaches the northern crossing. He hunkers in a makeshift shelter, his one good eye squinting at
the amber snowflakes and driving wind at the same time
a sleepless Lightning peers out of her cave, tormented by
a decision she cannot make.

Upon the storm's passing, Spike crosses the
wedge and goes in search of his chief—a white-spiked
bibija named Claw—scouting all the usual places and
conferring with every kezel he meets in what Redteeth call
the New Range. From a hunting party on the edge of kish
territory he learns that Claw has gone with his fancy on
a tour of the Old Range, far to the west.

You're welcome, thinks the leader of the party as

Spike moves on without thanks.

While Lightning and her companions are reaching the fringe of the plains and considering their next move, Spike hurries on. And now, feeling pressed by time and fearful his quarry will have escaped, he stops every thousand strides and howls urgently.

Did you hear that? Claw thinks to Eclipse, his black-spiked fancy, as they rub noses near a scenic waterfall. The Redtooth chief rises to two legs, and his ears angle forward. Eclipse, whose hearing is superior, doesn't bother standing.

It's Spike, she thinks, and she waits as Claw howls in reply, his voice rising above the wind. Not long after, Eclipse is proven correct, but she has no chance to gloat, for neither she nor Claw can believe the news they receive when Spike finally arrives.

+ + + + + +

Lightning and Joy make three more trips to the grassy fringe, cutting and gathering while Cliff keeps an anxious watch. Joy remains withdrawn, her thoughts sheltered. Lightning needs little effort to sense how uneasily this plan sits with her. If the bombas meet a bad end, she doubts she will be forgiven.

Once returned to the accrete, and after a quick meal—small by most standards, but the largest Cliff has had in moons—Lightning sets about weaving the grass into a square mat. Joy holds the loose ends to keep them from blowing away, lost in thought. Over, under, over, under, the mat grows blade by blade. But weaving on this scale is more difficult than Lightning had imagined. The grass cuts the tips of her fingers, and the wind refuses to cooperate. Her legs begin to cramp as the project draws on, and doubt grows in her mind. Cliff paces a worried, step-STEP-step circle, peering in all directions.

You know, thinks Lightning, *if you were planning to go to the Skull, you might want to think again.*

I wasn't, thinks Cliff, an easily read lie.

Good. Because Gami-kan told me a rogue kezel lives in those caves. Killed his apoliwot and ate his wabis. Or was it ate his apoliwot and killed his wabis? I can't remember. Anyway, no one could catch him, and now he shelters in the Skull.

That's not true.

If you say so.

Not that it matters to me, thinks Cliff. *I'm going east. I've got a friend on the Bristle range.*

Sure, thinks Lightning.

You said north before, Joy points out.

Did I? Well, I meant east.

Cliff watches the first grass mat take shape. Lightning wraps it around Gami-kan's pack, swaddling it in yellow. She has no concerns about Joy's sling, so faded it is already nearly white.

That's never going to hold up against the wind, thinks Cliff, mustering a confident tone as if trying to banish thoughts of a rogue kezel.

It will once I tie the ends, thinks Lightning. *Which will happen a lot faster if you stop bothering me.*

The wind shifts, its voice changing as it whistles through the swaying accrete. Cliff twitches as if one if his spikes has been plucked.

Good grief. Now what? thinks Lightning.

Nothing. Nothing. Just the wind. But maybe... he hesitates. *Maybe I'll weave one of those too. I just remembered: my Bristle friend found a fancy after the last Red and moved to live with the Whitetails.*

Joy clicks harshly, unable to ignore the obvious deceit, but Lightning acts as if she hasn't noticed.

Then you'd better get started, she thinks. *You have a lot of grass to gather.*

Can I use your cutter?

But Lightning doesn't dignify this foolish question with an answer, so Cliff turns away, his thoughts poorly sheltered as he searches for a stone sharp enough to cut through grass.

+ + +

Neither Lightning nor Joy are terribly surprised when Cliff displays a legendary ineptitude at gathering and weaving. He mangles the ends of the grass with his clumsy hacking and fumbles with the yellow blades, fighting wind and poor training as he tries to coax them into a secure weave. In the end, Lightning must finish the project for him, prodded by pain and the certainty that they have spent too much time.

Stand still, she scolds as she drapes a mat of yellow over his back. *I need to tie this in place.*

This is never going to work.

So you've said. Stand still!

With Cliff's camouflage secured, she hoists the pack to his shoulders, wrapped in rustling yellow. Her own cover she ties in place over her vest. The entire outfit feels awkward and uncomfortable, and she fears Cliff's doubts will end up being warranted.

OK, she thinks. *Time for a test.*

Cliff hunches near the accrete.

I'll keep a nose open for trouble, he thinks.

Fine. Keep your nose open, but keep that pack closed—and don't try leaving with it, or you won't like what happens. Lightning peers upward, her gaze sweeping the sky, and she nods. *Well,* she thinks to Joy, *you wanted to see it. Here's your chance.*

They make their way out toward the Thing's burial mound, Lightning's eyes cast ever skyward. Walking on top of the crusted snow as Joy does, instead of laboring through it, would be nice. But at least the camouflage stays in place, and the hasty weaving maintains its integrity—though its edges thrash and worry. More important, the first derka they see circles them initially, but when they stop moving, it flies on its way.

OK, thinks Lightning. *Good to know.*

They wind around tussocks of yellow and arrive at the bank of the River Tongue and the mounded snow nearby. All told, the place appears harmless enough, but

Lightning's nose works as hard as her eyes, and it tells her things they can't. She stops.

What do you smell? she asks.

Joy buzzes a quiet tune.

Old kezel. Very old.

Yes. And what else?

Something I don't know, thinks Joy. *Old too.*

Yes. The blue things, I'm guessing.

They make a slow pass around the mounded snow. No portion of the Thing rises above the white; as intimidating as it had once been, fire has laid it low. Lightning checks the sky again and peers across the endless plains, following the course of the Tongue as it flows toward the sun. She dreads to imagine how far away her enemies might be.

You found me here? thinks Joy.

This very spot. It used to be more exciting.

Joy scratches away some of the snow, pulling bits of charred items from the mound, remains of the Thing itself or unknown objects melted to slag. She examines each of these, chunks of shapeless black that seem to float above the ground. When they fail to answer her questions, she casts them aside, her eyes dim.

We should get back, thinks Lightning. A second derka appears, and they freeze, glad when it passes overhead, as unaware of them as the first.

Wait, thinks Joy. *I feel something here.*

Feel something? What do you mean?

But Joy doesn't answer. Instead, she digs deeper into the snow, throwing white behind her in a glistening arc. When she backs out of the hole, something floats before her. It is flat and black, a rectangle the size of Lightning's head and thick as her hand, covered in dirt, snow, and smudges of gray soot. But despite its soiled condition, it shows no dents or scratches, and where Joy wipes away the snow and soil, it gleams in the sun, smooth and free of blemish. Whatever it is, it avoided or was impervious to the fire.

What is this, now? Joy wonders.

A.P. Malloy

I don't know, thinks Lightning, peering closely. *I never noticed it any of the times I was here.* The object's perfect planes and exact right angles stir vivid memories. *It looks like something from the maison,* she thinks, and worried what unforeseen properties it might have, she moves to take possession of the object.

It doesn't smell maison, thinks Joy, but she surrenders her discovery. *It doesn't smell anything.*

Lightning quickly confirms this. Unlikely as it seems, the object, whatever it is, has no smell of the maison—or anything else. It is no wonder she overlooked it on all her previous visits.

That makes me like it less, not more, she thinks, and she casts it back into the snow. Joy moves quickly to retrieve it, but Lightning refuses. *Leave it,* she thinks. *We've had enough trouble.*

As she thinks this, a new sound comes to her ears, at first harmonizing with, then rising above the wind. It is a sound she has not heard in a long time, and a thrill races down her spine: the howling of a kezel band in the west. A moment later, Cliff hurries from his shelter, struggling through the snow as he limps toward them. He doesn't slow his pace until he reaches the mound.

Redtooth party! he thinks. *Old One Eye and his chief, plus others.* He looks back at the accrete and up to the sky, as if unsure which holds the greatest threat. *I've decided,* he thinks. *I'll come with you.*

The howling grows louder.

Not until that pack is secure, thinks Lightning. *Stop fussing with the straps!*

They were too tight.

Cliff fidgets as Lightning strives to fasten the wobbling pack in its place. She reads the shifting wind as she works, trying to gauge the distance of the Redtooth party. Thus occupied, she doesn't notice when Joy eases close to the mound, retrieves the black object from the snow—she is surprised by how heavy it is—and tucks it into her sling.

+ + +

Glancing up and behind, nose straining, Lightning leads them away from the mounded snow, following the southbound Tongue. The howls of the Redtooth party grow closer, rising eagerly. Still, Cliff refuses to move faster than a walk until Lightning orders them to freeze and another derka passes overhead, baffled by their camouflage. Once convinced they are in no danger of being plucked from the ground, he does his best to match Lightning's pace.

It is good that he does.

The next time he looks back to the accrete, now a thousand strides behind, movement near its apron tells a worrisome tale. First one, then three, and finally eight large shapes step from the shadows. Several rise to two legs, seeking news.

They don't need to see us, Cliff thinks to himself, and he hurries forward. *They know we're out here.*

To Lightning he thinks:

They're going to follow us, just watch.

Watch she does, turning a wary eye behind them even as she increases her pace. But the Redtooth hunters hold their position along the edge of the accrete. They seem to believe their mission accomplished, having driven the jabis onto the plains where nothing but a bad end can await. Or perhaps they suspect their quarry will try to re-enter the accrete farther to the east or west. Cliff imagines them wrangling with a plan as they spread out along the fringe. He loses sight of them soon after. But for another five hundred strides, their howling voices chase after, a sound that harries his imagination though it fades with each passing step.

Wrong again, Lightning thinks to him.

He trudges through the snow, his ears pinned back and his tail held low. Struggling to stay close, he aims fearful glances at the sky.

Sometimes, he thinks, *it's nice to be wrong.*

A.P. Malloy

+ + +

With two of them wearing grass mats like a caepod wears a shell, the companions follow the Tongue as it meanders south between snowy banks, matching the course of their enemies—though their trail is faint and often disappears altogether for hundreds of strides. Cliff's memory is their only guide as they march into the biting wind, but that memory is simple and clear: the blue creatures stayed near the river all the way to the horizon. What they did next, none of them can guess.

We'll find out soon enough, thinks Lightning.

They start out with Joy as a passenger, riding on Lightning's back for the first few thousand strides. But as the fear of howling Redteeth fades, she hops to the ground and makes her way on foot.

Thank you, thinks Lightning, glad to rest her legs.

I like to walk, thinks Joy, and she skips away, whistling in time. *The snow feels—*

She stops. She screams!

From out of the ground a probing, whiskered tentacle has emerged and wound itself around her ankle. It pulls her downward, as if trying to drag her beneath the snow and into the ground itself.

Ami-kan!

Lightning leaps snout first into the snow and chomps down on the whiskery tentacle. It has a taste like newly turned soil and someone's wet boots, but she hangs on and gives it a good shaking until it releases Joy's ankle and shoots back into the ground.

What in Weaver's name was that? asks Cliff, and his eyes dart side to side.

No idea. Lightning scowls as she runs her tongue over her teeth. The thing hadn't bled, but her mouth is filled with its grimy whiskers.

Will it come back? Joy wonders.

They stand expectantly, waiting to learn the answer. But their heartbeats have returned to normal, and Joy has rubbed away the blue welt on her ankle, and still there is no reappearance of the tentacle.

You taught it proper, thinks Joy.

Let's hope so, thinks Lightning, and she cleans away the foul taste with mouthfuls of snow.

Joy returns again to being a passenger, riding for several thousand strides until her fear diminishes. Then, longing to stretch her legs—and give Lightning's a rest—she climbs down and walks alongside. She treads nervously at first but relaxes as another thousand strides pass with no grasping tentacles.

Oh, look! How pretty, she thinks, noting the appearance of bell-shaped flowers several strides away. They appear related to everlasting skyrnak, but as she steps from Lightning's side and approaches the flowers, she notes at once they smell nothing like skyrnak.

Mmm...that is delightful, she thinks, bending low to get a good whiff. She picks a bouquet to bring to Lightning when—

Snatch!

Up darts a whiskery tentacle and wraps itself around her ankle, pulling frightfully hard.

Ami-kan! she shrieks, and bound, bound, pounce! Lightning arrives to give the tentacle its due. One hard bite and some serious shaking, and it retreats silently into the ground, quick as a blink.

Ri-stinking-diculous! thinks Lightning, spitting whiskers and gobbling snow. *Are you OK?*

Yes, it doesn't hurt. Joy rubs her ankle.

Ever heard of anything like that? Cliff wonders.

Yes, Lightning replies, scowling. *I'm an expert.*

Well. Do you think it smells us? Or hears us?

But why only me? Joy wants to know.

A good question, thinks Lightning. *And why only when you're not walking next to me?* She hands the cutter to Joy. *Looks like we've got a mystery to solve.*

It only takes a few thousand strides for the solution to present itself. As long as Joy stays close to the two kezel, she is left alone. But when she strays more than five strides away, slither and snatch, here comes trouble.

One good slash with the cutter is all it takes to free herself from the ferocious grip, but she retreats to Lightning's side, her heart racing.

That's enough of that! she thinks.

Smell, thinks Cliff. *Or sound. That's my bet.*

But Lightning has a different guess.

Pressure, she thinks. *Like a sneer. They can feel what's above them. Who knows? Maybe they're related.*

And what? We're too big?

Maybe. Joy walks next to me, and it feels like one big thing with six legs. She goes off on her own and...

Joy shudders, and her antennae go limp. Whatever the answer, from that moment on, she travels either on top of or directly beside Lightning, and though there are no more tentacles, she holds the cutter close.

+ + +

They cross thirty thousand strides in the first blustery stage of their journey, a monotonous affair now that the fright of clutching tentacles has passed. Though not a great distance for an able jabi, it puts Cliff to the test. Moons of malnutrition and the weight of the pack take their toll, and the rangy kezel often falls behind. He raises his weary head to watch Lightning's tail swinging side to side before him. It mocks him, marking a time he can't keep. And yet, even as Lightning chafes at his pace, her sore legs are grateful.

I'll be an ibiwa by the time we find them, she thinks, and she pauses to allow Cliff to catch up.

Hindering their progress is the need to stop every time they spot a derka. But beyond that is the deceptive nature of the terrain itself. In spite of their reputation as a flat place, Lightning soon discovers that when experienced up close, the snowy plains are everywhere pocked and lumpy. The tussocks of grass, bent by the wind, hide tangled roots beneath the snow, waiting to trip them up, and where they grow in quantity, the frozen soil is perforated by the entrances to small burrows. Whatever beasts live inside make guttural noises as they pass but do not show themselves.

Probably for the best, thinks Lightning, and her nose twitches. *If they taste as bad as they smell.*

They do encounter a remarkable type of creature, one that smells delicious. They have no name for these new additions, but their color and behavior make that easy enough: they are soon dubbed Yellow Hoppers. Lightning guesses they are related to cremlins, for they have round, flat bodies and long, springy legs sprouting in five different directions. They apparently don't expect a visit from kezel, for they are often caught unaware, sunning in the grass. But the element of surprise is no benefit. They are superlative leapers, springing a full two or three strides into the air, their direction random and different every time. Chasing them starts out as hope for a novel meal, but in time, it ends in frustration and wasted energy. Cliff curses like a professional as he guesses wrong and misses once again.

Fine! he thinks, scowling. *Hop on, you dirty turds. But I'll catch one of you yet!*

He never does.

For her part, Joy makes the passage largely in silence, her thoughts sheltered. But some time not long after she has lost count of the strides she has ridden—and walked—she becomes aware of something new, a tingling sensation, barely perceptible. At first, she thinks her stomach is calling for a meal, but she realizes the cause is not her, but what is in her sling. The artifact, up to now inert and forgotten, is generating a very faint signal. The feeling it creates is difficult to categorize. Later, thinking back, she describes it as the sense of being near a sleeper who has wakened. She peeks inside the sling, careful not to alert Lightning. The artifact appears as lifeless as always.

But the sensation continues.

So does their march, lumpy and rough, until, though it irritates her to do so, Lightning halts for their first real break since entering the plains, convinced that

Cliff will never catch up if she doesn't.

We're not resting long—a bite and a nap, she thinks to Joy, who climbs from her back, her skin turning from grass to snow.

+ + +

The second stage of their journey is no faster or less tedious than the first, and never once, as they follow the river over another thirty thousand bumpy strides, do the plains change their face. No matter how far they walk, they are eternally in the middle of a yellow-dotted sheet of white stretching out as far as they can see in every direction. Ancian had always claimed there were fewer derkas now than in the time of keel, and she had given the Moondwellers credit for this. But if so, how awful that world must have been. For the three travelers encounter all the derkas they care to, and the farther they go, the worse each sighting feels—though as long as they remain motionless when the creatures appear, they continue to sail across the sky blind to their presence. Once, to Cliff's great terror, a derka descends southeast of them like an emerald bolt and snatches something from the ground, raising a cloud of snow. It has retaken the sky before a faint scream reaches their ears.

Ooh...what was it? Joy asks.

But Lightning has no answer.

Doesn't matter. Cliff shudders and looks away. *It's derka food now.* He struggles to adjust his camouflage. *How I hate this place!*

And no one can disagree.

Still, in spite of the many demands on her attention, Joy has become preoccupied. The artifact, since its waking, has continued to generate the faintest of signals, though she appears to be the only one who senses it. In fact, she believes it is no longer simply awake, she believes it is now aware, as if it knows she is there and is somehow glad. Although she recognizes how silly this is, as the plains unfold stride after stride, she begins to think of it as another member of their party, and she traces her finger across its smooth face, taking comfort in its presence, heavy and hard against her side.

But her companions have no such comfort. They are drawing near the limit of their aching legs—and their patience with this never-ending landscape. Worse yet is the uncertainty that grows each time signs of their quarry vanish beneath the drifted snow. Hundreds of strides might pass before one of them picks up the trail again, and during the interim, they imagine the worst. Perhaps their enemies have moved off to the west, or even crossed the river. How would they know? But time and again, when they relocate the trail, they find it continues adjacent to the Tongue, as if mocking them for their doubt. This is why, when the river suddenly angles to the southeast, they at first assume they must do the same. But a faint scent like a beckoning finger tickles Lightning's nose, and she turns due south instead.

Hey, thinks Cliff. *Where are you going? You're never going to catch one of those hoppers.*

But that is not Lightning's goal. A hundred strides west of the river, buried in the snow, she finds something much better than a fresh meal: she finds a Sugarfoot glove, filthy but unmistakable. One good sniff and she knows beyond doubt it belongs to her amoti Pounce.

Good smelling, thinks Joy.

Lucky, thinks Cliff.

But the credit goes to Pounce—or whoever had the wits cast away the glove. For by doing so, they have told a clear tale. At least one of their clan is still alive, and their enemies have continued due south, no matter what the Tongue is doing.

Cracking crystals, thinks Lightning, and she stows the glove in her vest, praying she will have the chance to return it. *I would have stayed with the river. Who knows how far off course we would have gone?*

But their gratitude is tempered, for while they redirect their pursuit to the south, the River Tongue stubbornly continues moving southeast, and it isn't long before it abandons them altogether, disappearing to their left. Without its homey chatter, the plains become an even more lonely place, with the guttural warning of burrowing animals the only competition for the wind. Lightning and Cliff squint as they march into the sun, unhappy at its brightness, Weaver or no. Only Joy seems pleased by the light, and she stares at the pale fire, her lidless eyes glittering. She buzzes in a low, conversational murmur, as if to a friend.

They have traveled another five thousand strides, when, to the southeast, rising above the horizon like a mountain range of light, Father Blue, the Api-kan, comes into view, regal and stern. He is soon joined by a billowing train of heavy, gray clouds.

This will have to do, thinks Lightning to Joy. *We're not going to find anywhere better to make shelter, and you're going to fall over before that storm gets here.*

Joy buzzes a sleepy tune, her antennae drooping. *I'm hungry,* she thinks.

Yes, Lightning replies. *When our baggage gets here, we can eat.* She looks back at Cliff, who has fallen behind again. His head hangs low, and each step-STEPstep of his uneven stride appears slower than the one before. He doesn't bother to greet them with an insult or a complaint when he arrives. Instead, he flops down in a heap, disregarding them as they tug the pack from his shoulders. Lightning tosses him a portion of awl which he consumes without rising from the snow.

Tiny flashes of electricity dance along the horizon.

Let's go, thinks Lightning. *We have holes to dig.*

+ + +

They determine the east side of the trail to be the least exposed location, and Lightning puts her claws to work, throwing snowy dirt in a brown arc. The grass mat shifts awkwardly, but she doesn't dare remove it. Despite the encumbrance, she makes good progress, for the sun touches this land in a way not allowed in the accrete. After penetrating the frosty surface, she finds soil that is sticky and dense but not frozen.

Cliff! she thinks. *Start digging!*

He rises to weary feet and grumbles.

Why?

You want to sleep on the surface?

No. I mean why dig two holes? I'm no threat.

Lightning hasn't the energy to ridicule this idea.

Dig or die. You're not sleeping with us.

Cliff chooses the former. Few creatures on Aranae can dig like a motivated kezel, and once they settle into their rhythm, the jabis excavate their weight in soil every few hundred heartbeats. Panting with the effort, they have soon burrowed out of the sunlight. At this point, they slake their thirst with snow and remove their camouflage, returning to their work as Joy stands watch. Whether frightened by the digging or too far from their riverside habitat, the whiskery tentacles make no appearance. Eventually, the holes are widened until there is room for two in Lightning's and one in Cliff's, who collapses inside soon after, sinking into deep slumber.

+ + +

But before he does, and while Lightning attends to her own labor, Joy sits surreptitiously caressing the artifact—and thinking to it.

She doesn't expect a response, and so is not disappointed when she doesn't get one. But her thoughts do seem to have some effect. The device's signal strengthens, just a bit, and it is joined by a new sensation, one Joy feels not in her gut but in her head. It is as if she had, to that point, been sensing the thoughts of the kezel filtered through snow which the device has somehow melted away. Lightning's mind has always been open to her, but now it is laid bare in bright detail, each worry, malediction, and hope as clear as if they were her own. This, maybe, she could have overlooked, but the device has a similar effect on Cliff, someone whose mind is new to her and often veiled in secrecy. Now, it seems as familiar to her as her old dow coat, its thoughts easy to read whether sheltered or not.

Not silly at all, she thinks, running her fingers across the artifact. But she quickly removes her hand and adopts a neutral posture when Lightning finishes her work. Thickening clouds cast a pall over the land.

I'm going to stand a watch, the jabi kezel thinks, and she shakes the dirt from her spikes.

Are you not tired?

I'm exhausted. But I need to think. Don't worry, she adds. *I'll be in soon.*

Joy needs no persuasion. She crawls into their hole, clicking quiet and slow as she disappears underground. Moments later, she has fallen asleep.

+ + +

Lightning keeps a cautious nose to the rising wind and replaces the camouflage across her back as she begins her patrol, keeping both holes in sight while she explores. In the face of the coming storm, derkas have abandoned the sky, returning, she supposes, to their home in the northern mountains. This reminds her of the bombas, and she sighs.

I keep saying "I'm sorry" for things, she thinks.

Her patrol reveals nothing threatening outside of the storm. She can smell no signs of the six-legged creatures aside from their old trail, and notices no other life forms, burrowing, hopping, or otherwise. Whatever else lives on the plains has found shelter long ago. Before taking their cue, Lightning allows herself to sit musa, hunkered inside the mouth of their hole. As usual, her effort meets with mixed results, as her mind wanders. She removes the thrower from her belt, unsurprised to find that its parts remain frozen in place.

She curses it.

Not going be much use against those blue things anyway, she consoles herself, and she tucks the weapon away. *Not if I can't see 'em and they're traveling in numbers like Cliff says. But if a derka came calling... Mmm, I'd show it something!*

The pleasant thought of downing a mighty derka has a seductive lure. Sitting musa turns into simple daydreaming, and the jabi kezel loses focus. Her snout dips, and her eyes close. When she jolts awake, the plains have begun to glow a sickly blue, as the Api-kan moon begins eating the sun.

Had she heard something?

Had she seen something move?

She rises to four limbs, stretching cramped legs and peering from the ground to the sky.

One more sweep, she thinks.

But the wind disagrees, its tune becoming discordant, and icy snow appears, sudden and chaotic, as if uncertain which way it should fall. Seeing no time to be lost, Lightning foregoes her survey and takes shelter.

+ + +

When Joy wakes, Lightning is wrapped around her, snoring in the darkness. She extracts herself from the embrace and exits the hole, taking her sling and the cutter. Lightning remains asleep, eyelids twitching.

Tunneling through the snow, Joy steps outside to find the storm has passed—though the wind continues its noisy tale, speaking of all the places it's been. Her skin turns to white, and her eyes welcome the sun, if not the land it reveals. Featureless, flat plains stretch as far as she can see, bright, blinding white that ends at the horizons and the blue of the sky. The snow is not deep as much as heavy, and the driving wind has bent and covered every blade beneath it.

She clicks quiet disapproval.

The maison's plateau had been open like this, but it had not been so hostile and exposed for so many uncountable strides. Whatever type of creature she may have been by birth, Joy is kezel by upbringing; this shelterless expanse disturbs her.

Still, the sky is free for the moment of clouds and derkas, allowing her to stare at the low-riding sun and relish its warmth. Already the snow has begun to melt, softening the face of the plains. Buzzing idly, she moves away from the entrance to relieve herself, downwind and several dozen strides away, her unshod feet oblivious to the cold. Many thoughts jostle in her mind as she squats to do her business, from the fate of the bombas to the nature of her existence.

I am a kezel, she thinks. *Despite how I look.*

But Cliff's revelation of the six-legged creatures, a blue swarm of them when they weren't camouflaged, with large black eyes and antennae, worries at her. Are these the scion bombas had been so reluctant to discuss? She hopes she is not related to them, as they sound horrible, but the coincidence is too great to ignore. Would she be able to understand them if given the chance? Would they recognize her? She tugs and twists at her hair.

They are Ami-kan's enemy, she thinks, arriving at a simple conclusion. *They are my enemy.*

And she completes her task, using snow to cover the signs. Staying to the downwind side of their holes, she finds a spot where the sun has exposed yellow turf. Thinking to take her mind off the bombas and the strange blue creatures—and trying to suppress the guilt she feels at her disobedience—she removes the artifact from her sling, flat, rectangular, and surprisingly heavy. She rubs its smooth, dark faces, cleaning away awl grease and the last bit of dirt and snow. It is harder and more dense than stone, but in spite of its weight, its feel is seductive, as if it likes to be touched and wants to be held. Its fit in her grasp is familiar and pleasant, natural as breathing.

She raps it with her knuckles.

Do something, she thinks.

But the object remains unresponsive, its signal so faint it could have been her imagination. She turns it over in her hands, examining both sides, the facets of her eyes reflecting tiny ebony rectangles. Both faces are identical, swallowing light and refusing to mirror her image. In search of a clue, she runs her fingers along its perfect edges, feels its exact corners, and smells for a scent that doesn't exist. She finds nothing useful.

You can't fool me, she thinks, bending her antennae forward. *You must do something.*

But if the object has a secret, it does not share.

Whistling disappointment, Joy returns her attention to the sun. She intends to place the artifact in her sling, but she senses—or imagines she does—that it prefers to be allowed out. So, she places the cutter in the snow at her side and holds the artifact on her lap. Together they bathe in the light. Of all the things she finds odious about the plains, its exposure to unbroken sun is nearly redemption. She clicks a quiet, steady rhythm, and her antennae wave listlessly. As she sits, her heartbeat slows, her breathing grows relaxed, and the sparkle dims in her eyes. She thinks: *Stay awake,* one time before falling fast asleep.

Almost at once, she plunges into dreams of strange voices and blue creatures with six legs. She imagines smells both foreign and familiar, and a restive jumble of someone else's perplexing thoughts.

And as she dreams, the object begins to glow.

+ + +

The dozen six-legged creatures, each as large as Joy, who creep toward her from downwind, are impossible to see aside from shadows, the sparkle in their eyes, and tracks zig-zagging across the snow. Silent and stealthy, six of them fan out in a wide arc, surrounding her as she sleeps unaware. Three others move to Lightning's sleeping hole, and three to Cliff's. Both latter groups bear between them broad swaths of a translucent, woven substance, which they lay across the openings. This done, they re-join their companions.

Joy stirs. A strange smell disturbs her sleep.

Just as a tiny spark rekindles in her eyes, the six-legged creatures attack. They grip her with strong, bristly pincers and bind her with webbing extruded from their mid-sections, covering her mouth before she can scream. She thrashes and kicks to no effect.

Ami-kan! she thinks. *Help!*

But one of her attackers bites her on the back of the neck, and a sudden numbness spreads from there to the rest of her body. She attempts a second warning, but her mind has turned to mush, and her muscles refuse to obey. Her captors scurry across the snow, back the way they came, bearing Joy, her sling, and the artifact they have torn from her grasp.

But they overlook the cutter, hidden in the snow.

+ + +

Curled in a spiky ball, Lightning twitches and grumbles as a vague warning intrudes on her sleep. She reaches out to pull Joy close, grasping empty space. Her eyes blink open, but it is her nose that tells her Joy is gone, along with her sling.

Growling, she rises to her feet and hurries from the hole—and into the invisible sheet lain across the opening. She is soon entangled beyond hope, falling to the ground in a sticky, snowy mess. Her fury is as terrible as it is futile. The more she struggles, the worse her situation becomes, until she lies helpless, arms stuck to her sides, her face half buried in the snow. Heaving mightily, she rolls over, struggling to look to the south. Joy's scent rides the wind, moving away—or being moved, by the creatures whose scent fuels Lightning's rage.

Joy! she thinks, *I'm coming for you!* She looks to the second hole. *Cliff!* she thinks frantically. *There's a trap across your entrance!* Afraid that his slumber might exceed the reach of mere thought, she calls out in desperate, howling cries.

But Cliff does not respond.

Moments later, three hundred strides away, Joy's captors become visible, like a pool of the bluest water.

They move south toward a small hill jutting above the snow. Lightning registers numb surprise when the hill rises onto four massive legs like pillars, shaking snow and grass from itself in an awesome spray. Covered in plated armor and trailing a club-tipped tail, the beast is many times larger than a babelrack, with a viper's nest of orange tentacles sprouting from its head. But fierce as it seems, the giant thing bows to the blue creatures who clamber aboard its bony prominences. It makes a dreadful, ululating call then lumbers away to the south. Long after it passes from sight, the drumbeat of its stride jeers at Lightning through the ground.

Joy! She calls out again. *I'm right behind you!* And then: *Cliff! Wake up! Cliff!*

+ + +

But Cliff is not sleeping. He is far out of thought range when the blue creatures attack, limping step-STEP-step through the snow under cover of his fraying camouflage. North is his direction, the accrete his goal.

Enough, he thinks, *is enough.*

When he had awakened earlier to find the storm passing and both Lightning and Joy asleep in their hole, the notion of slipping away had sprung to his mind unbidden and sorely tempting. His courage, never abundant at the best of times, had been ready for this decision thousands of strides ago. It was only waiting on his irrational fancy for Lightning to succumb to reason. The sight of the animal being taken by a derka is what had done it; the horrific sound will be forever scored in his memory. The opportunity to flee without the shame of explaining himself had been too much to refuse. He had acted without a second thought. Now, plodding along, he attempts to soothe his guilt, marshaling excuses.

I did everything I could, he thinks. *I told her: an impossible cause...suicide!* He shakes his head. *I'm not getting eaten by a derka, not even for her.*

He imagines the security of the accrete, now that

the Redtooth party has surely given up hope of their return and moved on to other parts of the range.

Security, sure, but loneliness, too, he has to admit. *Still, better lonely than dead.*

Hunger reminds him that hunting solo all these moons has been tough go. But Pride has a quick retort:

Being awl bait isn't so wonderful either.

And yet, his head sags, and he pauses for a moment, making as if to tighten his camouflage straps. He looks back to the south. What was that sound? The sleeping holes are already out of sight, but beyond them, at the limit of his vision...

He squints, doubting what he sees.

A mote, a tiny, four-legged dot in motion, appears for a moment near the southern horizon. To be visible from this distance it must be enormous, but in spite of its size, it moves very fast, away from the holes, and it soon disappears. Cliff scowls.

What do you suppose that was? he wonders.

Fear has a ready answer.

Another reason to go home, it thinks.

But some other part of him isn't so sure.

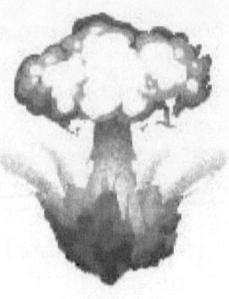

CHAPTER FOUR
River

BOUND AND HELPLESS, Joy floats in a venomous haze teetering near the brink of unconsciousness.

The world flies by on either side, yellow bleeding into white, and the wind howls in her ears. But louder still are massive, thundering feet, hard as stone, hammering a ceaseless rhythm against the ground. The beast smells worse than rotten awl, and its jarring gait churns her guts. They travel for thousands of its giant strides as she wavers on the edge of torpor, a foggy condition that is immobilizing but not anesthetic. By the time they stop moving, her last meal has found its way out and her head pounds though the monster's feet are still.

Her captors bear her to the ground, where she lies quivering in ropes of pale, sticky webbing. The world around her seems to continue moving, and the smell of strange creatures and the bewildering sense of their foreign thoughts assails her from every direction. The sensation is too much to bear, and she slips into blackness, the spark fading from her eyes.

+ + +

When she wakes, she finds herself lying on the ground in a small, gloomy hole. Most of the webbing has been removed, but she remains bound at the wrists and ankles. The hole is no more than five strides across and dark but for the light passing through its lone entrance, a small, rough circle. Menacing shadows crawl across the far walls when her captors walk in front of this opening. They are thinking to one another, that much is clear, but Joy can make no sense of their thoughts.

Gradually, the effects of the poison fade, and they are replaced by a growing claustrophobia approaching panic. Her breath comes rapid and shallow, and cold hands of fear clutch her heart. As she feels a whistling shriek rising inside, the memory of Lightning comes to mind, along with a fragment of her inherited wisdom:

Breathe calm, is the thought, *smell calm.*

Imagining the jabi kezel's advice provides some comfort. She will not let enemies smell her fear. So thinking, she breathes deep and exhales, holding for a time before repeating, again—and again.

Musa, she thinks. *Not useless after all.*

In this way, she masters her emotions, her mind slowly clearing of poison and the cloud of fear. When these two beasts have been tamed, she manages to sit up, stretching her arms and legs and appraising her situation. Though she is sore and sick, she doesn't appear to have suffered any permanent damage. The bite at the base of her neck throbs, but she can move her head with less pain than before, and the worst of the nausea has passed. She can see neither her sling nor the artifact, and there is no scent of kezel.

If Lightning is free, she thinks, *they will regret it.*

But perhaps she and Cliff have been captured as well and are being held downwind. This thought threatens Joy's fragile calm, so she turns her attention elsewhere, trying to sense the thoughts of those who pass outside. As she recovers, their ideas coalesce into lucid notions. Her captors are skilled at sheltering their thoughts, but she catches a word here and a phrase there. Some of the creatures appear to be referring to her, but their intent is unclear. Still, now she has something to work on; if she attends carefully, she might learn some useful information.

Can't keep secrets forever, she thinks, imagining the curse Lightning would choose. She strains to muster a few drops of urine. *Please, someone smell that.*

Just then, three of her captors enter the hole, each as large as she, walking six-legged and blocking the sun. Their antennae quiver in a way Joy senses as much with her mind as her eyes—eyes that sparkle just as theirs do. When the largest of them reaches for her, she doesn't try to avoid it. Instead, she allows it to grasp her, pulling her to her feet. Then, using its momentum against it, she swings around behind it and throws her arms around its neck as if offering a hug. Whistling rage, she hurls her weight sideways and twists. A terrible cracking sound follows, and the creature's body falls slack. Joy half hops, half falls onto a second enemy, bloodying her elbows as she drives it to the ground. It shrieks in pain, but its remaining companion leaps on her back, and its fangs sink into her shoulder.

Numbness precedes cold, and darkness follows.

+ + +

More thundering, jarring strides, more howling wind—but the blur of color now changes to infinite yellow. They have moved to a land beyond the reach of snow, a waving sea of grass.

Joy has no idea how far they travel in this second stage, but when she wakes from the sickening motion, she finds herself lying in the center of a much larger hole, this one dozens of strides across. Sunlight shines through three entrances, the brightest of which faces south. She smells water but hears neither babble nor fall. Though her cramping muscles yearn to stretch, she is bound and gagged with vengeance; the only way she is going to move is if someone carries her.

They fear me now, she thinks, but she is in no condition to be comforted by the thought. Her poor stomach has been so badly joggled she can't even think about

A.P. Malloy

food, but oh! what she wouldn't do for some water. Worse yet is the second bite, two small punctures on her left shoulder. It spreads heat and pain from the tips of her fingers to the top of her head.

As she lies helpless, blue creatures singly and in pairs take turns peeking into the hole, casting hideous shadows as they stare through glittering eyes. They never step inside, and they don't stay long, but their surprise and wonder are unmistakable. As one group turns away to be replaced by others, emotion overwhelms care, and they forget to shelter their thoughts. Joy does not like what she senses.

Blue! Scion!

No. It walks on two legs. It is vumierre.

No! See the antennae. Scion!

Yes! See them. Scion! What else?

No. See the limbs. Two and two. Vumierre.

Yes, see them. And see the ends. Wrong for scion.

Yes. Wrong. But see the eyes. Correct for scion.

Yes. Correct. But see the head!

Yes. See it. The head is most wrong for scion.

Yes, most wrong. And see the hair!

Yes. Like black grass.

Yes. Growing in the wrong place. Vumierre style.

Yes. And smell it.

No. It disgusts. It is a deformity.

Yes. It repels.

It killed Seven Hundred Twelve.

Yes. It is a murderer.

And they buzz a harmony of threat.

On and on this continues, until either everyone who cares has seen her, or the novelty has faded. Whatever the reason, Joy receives no more visitors for a long time, left alone with nothing to distract her from thirst and the pain of bite and bonds. When she thinks that only unconsciousness will ease her suffering, two of the creatures enter the hole, their legs bristled and their steps confident. They are followed by a third. The first two defer to this new arrival. They step aside, antennae bent low. The new creature is very old; Joy can see this at once. Time has faded its blue skin to gray, its eyes are lit but do not sparkle, and one of its antennae is missing. As it draws near, it walks with an awkward, stuttering limp in its four back legs.

In its front two, it carries her artifact.

Joy's heartbeat quickens, and she tries to dispel the fog in her mind. She needs clear thinking; she needs a strategy. But at the moment, she is simply afraid.

The old creature stops just out of reach, gazing at her as it makes a faint whistling sound whose meaning is unclear. If it thinks to itself or the others, Joy is unable to sense; its mind is sealed tight. Its attendants, however, are more transparent, and their thoughts are rife with hopeful speculation.

The profit is theirs, yes, Old Magister?

Yes. The profit. They found it.

Yes, Old Magister. They found it and brought it.

They buzz in harmony, apparently pleased with themselves. But the creature they address as Old Magister clicks bitter disapproval. It doesn't bother to shelter its thoughts when it replies.

Did they transport it this way? Uncovered for the entire hive to see?

The attendants rub raspy forelimbs together.

Old Magister did not say it was a secret.

No, he did not.

He said haste was the priority.

Yes. And avoiding the spiky ones—the sharksha.

Yes. There were two sharksha.

Yes. With large teeth. And claws.

They should have brought the sharksha as well! thinks Old Magister. *Fools. What were they thinking?*

But they were only twelve.

Yes, Old Magister. Such a small number.

Old Magister is dissatisfied? He is displeased?

He is very displeased! Have they no wits? Clear the hole! And the gray creature waves the artifact in dismissal. The attendants do not need a second order. Their antennae bending low, they turn and scurry away.

Old Magister stares at Joy after they have gone, the facets of his eyes cloudy. He limps around her out of reach, and he shelters dark thoughts. As she struggles to sit upright, her captor's lone antenna twitches.

Can it understand him? He buzzes a low note. *Does it know who he is?*

Joy considers responding, but perhaps there is an advantage in feigned ignorance. She will let the old one do the thinking and keep the hope of surprise alive. As well as fear and pain allow, she imagines all the inert things she can, things dense and unreadable. Her mind goes to deep water and dark holes, rocks and frozen soil. But Old Magister has survived many storms and is wily and skilled, as strong in mind as he is weak in body. His thoughts probe like grasping fingers.

He can tell it is scared. Why else stay camou-flaged? Tell him what kind of a creature it is, and what business it has, and he will release it. But his thoughts are like an eclipse, and when he adds, *There is nothing to be afraid of,* Joy knows he is lying.

She thinks about ice and piles of dead grass.

It was traveling with sharksha, Old Magister thinks. *How? For what reason?*

Snow, wet and thick.

The bottomless black of the nacht.

Old Magister stops his limping circle. He holds the artifact for her to see.

What is it? His soldiers say it was looking at the object before they took it prisoner. They say a glowing light came out of it. What purpose does it serve?

Derka droppings.

Awl bones.

Fallen feathers, gathered in dust.

The probing fingers in her mind grow to claws as Old Magister mines for her secrets. His eyes brighten to a brief sparkle, and without warning, he steps forward and strikes her across the face with the artifact. Pain blinds her for a moment, and her ears ring—but the blood on her lip tastes like a victory. She thinks about the high, lonely wind on the upper plateau, and the maison, gray, cold, and unreadable.

Old Magister clicks a slow rhythm.

Stubborn? he thinks. *Not for long.* He waves the artifact at her. *It will tell him what he wants to know, or hunger and thirst will be its end.*

His lone antenna bending with the effort, he makes a last attempt on her mind. When that fails, Joy feels certain he will strike her again. Instead, the gray creature grows cold, his rage extinguished. He watches blue blood run from the corner of her mouth, then turns and limps from the hole. Joy is left alone and remains that way until sleep claims her.

+ + +

When she wakes, the gnawing complaint of her stomach tells her that much time has passed.

Her eyes sparkle to life as six of the blue scion enter the hole, approaching with great care. Two carry an opaque sheet, woven from something similar to what binds her, though not adhesive. Another carries a long, slender shaft, pointed at each end. This the creature lowers at her. While its partners prevent her from resisting, it slides the pole through loopholes in the bindings around her hands and feet. Four of the creatures hoist her between them, two at each end of the pole, and there she dangles in the middle. The others drape the sheet over her, buzzing satisfaction.

Their treasure hidden, they bear her away.

She is carried out onto the plains, where the wind greets her with the smell of exotic beasts. But she can see only hazy sunlight through the shroud and a parade of yellow grass beneath her. The bindings eat into her wrists and ankles, and her captors take little care in providing a smooth ride—but they don't travel far. Soon, Joy hears a strident, ululating call. She doesn't need to see its maker to know its form; she will never forget that horrible sound. Does this mean another move?

She cranes her neck to look at the ground, and sudden inspiration strikes. Ignoring the pain it causes, she throws her weight to one side. Caught off guard, her captors lose their grip, and she is dropped to the yellow turf, tangled in the woven sheet. The scion whistle angrily as they scramble to regain control. One opens its beaky mouth, exposing a pair of fangs.

No! thinks another, its thought so clear and unguarded Joy could have sensed it from twenty strides. *It already has two bites!*

Yes, thinks a third. *Not to have any more!*

No more, others concur. *Old Magister's orders.*

Yes, thinks the first, regaining its composure and closing its mouth. *Very clear.*

And so, the creatures settle for subduing her with their pincers. This is more difficult than expected. Joy thrashes wildly, for a moment escaping the shroud and glimpsing the world around her. A bustle of six-legged creatures, several of the giant carrying beasts, and the serpentine course of a mighty river are all she sees before the sheet is returned and she is hoisted aloft.

But she is not disappointed. Escape had never been the plan. Had her captors been more observant and less worried about concealing her, they might have noticed the small, sharp rock she hides in her clenched hands, one of many littering the plains.

+ + +

The final leg of their trek is downhill, and Joy's captors, instead of bearing her between them in single file, must walk abreast to keep her from slipping forward on the pole. When the wind allows, she can hear their buzzing and clicking. That it reminds her of herself makes them more repellent, not less.

Soon, the scent of fresh, flowing water grows, joined by the sound of splashing. Several strides later, they pass from the yellow turf onto a hardened surface of grainy brown. Pincers clatter as Joy is borne to a place hidden from sun and wind. Her captors drop her to the floor where she lands with a painful thud. One of them removes the shroud, the other, the carrying pole from its loopholes. The only light comes from a small opening which her captors seal behind them upon exiting. Any thoughts they have remain sheltered.

And there she lies, alone in darkness.

She retches at the scent. Damp and fetid, the floor seems to have been soaked for ages in filth. Its stink overwhelms all other smells. She struggles to sit up, her antennae bending forward in the dark. The slap of water against a hard surface keeps a regular tempo, and the room bobs lazily side to side. Lingering in the distance, the muted sounds of her enemies can be heard, but aside from that, her ears tell her nothing.

Unless...

Something in the dark inhales, its colossal, rumbling sigh warm like fermented grass. Joy squirms and wriggles to back away but meets a solid wall; she has nowhere to go. Straining to see a hint of motion, she hears a heavy shifting sound, and then a settling of weight, as if a giant sleeper rolls over and resumes slumber—or has wakened and sits staring at her in the dark.

A fresh wave of its stench wafts her way.

Joy clutches her rock and holds her breath. Her antennae lean into the blackness, seeking answers, and every nerve in her body sings as she braces to be pounced upon. And yet, nothing happens. Taking great care, she reaches out with her mind, probing for a readable sentience. The results are puzzling, and she doubts what her mind tells her. Thoughts are indeed brewing in the darkness, deep and slow, and the mind that thinks them has a peculiar quality, one she can't fathom. Then, sudden and dreadful understanding:

She faces not one, but *two* alien creatures.

They debate with one another in the dark, and she is the subject of their discussion. Her gag prevents her from biting, not making sounds, and she begins nervously clicking, quiet but rapid, certain that at any moment two hungry terrors will rush out of the dark, evils she will hear, smell, and feel, but never see.

Mmm...hunter? the first mind thinks.

Mmm...no, the second mind replies. *Kezel.*

Not kezel, the first mind is certain. *Smell some kezel, mmm...but not kezel. Smell more hunter.*

Smell more hunter, mmm... the second mind agrees. *But not smell* all *hunter.*

Mmm...but sound hunter, the first mind is quick to point out. *"Click, click, click."*

The second mind pauses to consider this.

Mmm...

Joy forces herself to stop clicking. She hunkers, taut and attentive. If this is how she is to meet her end, she will do so in a brave fashion. The first one to make a move will receive a sharp rock for its trouble. Still, they do not attack.

The second mind arrives at an answer.

Mmm...sound hunter, it concurs. *Smell hunter too. But not hunter. Smell kezel too. But not kezel. Smell something else. Smell...mmm...different.*

Mmm...smell strange, its companion agrees.

Joy can stand the tension no longer.

Better strange than revolting! she thinks.

The creatures' response to this is immediate and explosive. Whatever they are, they stomp and snort in the dark, clattering and thumping as they call out surprised exclamations like a hundred horned dows all blowing at once. Hot breath and spittle reach her in equal amounts, and the more they move the worse they smell.

Mmm...not hunter! thinks the first mind.

Mmm...not kezel! its companion adds. *Thinker!*

The amazed creatures settle their commotion; Joy imagines them staring at her, contemplating. The second mind reaches out, as if fearing duplicity.

Thinker? it asks. *Mmm...not smell Thinker.*

I'm sorry to disappoint, she replies, buzzing.

Mmm...sound hunter, the first mind thinks. *Smell*

some hunter, too.

Also smell some kezel, the second mind adds. *And smell strange. Mmm...smell three things.*

I am a kezel, thinks Joy, clenching her rock.

Mmm...smell some kezel, the first mind concedes.

Mmm...but not kezel, thinks the second.

Then approach! thinks Joy, clicking, though she hadn't meant to. *And learn your mistake!*

The creatures do not accept her invitation.

From outside their cell, many piercing whistles become audible and the muted thoughts of the scion call to one another. As if responding to this signal, the floor shifts beneath her, and Joy has the disquieting sensation of ponderous motion.

Now what? she wonders, but she guesses the answer in a heartbeat: they are moving on the river.

+ + + + + +

Many thousands of strides to the north, Lightning attempts to nibble a hole in the sticky webbing that binds her. But her snout is wrapped nearly shut, and the angle is awkward. The portion she can get her teeth on resists, its stubbornness infuriating. She pauses to call once again for Cliff, her frantic thoughts cast as far as her mind is able. She howls in wrath but receives no reply.

Worthless, shameful coward!

Her eyes sweep from side to side in increasing desperation. Not far from her, she spies a corner of stone peeking above the melting snow. And to its side, half-buried in the snow, something gleams.

Her cutter!

She rolls like a fallen accrete, face down, face up, face down again, until she has reached the outcropping. Hoping to free her hands and so use the cutter, she scrapes the webbing across the stony teeth, grim and persistent. She has liberated two fingers when the clear sky betrays her. A speck of green floats high above. She blinks and squints. The speck is no illusion; it soars with purpose, tracing a huge, emerald circle. She presses up against the outcropping and remains motionless. Will the webbing hide her in the snow? Should she attempt to roll back to the sleeping hole?

No, a mind thinks to her.

Lightning struggles to turn her head. Creeping awkwardly toward her from the north is Cliff, covered in yellow and looking to the sky.

Where have you been? she thinks. *Didn't you hear me? Grab the cutter! Pull me to the hole!*

Working on it, thinks Cliff as he holds the cutter between his teeth and grips the webbing at Lightning's nape, dragging her across the snowy ground, scraping and sliding on her back. She looks to where the derka has begun to spiral downward.

Not to add pressure, she thinks, *but it sees us.*

Cliff slips and stumbles, surprised and distressed at how heavy Lightning is.

Blasted sun! he curses as he squints. *How does anyone live in this light?*

Pay attention! The holes are close. Don't fall in!

Groaning and panting, Cliff pulls Lightning the final few strides, backing into the larger of the two holes and tugging her after—almost.

Straighten your legs! he thinks. *You're too wide!*

If I could straighten my legs, I would!

Cliff renews his grip, digging in and leaning back. A final heave pulls Lightning into the hole, filthy and enraged. A shadow sweeps across the opening. For a heartbeat, the sun is blocked from view then reappears, and as it does, a gust of wind blows snow into the hole along with the sound of a massive object in flight. A harsh, deafening cry is accompanied by a foul smell that lingers after the sound is gone. The snow settles. The smell fades. Soon, they can hear only their own breathing and the perpetual complaint of the wind.

Will it come back? asks Cliff. *Will it try to get in?*

Derkas don't land on the ground, rockhead. They need mountains or accrete. Hurry up! Free my hands.

Book of Dreams

But Cliff does not obey at first.

You're welcome, he thinks.

For what? is Lightning's bitter reply. *They took Joy! Where were you then? Running back to the accrete, I suppose. Start cutting, coward!*

I was exploring! I thought I sensed trouble. And it's a good thing I did, or we'd both be trapped.

More cutting, less lying!

Cliff shelters his thoughts and does as instructed. He must take pains to avoid injuring Lightning, as she squirms impatiently and the webbing is wiry and tough. The moment she is able, she reclaims the weapon. Against its bright edge in the hands of an experienced user, the bindings have no defense, and she is soon free, though strands of webbing continue to cling to her vest and mat her spikes.

Next time you go "exploring," she thinks, *see if you can find your honor.* She secures the contents of her vest, gulping some awl from Gami-kan's pack. The smallest piece she gives to Cliff. *It's twice as much as you deserve.* She covers herself with her grass mat, tying it in place, her fingers anxious and trembling. Cliff's ears pin back, but he accepts the food, snap and swallow. He follows her outside, his eyes drawn to the sky.

I suppose you're going to follow them, he thinks, though he already knows the answer. Lightning doesn't waste energy on a response. She checks that the pack is securely closed and lifts it to her shoulders, fastening its straps and plucking troublesome webbing from around her eyes and ears.

Cliff wrinkles his snout.

Any chance you have a plan?

A plan? Lightning squints at the cloudless sky. The next derka passes without incident. *Obviously. Catch and rescue. Kill if necessary. What other plan is there?* She adjusts her mask. *Keep up!*

+ + +

The trail is unmistakable and unerring. It moves due south, using the way taken by the captive kezel moons ago. For twenty thousand strides, the pursuers travel sharing few thoughts. Lightning ignores most of Cliff's attempts at conversation, and he makes fewer of these, forced to concentrate on maintaining her pace.

It travels fast for how big it is, he thinks as he limps through the melting snow.

It travels fast, thinks Lightning, *but it leaves a trail a blind wabi could follow. It can't run forever. Keep your nose down and your eyes up!*

Twenty thousand strides grows to thirty, at a pace Cliff hadn't believed himself capable of. They alert one another at the sight of derkas—too many, for either's taste—but are seen by none, pressing on long after hunger and fatigue have come to call. Cliff tries to fill his belly with wet snow, but there is less of this with each stride, and soon, patches of yellow turf show through the white. His tongue wags as he marches.

Are we going downhill? he asks.

Yes.

Is it getting warmer?

Yes.

Still, their quarry shows no signs of slowing. It has made good use of its head start, and Lightning believes it is farther away now than ever. She looks back, growling frustration; Cliff has fallen far behind. As she considers a respite, her impatience simmering, she catches scent of Joy. The sign is not a vague hint woven in with the smell of their enemies, but concentrated, localized, and close at hand: urine—and blood. She hurries toward the source, off the trail and to the west. A hundred strides away, she discovers a network of holes, constructed with skill and connected by narrow tunnels. These are too small for her to enter, but she can smell Joy has been inside and stayed for a time before being moved again.

And injured, she thinks, mad enough to howl.

When at last Cliff limps up to where she stoops, her snout thrust into one of the holes, he is too tired and hungry to comment on the discovery.

Ten thousand strides ago, Lightning calculates, rising to scan the horizon. *We're falling behind.*

Cliff reads the incrimination in her tone but has no energy to defend himself. When she doles out one small piece of awl for each of them, he chews the meat to a pulp before swallowing, savoring the taste and sheltering his thoughts as he gazes to the south. The world ahead is more yellow but just as featureless as the one behind. And yet, his nose speaks of change in the air.

There is water in the distance—a lot of it.

I smell a river, he thinks. *They're heading for it.*

Yes.

And more of those creatures. Four-legged and six.

Yes.

How far away, do you think?

Fifteen thousand. Maybe more.

Another fifteen... Cliff groans.

Lightning scoops some of the last remaining snow into her mouth and tightens her camouflage before taking a deep breath.

Maybe more.

+ + +

In the end, the most pessimistic estimate is also the most accurate. A full twenty thousand strides have passed under their weary feet before the smell of both the water and the beasts they track grows strong.

Soon after, Lightning comes to a modest ridge running east to west, a hedge of rust crawling across its yellow shoulders. Once again, she pauses to close the gap between herself and Cliff, and when he arrives, his tongue hanging, they climb the ridge side by side. The draping hedge grows until it becomes a forest of thorn and vine. They peer around its western edge, to the broad valley sloping away below them to the south. Lightning's eyes widen at what she sees, and Cliff's sudden gasp gives voice to her surprise.

At the bottom of the valley, a shallow decline of a thousand strides, rolls a powerful river, blue as the sky and winding like a sneer until it vanishes behind thorny hills to the east. On the far bank, four-legged beasts, enormous even at this distance, work in concert, their ululating calls awful to hear. Under the direction of blue riders, these giant creatures pull—upstream—floating objects to which they are lashed. The objects are long, hollow, and empty, but similar vessels float back downstream in caravans steered by the blue creatures, and these have their hollow sections filled with indiscernible items bound in webs.

So many, thinks Lightning.

Like I said, Cliff scowls.

The ones we're after went straight to the river. Lightning points to the trail. *There, on the bank, where the blue things are loading those...those floaters. Even you can smell that, yes?*

Yes, so? You think they put her on a floater? Cliff shakes his head. *Why would they do that?*

Why do they do anything, Cliff? But look! Whatever they carry to the river they put on a floater, and away it goes. Lightning massages her aching legs. *Can you think of a better answer?*

Cliff cannot.

We need to get closer, thinks Lightning.

They pick their way through the thorny fringe of the vines, moving south, their noses open to the wind that rises up from the valley. Prickly tendrils scratch at their ears and litter the ground with tiny needles. By the time they reach the end of the vines, their toes and fingers burn as if they have been walking on slivered crystals. But their stealth is rewarded; they are now twenty strides from the river. Cliff plucks thorns from his toes as Lightning peeks out from the vines. She has a clear view of her enemies. There are fewer of them now, as most have disappeared down or upstream, steering the caravans of floaters or riding their giant steeds. The remainder work near the river's edge, where they load the last of the vessels. Her nose twitches; Joy is close.

Where are you? she thinks. *Give me a sign.*

There, thinks Cliff, and he points downstream.

There, moored to the stony bank, is a much larger floating device, big enough to house a babelrack and riding low in the water. A dozen blue creatures clamber across its deck. Another scurries from the bank, crossing over a woven lattice to reach the craft. In its front limbs it carries a talihew hide, faded and stained: Joy's sling. It disappears inside the vessel as others of its kind roll up the woven gangplank and unmoor the craft. It moves, ponderous but sure, out into the current, gaining speed as it goes. As Lightning watches, her enemies on the nearby bank launch one of the last small floaters from shore. It drifts away unpiloted, but riders on the next caravan sling a web as they pass, and it is pulled into line, becoming a part of the convoy, bobbing its way downstream. When another such caravan comes into view, approaching from far upstream, a flash of inspiration tells Lightning what she must do.

When he hears her plan, Cliff is incredulous.

We have no idea how to make those things work!

We don't need to make 'em work. See? We get that last floater and hide inside.

Worst idea ever. We need to stay on the bank. We can trail 'em from here.

Through these thorns? Are you joking? And if they land on the far bank? Even if we can swim this river—which I'm not sure either of us can—how big do you think the awl are in there? She pulls needles from her fingertips. *No,* she thinks. *Joy's in that big floater, I'm sure of it. We're following—and we're riding.*

Cliff is unconvinced. He begins to offer another objection, but Lightning interrupts, snarling.

Cliff! Get ready! She removes her camouflage, rolling it tightly, folding it in half, and stowing it in her pack. *They're almost done loading the last floater.*

Cliff grumbles, but he follows her example, cramming his frayed camouflage in next to Lightning's.

A.P. Malloy

I'll go first, she thinks. *Strike and drive. You come in from over there. There's only a few, and their position is sheltered. If we act quick, no one will see us.* She turns to Cliff and bares her teeth. *No survivors...*

+ + +

The last of the floating vessels, eight strides long and three wide, is filled near capacity with dead virbles and lashed by two woven ropes to an outcropping of stone. The current pulls at the craft, and it strains against its moorings, creaking impatience.

Four blue creatures onboard secure the virbles using sticky thread excreted from their mid-sections. Two of their companions wait by the outcropping, while farther up the bank, a dozen others haul the last of the virbles from nearby holes to the river, chittering to one another. One of these stops its labor and turns to the north, to a viney ridge at the head of the bank.

A sound, yes? it asks.

Its companions also pause and grow silent.

A sound, no, one of them replies.

But then the hoarse objection of trampled vines rises above the wind, and arcs of flying dirt appear. The creatures tilt their heads, confused for a moment, then terrified. Whistling fear, they recognize their danger, drop their burdens, and scramble away.

Lightning bursts from the vines, and two of her enemies die in her jaws without another sound. A third follows soon after. The others, clicking in dismay, change colors as they scatter, their quickness remarkable. Two choose poorly, running directly into Cliff, who dispatches them more out of surprise than intent. But their companions are masters of evasion. Camouflage is no use against kezel noses, and pincers leave tracks on the wet ground, but still they dance and jitter, buying time for loud, whistling shrieks before at last being silenced.

The damage is done.

What Lightning had hoped would be a stealthy affair had been clumsy. The cries of the slain have alerted those creatures near and aboard the last floater. Clicking high and fast, the two on the bank move to unmoor the craft, gnawing the ropes using their sharp, beaky mouths. As Lightning charges, their companions on the vessel shriek and whistle, their eyes glittering. One leap separates her from the hapless creatures on the bank, but as she gathers herself, six more enemies appear from a nearby hole, waving their antennae. They swarm over her, driving her to the ground.

Cliff! she thinks. *The floater!*

Cliff leaps awkwardly, reaching the nearest of the two moorings and killing the blue creature as the rope it gnaws gives way, loud and thrumming. The vessel swings out into the current, pulling against the last tether. The second creature stays at its task, gnawing and nibbling, but this is its undoing, as Cliff, with a sweeping slash of his claws, divests it of its head.

Nearby, Lightning regains her feet, dispatching the last of her attackers, splattered in blue from head to toe. She casts a quick glance upstream. The caravan draws into view. Bounding forward, she joins Cliff, and together they grasp the remaining rope, attempting to draw the vessel ashore. Twice as many kezel may not have been enough for this task. Fully laden and drawn by the current, the craft has a mind to go south and won't be denied. How long before the approaching caravan will see them or hear the warning?

Not long, thinks Lightning.

As she does, one of the creatures aboard the vessel begins biting at its end of the rope. Its companions encourage it, waving their antennae.

Time to swim! thinks Lightning.

She releases the rope and leaps from the outcropping into the shallows of the river. Cliff hesitates, but as pulling is futile, he releases what little slack he has. The rope snaps taut, and the force of the current ruptures its final strands. With a sound like cracked ice, the vessel floats free. The riverbed falls away from under Lightning's feet almost at once, but lunging and splashing, she dives forward and grasps the nearest trailing rope. A moment later, Cliff has jumped into the river as well and reached its partner, snaking behind like a tail. Bit by bit, they pull their way toward the craft. Bite by bite their enemies gnaw at the ropes.

Cliff arrives first, for he is not burdened by a pack. Struggling mightily, he pulls himself out of the water and into the craft. While their companion gnaws at Lightning's rope, the remaining creatures turn their attention to him. Three times he is bitten before he can end their noise. At once he grows dizzy. His ears ring, and numbness spreads outward from the punctures like a cold wind until he falls unconscious onto a bushy green pile of dead virbles.

But Lightning sees none of this.

As the last strands of her rope fray, she reaches for the cutter and makes a desperate throw. The creature gnawing the rope dies mid-bite, her blade buried between its eyes. With a final heave, she pulls herself into the vessel, stashes the cutter in her belt, and reels in the trailing ropes. Not daring to check if Cliff is still alive, she hides him, along with the corpses of their enemies, under a heap of virbles. She is quick to follow. Peeking out from under the pile, she can just make out the upstream caravan. At the sight of their lone vessel, blue riders snare it with webs, lash it to the others, and pay it no more heed.

It trails behind, obedient and unremarked.

Lightning turns to look downstream.

The vessel they pursue has already rounded the bend and is out of sight. But coming into view are two of the ululating behemoths, overseen by teams of blue riders. The beasts bathe in the current like living islands, one on each side of the river. They splash and wallow with a frightful noise and a force that fills Lightning with awe, churning the water white.

No fear of awl for these creatures!

We're going to crash, she thinks, but her drivers are unconcerned. They display a casual expertise as they steer the caravan straight at the channel between the two monsters. For five long breaths, Lightning closes her eyes as she is engulfed in the scent and sound of her enemies, whistling and clicking to their passing fellows. Their vessel bobs wildly in the riotous waves.

She covers her ears and waits for it to end.

And then they are through, the nightmare left in their wake, as Lightning and Cliff float on toward the river's southern bend and strange, sunlit lands beyond.

CHAPTER FIVE
Albion

JOY'S MYSTERIOUS CELLMATES are slow to adapt to the disturbing sense of motion. As the putrid floor of their prison rises and falls in a slow, regular fashion, on occasion tilting from side to side, the beasts bellow and stomp, their thoughts in disarray.

Mmm...moving! the one thinks.

Moving away! thinks its companion. *Mmm...*

Joy shares their anxiety but takes solace in the beasts' commitment or compulsion to remain on their side of the room. Are they bound as she is? Either way, their distress, and the noise it accompanies, worsens the pain in her head, straining her patience.

Please, she thinks. *That does not help.*

But her appeal is greeted by increased agitation, and many heartbeats must pass before the beasts accept that this turn of events is no signal of imminent doom. Their disgruntled snorting eases as they finally compose themselves, and as they grow quiet, Joy senses them thinking slow thoughts to one another.

Panic is not useful, she chastises in a weary tone. *Wastes lots of energy.*

At first, silence is their response. She imagines them observing her in the dark. Then:

How Thinker? the first mind asks, returning to its earlier line of questioning. *Mmm? Not smell Thinker. Think*

"I am kezel," but not smell much kezel.

Mmm...how not hunter? the second mind wonders. *Smell hunter. And smell strange.*

Says you, thinks Joy. She adjusts her grip on the rock and scrapes at her bindings, starting with those around her legs. They are thin but tough, chafing at her ankles, and she can see the effort will be difficult.

Kezel not thinkers, the first mind is quick to assert. *Mmm...kezel stupid. Kezel killers, not thinkers.*

To which the second mind contributes:

Mmm...kezel eaters, not thinkers.

You are wrong there, Joy buzzes. *About the thinking, anyway.* Scrape, scrape, scrape. *And the stupid part.* A series of low, rumbling inhalations comes from the direction of the first mind.

Smell some hunter, it thinks. *Smell some kezel, too. But mmm...also smell strange. Why smell strange?*

I could ask you, thinks Joy, weary of the circular questions. She feels the beasts through the floor, shifting and restless in the dark. Do they have eyes? Who knows? Maybe the dark means nothing to them.

My turn, she thinks. *Who are you, please?*

For a long time, she receives no answer. Are the creatures sharing hidden thoughts, pondering a suitable reply, or confused by the question?

It is not difficult, she thinks. *Who—what—are you?*

But the creatures shuffle indecisively, snorting to one another, and neither offers a thought. Joy gives up on the conversation, intensifying her efforts with the stone. Scrape, scrape, scrape with her left hand, scrape, scrape, scrape with her right. Both grow weary and sore before the first mind settles on its response:

Mmm... Thinkers. We Thinkers.

The creature's thought catches Joy by surprise.

Thinkers? she replies. *You are called Thinkers?*

We Thinkers, the second mind confirms. *You think, mmm...but you not Thinker.* The beasts make deep reverberating sounds of affirmation to one another.

No, Joy agrees, *I am not Thinker.*

Mmm...smell hunter, the first mind observes.

Joy clicks a harsh staccato.

The ugly blue things? she replies. *I am not hunter!*

Mmm...smell like them, thinks the second mind.

I can't help that!

Hunters tie, the first mind thinks. *Mmm...and bite.*

Yes, I have noticed, thinks Joy. *Are you bound too?*

The creatures begin to stomp and clatter as if noise alone was a sufficient reply.

Mmm...can't run, the first mind thinks.

Mmm...can't see, its companion adds.

Do you have food? Joy asks, though her nose gives little reason for hope. *Or maybe some water?*

But this question upsets the beasts all the more, their hot breath stirring the air as they snort and bellow.

Mmm...no flowers! the first mind wails.

No yellow grass! thinks the second.

No water! they think at the same time. *Mmm...*

OK, fine! thinks Joy. *Please, do be quiet!*

But her request goes unheeded, and the two beasts soon work themselves into another frenzy of fear and anger. When Joy believes she can no longer take the noise, a rectangle of light appears, and a dozen bristly scion enter the room, clicking and whistling. The sudden light dazzles Joy's eyes, but it doesn't touch the far side of the room where the beasts remain hidden. Joy conceals her rock, holding it close as her captors scurry by without pause to where the beasts make their clamor in the shadows. Not for long.

She hears a bellow of rage, then giant bodies slumping hard to the floor. Clicking pincers and satisfied buzzing follow soon after, and the scion return in single file, their task complete. By the time they exit the room and secure the opening, no thoughts come from out of the dark, and Joy's only companions are heavy snoring and the ongoing sense of motion.

+ + +

How long her cellmates remain unconscious is difficult for Joy to guess. If not for their deep, rumbling breaths, she would have feared them dead. Whether by their nature or the effects of the toxic bites, in sleep their minds are thick like clay. If they dream, they do so in vague emotions and dull color, and Joy isn't sure if what she senses is real or her own harried imagination.

We float on water, she thinks. *How will Lightning track?* But she has no answer, and so, while the beasts sleep, she works at scraping until her cramped fingers can barely maintain a grip. On the last scrape, one of the strands gives way with a tiny snap.

Victory, she thinks.

But the defeated strand is one of many. Fatigue, hunger, and fiery thirst overwhelm her at last. Waking life dissolves into a sleep world where she believes she still scrapes at the bonds, when instead she lies motionless, her eyes dim. Faceless minds drift through her dreams, thinking ideas that confuse and worry. One in particular comes into focus. It is unfamiliar to her, but its thoughts are clear and its tone seductive.

It is a fool to hide its mind. Divulge some simple information, just a hint—about the artifact, for example—in exchange for some water. What harm could come?

But a moment later, Joy senses another thought, more compelling than the first, from a mind she has longed to sense, and it dispels the fog.

Joy, thinks Lightning. *Can you sense me?*

Yes Ami-kan, she thinks. *Yes, I am here!*

Be strong, the mind thinks. *I'm coming for you.*

But where are you? Joy reaches out in her sleep, clutching nothing but empty space. The intensity of disappointment wakes her. Darkness prevails—and the awful smell of her prison. As her mind clears, she senses the languid thoughts of her cellmates, now awake and recovering from the effects of poison. A pang of fear and sadness grips her. It had seemed so real…

She buzzes low, mournful notes, and she wiggles her fingers, trying to coax life into their aching joints. As she resumes her scraping, one of the beasts sends out a groggy, tentative thought.

Mmm...strange smeller. You have name?

I... she is taken off guard. *My name is Joy.*

The beasts contemplate this.

Joy, the first mind repeats.

Mmm...Joy, the second agrees.

Yes, thinks Joy. *And you?*

I Female, the first mind thinks. *Mmm...*

I Male, offers the second. *Mmm...we Thinkers.*

Yes, Joy replies. *I understood that part.* She shifts the rock to her other hand. *We should work together,* she thinks. *Tell me about hunters...*

And so, through tedious effort, often frustrated by the density of their minds, Joy discovers how it is the beasts are familiar with kezel (some of their relatives have ended up unwilling guests at kezel feasts) and how they had been caught (trapped, bitten, and hauled away). They are not the first of their kind to meet such a fate.

Hunters take young, thinks Female. *Take old.*

Mmm...stomp Hunters! thinks Male. *Gore Hunters!*

Yes, that sounds good, thinks Joy. *But stay calm, please,* she adds. *They will bite again.* Then, although she doubts they will know, she asks, *Where are we going?*

Mmm...away, thinks Female.

Far away, Male adds. *Mmm...*

Moons will stop them, thinks Joy. Her antennae bend forward, hoping for confirmation. *Won't they?*

But if the Thinkers have an answer, they don't share it. Joy tries to reconstruct the passage of time. The last storm had roared overhead just before her capture, when they had sheltered in their hole on the plains. As troubling as that time had been, it now feels like a peaceful dream. How long ago was it? And which of the moons had it been? Or had there been more than one? She feels sure of nothing. Moons may stop the scion, but she is unable to guess when.

Tell me about Thinkers, she requests at last. *About stomping...and goring.* She clicks a grating staccato. *That sounds very useful.* Then, thinking of a potential escape, she adds, *Can you swim? Fly?*

Her cellmates attempt to unravel the questions, but their effort is slow. As they do, and as often as her weary hands allow, Joy scrapes at her bindings, cataloging the bits of information she gathers. Thinkers are experts at stomping and goring she learns. Many hunters had been mashed or speared during their capture. A second strand of the bindings surrenders.

Snap!

Yes, Thinkers can swim and run.

No, they cannot fly.

On this goes, questions and stumbling answers.

A third strand gives way.

At times, Joy drifts in and out of sleep, and as her hunger and thirst grow, larger portions of her time are spent unconscious. The Thinkers still their thoughts as well, brooding between themselves. In a last, lucid moment, Joy sees she will lose the battle to fatigue. She wedges the stone between her bound wrists and hides the broken strands in her clenched fingers.

Sleep consumes her a moment later.

How long she remains in her torpor she can't say. The scion named Old Magister visits more than once, but she drifts in a place that neither his threats nor his probing thoughts can reach. Failing in his last attempt to infiltrate her mind, he clicks in fury and strikes her again before limping into the darkness. She recalls his frustrated buzzing and his bitter smell.

At some point, she becomes aware of a change in the constant motion—a jolt, then a steady bobbing, accompanied by the nervous shuffling and stomping of Thinkers. Even this fails to wake her. She recalls blessed sunlight, then motion of a different type, minds exchanging veiled thoughts, and the ceaseless blowing of wind. The sound of it haunts her dreams.

+ + +

When Joy wakes at last, she does so startled by the unmistakable, tantalizing smell of fresh awl.

She lies on her side, still bound and gagged, but no longer in the dark cell with the Thinkers. Instead, she is alone in yet another hole, cramped and poorly lit but dug into solid ground, a relief after the sickening motion of the river. The aroma of awl wafts through a small, circular exit, along with evidence of rain. She senses her captors outside—guards, she supposes—but can read none of their thoughts. The rain speaks of a recent storm. Whether that is the cause of her relocation, she neither knows nor cares. Being on land increases her chances of rescue, that is all that matters. She is happy to see her captors have overlooked the damage to her bindings, but she is unable to muster a single drop of urine, and her mouth is dusty dry.

So tormented, she turns again to her bonds.

Scrape, scrape, scrape.

In time, she senses someone approaching, and she hides the stone. Near the exit, a low buzzing arises, joined by agitated chittering. Four, no, five scion are in angry converse—her guards and some newcomers. The noises escalate into what sounds like a fight; whistles become shrieks and crazed shadows play on the far wall. In the end, the ruckus subsides, and two of the blue creatures enter the hole. They slip the pole through the loops in her bindings and bear her into the light, bringing the shroud but not bothering to cover her. Once there, they drop her to the ground and step away. What their purpose might be, she can't say, but for the moment, she doesn't care, forgetting hunger and thirst as she takes her fill of the sun. It chases sleep from her mind, and as it fills her eyes, details become clear.

Like the plains, this new land is open and flat, spreading outward to every horizon—but its color has changed. Yellow tufts of waving grass have given way to patches of rusty moss. The ground is a pale clay, baked hard and cracked like a fallen sheet of ice. Rain has glazed its surface, but already the arid soil is yearning for more. Clouds of black dots, the tiniest winged creatures Joy has ever seen, blow this way and that, surfing the wind. They land like a thin blanket, then peel away again to ride the bluster.

The hole she's been taken from is one of many near the western bank of what at one time must have been a wide river. Now, its flow is so reduced she could easily swim across. It winds to the south, and near the limit of sight, it passes a tremendous basin to its east, thousands of strides from rim to rim, the remains of a wide but shallow lake. It was once fed by the dwindling river, but the last of its water now pools at the center, surrounding an island of rusty rock. As if growing from the top of this island, six rough columns, dirty gray and brown, rise above the horizon. In height, they rival the bomba's maison, but they lack any sign of the dome's symmetry. Instead, their irregularities and mundane colors make the towers a perfect fit for this environment, amazing but completely natural.

Everywhere, from the river to the island, scuttling bits of blue sparkle as six-legged creatures move about in lines and clusters. Joy's enemies are uncountable.

At last, her captors click to one another and look to the south, where a strange shape has appeared over a small rise, jogging toward them bipedally. Whatever they have been waiting for approaches, and tickling dread rises along Joy's spine. From a distance, the newcomer has a bizarre appearance. The two legs it runs on seem at first to be joined by many other limbs, sprouting from its side, and it appears to have two heads, one topped by a mountain of black hair. Slap-slap, slap-slap, the biped's feet mark out a regular time against the ground, squelching mud between its toes.

But as it grows closer, Joy recognizes the truth:

Two creatures approach, one rider, one ridden.

The rider is a scion, the brightest, bluest, largest one of its kind she has yet seen.

Its steed is naked and brown. It slows to a walk, then, mere strides away, comes to a full stop, allowing its passenger to dismount. The leash around its neck hardly seems necessary, for it is docile and silent, looking through two muddy brown eyes, its face inexpressive. An extravagant pile of black curls grows on its head and across most of its face. That same fur continues on, a black snow dusting its chest and thighs, between which dangles some type of organ. The creature's two arms are muscular, but it has no tail, and when it yawns, Joy sees two rows of white but unimpressive teeth.

Surely this is a rumidelchia? Have Moondwellers returned as Lightning's gami-kan had promised? But this is no time for speculation. Here comes the scion rider to join the others. He walks six-legged, but were he to stand upright, he would be a full head taller than Joy.

Does New Magister see? thinks one of the two smaller scion. *Did they speak the truth?*

Yes, thinks the second. *Is he pleased?*

The scion named New Magister steps toward Joy, her reflection playing across the facets of his enormous eyes. He tilts his brilliant sapphire head to the side, and his beaky mouth clicks a rapid cadence. His antennae, long and supple, bend forward.

They did, and he is indeed, he thinks. *They will not be Thousands for long.* His eyes glitter. *He predicts they have a future in the Hundreds. Would they like that? To be soldiers and not drones?*

The smaller creatures buzz and bow.

New Magister honors, the one thinks.

Yes. New Magister does, thinks its companion.

Where did they find it? asks New Magister.

It was being carried—hidden, thinks the one.

Yes, thinks the second. *It fell to the ground.*

Yes. Fell. They saw it before it was covered again.

Yes, thinks its companion. *Old Magister desired it to be kept secret, but they saw.*

New Magister moves closer still, as if to touch Joy, but the drones whistle in alarm.

Not recommended, New Magister, thinks the one.

No. More dangerous than it looks.

Book of Dreams

Yes. Already killed once.

New Magister accepts this warning but takes no pains to hide his fascination.

It wastes a great deal of energy, he thinks.

Yes, New Magister, it tries to stay hidden.

Yes. Always camouflaged.

New Magister sniffs through his nasal slits, his bristly, black forelimbs flexing as if anxious to touch Joy in spite of the others' warning.

Why, do they think? he wonders. *Why try to hide?*

But the drones have only guesses.

Maybe it is ashamed of its form, thinks the one.

Yes, thinks the other. *Ashamed of being vumierre.*

Yes. Of walking on two legs.

But how did it come to be this way? New Magister wants to know. *A scion in vumierre form?*

They do not know, thinks the one drone.

No. They do not, thinks the other.

No. If Old Magister knows, he does not share.

No. Very secretive.

Yes. Very. Perhaps it was forced breeding.

Yes. Or perhaps illness.

When New Magister bends his thoughts to Joy, they are curious but kind, their tone benevolent.

Welcome to Albion, he thinks, *home of the original Scion. It must be very hungry. Where is it from? Does it have a number? A title? A name?*

Joy tries to maintain the illusion of stupidity, concentrating on all things dense and dumb, but New Magister doesn't seem to mind. Unlike Old Magister, he doesn't attempt to pry secrets; instead, he admonishes himself in a tone of good nature.

Food and water first, he thinks, *conversation later. Bring the guest to his hole,* he orders. *And use care! He will be displeased if it is damaged.*

Old Magister will not like, thinks the one drone.

No, his companion agrees. *He will dis-like.*

Their loyalty commends, thinks New Magister, *but Old serves New, and New serves Queen.* His eyes sparkle.

A.P. Malloy

Do they wish to anger Her?

The drones click to one another, antennae waving to and fro. But in the end, they decide against further objection, using the pole to hoist Joy between them.

He would have it unbound, thinks New Magister apologetically. *But it might try to kill again—or get itself damaged. Which reminds...*

With a quick, easy motion, he drapes the shroud over Joy, occluding the sun. The last thing she sees is New Magister returning to his perch on the brown creature's back. His kind thought enters her mind.

It will be safer if it is less visible.

+ + +

Joy is carried at a brisk pace, accompanied by the slap-slap of the biped's bare feet. Though she can hear the chittering and buzzing of others, never once do her captors slow their steps. If they exchange thoughts with any of their kind along the way, she is unable to sense them. The bindings dig into her wrists and ankles, and her hands grow so numb she fears she will drop her stone. Her head lolls from side to side as pale, thirsty ground passes beneath her, soaking up the last of the rain that slicks its cracked face.

She is nearly unconscious when her captors come to a sudden halt. At the same time, thoughts, unsheltered and angry, fill her mind. Despite her weakened state, she recognizes their source, and the sense of it causes an inadvertent shudder.

Drones there! Old Magister seethes. *What are they doing? They will put that down now!*

Joy imagines she can hear the approach of a limping step, the dragging of pincers across the clay. The carriers begin to do as they are told, so commanding is Old Magister's tone. A moment later, however, the calm thoughts of New Magister smoothly order them onward. Their hesitation is noticeable but slight, and they proceed as instructed without question.

He found it, thinks Old Magister. *It belongs to him!*

All found things belong to Queen, replies New Magister, and his tone is congenial.

He was questioning it!

He was starving it, it would seem, when what he should be doing is preparing for the Circle.

Furious clicks and cool, composed buzzing soon fade beneath the wind. Joy imagines Old Magister trying in vain to stay close as his prize is borne away. He hurls thoughts after them, angry and futile, but these grow faint, eventually drifting beyond sense.

Three hundred strides later, they arrive at their destination. After a brief descent, Joy's carriers bear her into darkness again. They lower her to the ground more gently than has been the practice in the past, and on orders from New Magister, remove both the pole and the shroud. They are in yet another hole, more spacious than the others, with two exits and three slender columns running from the floor to the ceiling.

Food for the guest, thinks New Magister, and he dismounts, tethering his steed to one of the columns as the drones scurry from the hole. *It will be safe here,* he thinks, and he removes the gag from Joy's mouth. *Maybe after a time he shall free its extremities as well. Would it like that? Would it like to explore fair Albion?*

As he looks at her, antennae bent forward, Joy feels a powerful compulsion to trust him, seeing in his gaze the comfort of an ally. Maybe she should share information, like her name, perhaps, or where she comes from. But as she considers this, the drones return, breaking the spell. One bears a strange, flat object, pale green and floppy like a squashed virble, the other, strips of fresh awl. The smell is so powerful a tiny whistle escapes against her will. Taking care—not for her or the food, but for their own safety—the drones place their burdens near Joy and retreat the way they came.

It's not poisoned, New Magister thinks. He takes a portion of the awl and swallows it whole, then squeezes the floppy green thing, using his proboscis to siphon the fluid that drips forth. *It sees?*

But Joy looks away. If her camouflage is useless, she can still hide her mind. Her gaze is drawn to the brown creature, who has lowered to a sitting position and busied itself with scratching.

A handsome male of the species, thinks New Magister. *Wouldn't it agree? Perhaps he should let the two of them become acquainted.* His tone remains affable. *Show it can be trusted,* he adds, *and he will remove these bindings.* He buzzes in a gentle fashion. *Ceasing to camouflage would be a fine start—as would relinquishing this.* And, quick as the strike of an awl tongue, he snatches the rock clenched between Joy's palms. She tries to hide feelings of loathing as New Magister exits the hole, clicking a placid rhythm.

+ + + + + +

Lightning wakes with a small, unintentional yelp of surprise, startled that she has been sleeping—again— and disoriented by her foreign surroundings. Buried beneath a pile of dead virbles aboard a bobbing watercraft, she must blink her eyes several times to confirm that this is no illusion. The details of her circumstance flood back in an instant.

I liked the dream better, she thinks.

Cliff lies next to her, still unconscious. Hidden by virbles are the bodies of their enemies. Lightning estimates thousands of strides have passed since their clandestine attachment to the caravan, if measured on land, traveling in a straight line. How many more they've covered via the winding river, she can't guess, but her cramping legs and frayed nerves tell her it must be many. And yet, wind the river does, sweeping first to the east, then the west, but always in the end carrying them south at a brisk pace, into the sun and harrying wind.

The voyage has been singular in its unpleasant monotony, punctuated by fits of restless sleep. Virble has kept hunger at bay, but the bilge slopping at the vessel's bottom is undrinkable, cloggy with green hair, and Lightning soon grows parched. Peeking over the vessel's prow, she reaches the water with the tips of her fingers and licks these, reading the wind. The smell of their cargo hides the stowaways and fallen enemies, but she fears it may also mask signs of Joy. Since leaving shore, she has caught no scent of her, nor sight of the craft in which she believes Joy was imprisoned. She hears the blue creatures driving their caravan, but their vessel has been disregarded. They meet no upstream traffic and are joined only by other unpiloted craft, pushed out from the bank and tethered to the rest.

We must be quite a party by now. She squirms, attempting to stretch her legs. *Cliff! Wake up!*

But the gray kezel sleeps on. What she will do if their enemies happen upon them while he is still unconscious, Lightning can't say. In her current foul mood, the option of leaving him has crossed her mind.

Cliff!

She concentrates the thought, amplifies it, but the result is the same. She then pokes and pinches him, but as she considers jabbing him with the cutter, her nose detects a new scent mingling with the virbles. A storm gathers. Moons are rising.

Which ones? she wonders, but to her surprise, she can't recall the color of the most recent moon. Most likely Ami-kan the Green, but had she traveled alone?

Doesn't matter, she thinks. *They can't stay on the river in a storm, no matter which moons—can they?*

She soon has her answer. Amid loud whistles and rapid clicking, the drivers' steering poles splash in the water, digging in against the current. The caravan begins to change direction.

We're going to shore, she thinks, though what that means to the stowaways is unclear.

After much buzzing and scurrying, the creatures attain their goal, and with a bump and a lurch, the entire caravan comes to a halt, tethered, Lightning guesses, to the western bank. Up and down their vessel bobs as it resists the river's pull, and side to side it shimmies, thumping its neighbors with jarring reports that wear at the jabi kezel's ragged nerves. But Cliff remains oblivious in spite of the noise. Then, though Lightning can scarcely believe it, the sounds of her enemies begin to fade, along with their smell, until both are beyond sense. She waits, straining for any sign of them, and when she is sure they are gone, using the utmost care, she pokes her head out from under the virble pile.

Amber clouds creep across the sun, and the wind, moody as ever, shifts from pensive to hostile. Big Brother peeks above the horizon, but that doesn't tell the whole story. He may soon be joined by others. She couldn't have determined which had she the energy to try. Moon patterns were Ancian's specialty, and Ancian is...

Lightning clenches her jaws.

Oti-kan is bad, she thinks—*with or without the others. Don't need Ancian to tell me that.*

Their vessel is at the downstream end of the caravan, secured to a row of small, stony columns embedded in the bank. Upstream of them bob dozens of similar crafts, each fully laden. Some carry bales of yellow grass, others, bunches of the sweet smelling bell-flowers common on the plains. Several contain other creatures, including dead cremlins, and many bear items Lightning can't identify: a load of sandy powder, small rocks that glow, and sheets of striped skin, rolled up and bound in white. Far up the west bank to which they are moored, a single file of blue creatures walks six-legged away from the river and toward a warren of holes dug into a gentle slope to the south. These she judges to be the ones from their caravan by the burden each carries on its back. If her surmise is correct, they are unloading the vessels ahead of the storm. Anything not well-secured or underground will be blown or washed away.

Which means they'll be coming back, she thinks. *Well, we weren't staying here anyway.*

Her mind races. They must get to shore in time to find or make shelter. But where? Within sight of their enemies, that much is clear. Joy may be nearby or may have been here and left a trace. And yet, not so close as to risk discovery—nor upwind.

Looks like we're getting wet again, she thinks.

Retrieving the corpses of their enemies, stiff and cold, she drops them into the river, making quiet splashes. The blue bodies float away downstream, but not as fast as she would like; she worries she may have made their situation worse. If the corpses are still in sight when the others return...

Doesn't matter, she thinks. *Bodies can't stay in a vessel that's about to be unloaded, and neither can we.* She rubs life into her cramping legs. *Cliff!*

But the slumbering kezel remains insensate, dozing in his grisly bed. Lightning kicks him and yanks his ear, slapping him across the snout. Nothing serves. Growling her frustration, she hauls Cliff out of the vessel, a clumsy, splashing affair, half swimming, half wallowing ashore, the current tugging at her legs. The bank here is shallow, a fact for which she gives thanks, as Cliff's wet, dead weight is greater than his bony frame suggests. He refuses to wake even after his dousing, and Lightning pants heavily by the time she reaches dry ground.

She drops Cliff and turns to take hungry gulps from the river before again checking on her enemies. Most have disappeared inside the holes; once unburdened, they will be quick to return for the remaining cargo. Clouds rolling over the horizon thicken as they advance, and far to the southeast, a jagged pinstripe of electricity shoots from the sky to the ground. Lightning pauses, counting. Five heartbeats pass. Ten. At fifteen, she hears a long, low rumble, muffled by the wind.

Oti-kan's in a hurry, she thinks.

Taking a deep breath, she gets a firm grip under Cliff's arms and drags him away from the river.

+ + +

The journey is not long, but walking two-legged—

backwards—while dragging Cliff makes it very slow. Driving wind carries drops of cold rain, and the world turns a dusky orange. A thousand strides west of the river and another thousand north of their enemies' shelter, Lightning arrives at a broad stand of thorny vines clustered above a sharp rise. From here, she can see down to where the last of the blue creatures, nearly invisible in the gloom, haul the now empty vessels out of the river, lashing them to the stony pier.

Weaver! she thinks. *My poor legs.* And she curses as she drops Cliff to the ground, pausing to catch her breath and read the wind. Even from this distance, she smells her enemies in their holes. But there is something else. Is that...? It is. Mixed with the scent of various cargos is one that buoys her flagging spirit.

Joy hasn't been here, but kezel have.

Moons ago, she thinks, *but they were here.*

Renewed hope energizes Lightning, and she begins digging among the vines' gnarly roots. The soil gives way to her determined effort, revealing a root system both expansive and durable. She burrows down for a body length and then forward two more. Weary to the point of shaking, she exits the crude shelter filthy and grim, turning south to watch the sky.

Billowing, orange clouds fill the horizon, and the wind has grown frenetic, driving distant sheets of rain across the land as superheated air collapses in pealing thunder. And here comes Api-kan the Blue! He chases after his boastful woti, eager to gobble up the sun. All of this is very normal. But strangely, only scattered drops ever reach them, and the storm, as blustery and loud as it is, hides the Weaver but sheds little moisture on this part of the world.

Count your blessings, thinks Lightning, and she grabs Cliff by his arms, dragging him into the hole. No sooner has she done so than his eyelids flutter and blink before opening wide.

I should have guessed, she thinks.

In the ghostly, orange light, Cliff stares at her, his

gaze one of stark confusion.

Where are we? What happened?

You got yourself bit—repeatedly. And I had the decency not to dump you in the river. That's what.

Cliff considers this news. He winces at the angry voice of the thunder.

How long have I been sleeping? The last storm...

Was a long time ago, thinks Lightning. And she helps herself to some of the awl in Gami-kan's pack—with a grudging allowance for Cliff—while she relays the details of what he missed.

We're on the west bank? he thinks unhappily. *That means we're on the wrong side. How are we supposed to get back to the accrete?*

I'm doing the thinking for both of us, Cliff. I'll solve that problem when I get to it.

Cliff rubs the back of his neck.

How come you didn't fall asleep?

Because I had the sense to not get bit.

Cliff gulps the last of his awl, and he squints.

But you did. He points to her snout.

Lightning reaches up to touch the place he indicates, near her upper lip. There, indeed, she finds two small but unmistakable punctures. She frowns. Another bite marks her left ear.

Some of us are tougher than others, she thinks.

Then you're tougher than every other kezel they hauled away, thinks Cliff, though his tone says he doesn't believe this. Lightning hasn't energy to solve the mystery. With hunger dulled by the awl, she can't keep her eyes open another moment. She blinks and yawns, her tail hanging low.

You have to stand watch, she thinks. *Don't fall asleep! There are a bunch of those disgusting things out there waiting to bite you again.* She curls up and collapses. *Wake me when the storm passes.*

+ + +

She feels certain she has just closed her eyes and begun to drift away, when she is awakened by the unpleasant sensation of Cliff tugging at her vest.

Lightning, he thinks. *Wake up!*

She indulges the hope that these words are part of a dream, the tugging a product of her sleepy imagination, and she ignores them both. But Cliff insists, poking her shoulder.

They're moving again! he thinks.

Growling low and baring her fangs, Lightning opens her eyes and glares.

Poke me again, she thinks. *I dare you.*

You'd be a lot madder if I let you sleep, thinks Cliff, which is true but doesn't improve Lightning's mood. She rises slowly and adjusts her vest, removing her mask to rub at her weary eyes.

Wait here, she thinks, and she takes a careful sniff, stepping out into the sunlight. Very little water drips from the vines. Contrary to everything she knows about storms, there are signs of wind damage, but no snow and scarcely any puddles. To the north, a band of dark shadow rides along the horizon; the storm rages in other lands, possibly the accrete.

But to the south, all is bright and blue.

Cliff was correct: their enemies are on the move, but they are not reloading their vessels. Instead, they proceed from their holes, moving south alongside the river. As they march, they form a long, single file of blue, each individual carrying a burden on its back. Lightning estimates over a hundred of them, and still more exit the holes, joining the line. She watches until the last of them has moved away, then relieves herself and sips hastily from the lone rain pool before returning inside.

So, what's the plan? thinks Cliff.

Eating and thinking. Lightning gulps some virble, scarcely bothering to chew, and she takes her camouflage from Gami-kan's pack, unrolling it carefully.

Those thorns sure messed up my weaving, Cliff laments as he examines his own camouflage and tears into his portion of the virble. *Think it'll hold?*

My *weaving, you mean,* Lightning corrects, and she ties her mat in place, noting all the spots the thorns have snagged and torn. *Of course it will hold.*

Cliff wrinkles his nose in doubt.

What if we run into...company?

What if you stop asking so many questions? Lightning shoulders her pack. *They're not waiting for us.*

Sheltering his many reservations, Cliff secures his camouflage and follows Lightning out of the burrow as the last of their enemies fall in line and move south.

Hurry! thinks Lightning. *We skirt their holes to the west and then re-join the river.*

And after that?

But Lightning creeps out of the thorns without an answer, her nose down and her eyes up.

+ + +

They give their enemies' shelter a wide berth. The smells coming from the network of holes confirm Lightning's earlier discovery. When he recognizes the scent of other kezel, Cliff's ears perk up.

They were kept alive all this way, he thinks. *That's a good sign, yes?*

Lightning can imagine reasons why it might be anything but good, but she keeps these to herself.

Better than the alternative, she thinks. *There!* She points to the south, where a slender line of blue twinkles in the sun. *They're moving fast; let's go!*

Their enemies travel on a wide path bordering the river, a hundred strides from its west bank. Staying between this path and the river, Lightning and Cliff keep their upwind quarry in sight, wading through the long, yellow grass. Occasional stands of thorny vines greet them with clutching, prickly hands, but whatever creatures inhabit this part of the plains seem unwilling to accost them. The worst obstacles are small pits of rusty mud, well hidden. When they plunge into these, they are released with great reluctance and loud slurping. But they occur less frequently as the land becomes drier, harder, and less colorful. Bell-flowers disappear, and beaming yellow grass grows brittle and pale.

They have travelled several thousand arid strides when they are overtaken by one of the monstrous four-legged beasts, also traveling south, driven by many blue riders, chittering and buzzing. Their noses provide no warning of its downwind approach, but the beast hammers along the path causing such a noise they have ample time to take cover. They watch as it passes by, covering their ears as it bellows its strident call.

What a horrible sound, thinks Cliff as he pulls his foot out of a mud hole. *What a horrible, awful place!*

Not long after the beast has gone its way, another sound reaches their ears.

What is that? thinks Cliff.

Lightning pauses to listen. Beneath the wind, comes a low throbbing, sensed through the ground as much as the air. Memories of the Gnashers stir.

I've heard a sound like that before, she thinks. *Come on. Things are about to change.*

They cross the path, stepping away from the river and continuing south through grass grown faded and brittle. They don't have far to travel. The throbbing grows until it fills the air. Cresting a rise, they gain a clear view of the convoy, which has come to a stop. The river disappears as if cut by a blade.

A fall, thinks Cliff.

A huge fall, thinks Lightning.

Their quarry makes its way to where a pair of babelracks labors under command of a dozen of the blue creatures. Their purpose is unclear, and if either they or their masters make a sound, it is buried beneath the ceaseless roar of the waterfall.

What are they doing? thinks Cliff.

That's what I want to know. Carefully now. We can't let them see us...

Creeping forward with Cliff following close, Lightning moves down the hill, keeping the river to her left. Her wary pace may be what saves her life, for, a hundred strides later, the land comes to a sudden, shocking end. She backpedals quickly, bumping into Cliff and cursing. He is about to apologize, but what he sees drives all other thoughts from his mind.

They stand at the edge of a sheer landfall unlike anything either of them has ever seen, a ledge that stretches out to the east and west as far as they can see and which towers hundreds of kezel-lengths above the land below. The river pours from its cleft and cascades in a dizzying arc, striking the lower land with audible force. There, in a frothing tumult, it pools and churns before continuing south. The terrain it divides is grassless, arid, and pale. It spreads out before them without visible end, disappearing into a foggy haze. A smell like a belching fumarole wrinkles their snouts.

You were right, thinks Lightning. *An awful place.*

Here, at least, is an answer to their question about the babelracks. Their enemies have strapped the creatures to a huge, circular device and compelled them to walk around it, turning it like one of the net wheels in the maison—only many times larger. Their muscles bulge beneath their spotted carapaces, and their tusks glint in the sun. Thick ropes run from the device to the edge of the landfall then to the lower land, and from these hang empty containers like woven baskets. One by one, the blue creatures unload their burdens into the containers, and as the octopods turn the wheel, the ropes and the containers they bear are lowered to the land below, emptied by dozens of tiny blue dots and sent back up, waiting to be refilled.

Cliff groans at the sight.

There's no way we're climbing down from here, he thinks. *If only we were derkas!* As Lightning considers their dilemma, Cliff casts his gaze to the open sky. He catches his breath. *Derka!* he thinks.

I heard you the first time.

No. There's a derka!

A.P. Malloy

Lightning pins her ears and casts a darting glance to where Cliff points. Above them and to the south, close enough to flash in a blaze of color, something large and winged swoops down, for a moment blocking the sun.

Sweet dow for dinner! thinks Lightning. *That's not a derka, you fool. That's a bomba!*

CHAPTER SIX
Wings

THE BROWN CREATURE—Rumidelchia, Moondweller, or whatever it might be—remains on its haunches, tethered to a column but just within reach, its expression impossible to read. Joy returns its gaze, poised to defend herself, but for the moment, seems content to sit and stare, on occasion scratching its head or running fingers through the tight curls on its face. Can it see through her camouflage, or is it merely attending to her smell or the sight of her hands and feet? For the bindings have so restricted circulation that these are no longer hidden but are instead a pale, unhappy blue.

Irrelevant, she thinks, recalling a bomba word.

She turns her attention to the food, hesitating one last time, worried about deception.

Either starved or poisoned, she finally decides. *Neither one is good.*

And so, keeping wary eyes on the brown creature, she attempts to relieve her thirst. She can't wring fluid from the spongy thing as New Magister had, but she bores it with her proboscis, extracting enough to swallow. The cool liquid pioneers a trail down her dusty throat, and for several moments she can think of nothing else. It has a subtle, earthy smell and is mildly sweet, tingling her antennae and brightening her eyes.

Save the rest, she thinks, but this wisdom stands

no chance. Soon, nothing remains but a shriveled green skin. The awl suffers a similar fate. Nothing she has eaten has tasted so good, not since she was very young and Ari had found the lost pack. She forces herself to eat slowly, alert to any ill effects, but there are none.

That's one promise kept, she thinks of New Magister. *Doesn't mean he's friendly.*

With this new energy, Joy attacks her bindings, taking advantage of what she perceives as her captor's foolishness. She gnaws using her beaky mouth, and the brown creature stops its scratching and leans forward, its eyes squinting.

"Blarby moona katza koo," it says in a low, mumbling voice, imprecise like a mudslide. Joy twitches in surprise, and her antennae quiver as she braces for trouble. But the creature remains seated, looking at her as if expecting a response. As the sounds mean nothing to her—she couldn't replicate them even if they did—she chooses to ignore them, returning with renewed intensity to biting, working until her jaws ache. She had made better progress using the rock! She halts to rest her weary mouth and stretches her limbs, cramped and sore.

"Om nomna rumm wor," says the creature, and it leans in closer as if working to penetrate her camouflage. It reaches forward, extending a finger to touch her, but she whistles a clear warning, and it pulls its hand away, making an odd hooting sound.

"Dona rilly gerta soo," it says. "Issa nom nom."

Should she attempt a response? If a spy, the creature will divulge anything it learns. But perhaps it is, like the mysterious Thinkers, a potential ally who hates their captors as much as she. Maybe it does not care to be ridden by a disgusting scion, and by keeping her thoughts to herself she is wasting an opportunity.

She chooses to take the risk.

I do not understand, she thinks, and then adds for clarity, *Mind, not mouth, OK?*

The creature stares as if nothing has happened.

Are you...a Moondweller? she asks, concentrating

to get its attention. *Are you a Rumidelchia?*

But her thoughts fall unheeded like a stone into the nacht. She buzzes her disappointment. All the descriptions she had been given of the mythical bipeds had created an image of great intellect and vitality. How could a creature like this have built the maison? What possible use could it be as an ally?

"Sana aga moona pok," it says, and it gestures broadly, waving at one of the exits. "Bung porta kata ding, lundin fallundin. A porli poo. A porli, porli, poo."

Yes, thinks Joy, clicking. *Porli poo to you.*

At this, the creature makes clicking noises of its own, though its mouth is not well formed for the task. The effort is simple mimicking, Joy is sure, and yet it is somehow endearing. She buzzes in response, and the creature, seemingly pleased with this, makes its best attempt to copy her. Buzzing, it claps its hands.

For the first time, Joy examines these in detail. Despite the difference in color and size, they are just like her own. So are the feet. The sight of them brings to mind memories of peaceful days near the maison, when Lightning had taught her to identify creatures by the prints they made. A kezel's four clawed toes and fingers had been the easiest to learn, but all creatures made their own unique marks, and Joy had learned many of them. There was the sneer with more legs than she could count, weaving its way across the world, the bombas' three long, splayed toes, the cloven tread of curly-tailed talihew, and the flippers of a waddling dow. But not one had prints like hers—unless she counts the hand of light discovered deep inside the maison.

What does it mean? she wonders.

But she has no answer. Maybe it means nothing. Maybe digits like hers abound in the world. Still, if there is no connection, why did the one called New Magister place them together? What was his goal?

He will be disappointed, she thinks, and she returns to biting, delighted when a strand snaps away. She is about to congratulate herself when she senses a familiar tickling in her mind, unpleasant and insidious, like invisible fingers sneaking through her brain.

Someone is trying to read her thoughts.

She glances from one entrance to the other, where she catches the slightest movement, a hint of fleeting shadow. Had someone been standing there, hiding? If so, they are gone now. She scolds herself. She had been foolish, allowing her mind to wander to thoughts of Lightning and days gone by. She suspects the brown creature of participating in a ploy to distract her—or being someone's witless tool.

Either way, she thinks, and she closes her mind, determined to be unreadable.

Moments later, New Magister enters the hole, whistling a pleasant tune, his thoughts inscrutable. He is followed by six others.

He keeps his word, he thinks. *It wants to be free? It will be. But first, some sun!* He buzzes low and long, his eyes sparkling. *Would it like that?*

Joy drops her gaze to the floor.

Excellent! thinks New Magister. *But they must keep it safe. It has seen how others respond when they encounter it. Old Magister is not the only scion whose motives are suspect. It is...a curiosity.*

He clicks a complex rhythm.

Will it think nothing? He feels certain it can.

But his antennae quiver in disappointed hope.

Well. He supposes it's to be expected. It has been through a traumatic time. In a similar situation, he might do the same. He gives a terse order to the others. *It will please forgive him,* he thinks to Joy. *A bit more of being tied and blind, then freedom.*

He untethers the brown creature and leaps to its back. The creature bears this as if nothing could be more normal and makes no complaint when New Magister prods it with his pincers. As she watches them exit the hole, Joy is hoisted in the air and is once again shrouded.

+ + +

Book of Dreams

Pincers scuffle the hard, dry ground, and sunlight grows, along with various unfamiliar sounds and smells. Master of them all is the wind. Outside the hole, it howls at one moment, then drops to a moan, shifting directions and speeds as if confused. The farther she is carried, the more distinct its messages: they are approaching a place where many foreign creatures congregate.

Her captors pause. She hears the clattering of pincers on a new surface. The pale land passing beneath her changes, as if viewed through ice, and the scion place her with care on the ground. Except it isn't the ground, it's a clear, curved surface through which the ground can be seen but not felt. The soldiers remove her shroud and with a quick snip! snap! they bite using their beaky mouths—much sharper and stronger than her own—to sever the bindings. Dazzled by sunlight and too sore to move, she has no chance to attack before they move out of reach. What is this now? She is enclosed in a translucent globe, like a giant bubble, twice her height in diameter. It is scored with many small holes, each no wider than one of her fingers, allowing sounds and smells to flow, but baffled. The scion close and lock a hinged opening near the ground, sealing her inside. The door blends with the curved wall, becoming almost invisible, and there she is, trapped.

They are still scared of it, thinks New Magister. *But he doesn't believe it means any harm. With time, it will come to see them as family.*

Joy looks away, sheltering her disgust. The globe distorts her view, but she appears to be in a small vale, parched and rusty. The vale's outer rim slopes upward to form a steep berm. This is marked by two sealed openings, the one they entered, and another, a hundred strides to the east, near which a trickling fall spills, drip by drip, into a shallow basin.

There is no one else in the vale, but the wind carries clear signs of many creatures gathered outside, most of whose scents Joy is unable to identify. There is occasional ululation—no mystery there—but also squeaking, braying, roars and shouts, barks and chirps of all types. Waves of emotion come from the direction of the sounds, bending Joy's antennae. So much fear and hate! But there is a profound reservoir of sullen apathy as well, like a tarry pit. She lowers her head and stares at the ground, aware of New Magister's mind hovering. How well can he penetrate her defenses? Is he ridiculing her feeble attempt? Has he been reading her from the first?

He taps the globe with his pincers.

Clever vumierre device, yes? Created ages ago for the recreation of their two-legged young, but now put to scion use in the service of Ozag, Abundant and Baleful.

Bubbling curses rise in Joy's mind. Oh! The thoughts she wishes to unleash.

Very well, thinks New Magister. *He can see it needs time to adjust to its surroundings.* He preens his antennae casually. *He will leave it to do so.*

And he dismounts, running his pincers up and down one of the brown creature's legs. His buzzing is low and fluid as he examines it from head to toe. It doesn't resist, but its lip curls in what Joy reads as a scowl.

Wash it, New Magister thinks, giving the tether to one of his escorts. *Make it shine! And clean the hair—mind they don't pull it but do make it stand up proud.* Clicking to himself, he turns away and scuttles from the vale, trailing a line of dust that is soon blown from sight.

+ + +

As Joy watches, trapped inside her globe, the remaining scion usher the brown creature to the water basin and remove the leash from around its neck. It was unnecessary in any case, for it remains as docile as ever, never threatening its handlers or seeking escape. Using their proboscises, they transfer water from the basin and spray the creature from top to bottom. Its tower of hair hangs in a black mess about its face and shoulders, and two of the scion run pincers through the dripping locks, untangling snarls and massaging the scalp. It lowers its eyelids. Does it enjoy the experience or simply tolerate it to avoid being bitten? Joy can't tell. Its skin glistens as it dries, and it makes no sound.

Their work complete, the scion exit the vale—but they are quick to return. The first carries something like a pair of skins, one white, one black and sleek. Its partner bears a hollow, ebony sphere, larger than Joy's head. These they lay on the ground. To her amazement, as the scion exit the way they came, the creature steps into the skins, white first, then black. This latter it fastens by small devices that slide, zzzip! zzzip! until it is clad neck to toe in a form-fitting suit of black. The globe it places over its head, though it is no easy thing to squeeze over its prodigious mane. Joy wonders if it can see but soon learns the answer, for it looks her way and waves before approaching. It walks in a stately fashion, as if proud of its new attire, and when it arrives, it pokes a finger into one of the holes scoring her prison.

"Wanadilly inna duzzle tink," it says, its voice muffled by its new headgear. "Saratona saradun duzzle."

Whatever, she replies. *Please do go away.*

But the creature merely stands watching as she rises to her feet, stretching her aching limbs and wiggling her fingers and toes. As she shifts her weight, the globe moves beneath her. She takes careful steps forward, as if climbing the curved, inner wall. The globe is forced to roll under her, trundling across the arid ground. Had New Magister called this freedom?

Just a moving cage, she thinks. *That's what it is.*

She walks the globe into position so she can reach its door. But she is not surprised to find it can't be opened by either kicking or cursing.

"Simmin blong anta blong," thinks the brown creature. "Anta winnidunnit, thassa duzzle tink."

Fine, thinks Joy. *Let's try something else.*

She walks the globe to the far end of the vale, struggling to maintain her balance. Her progress is slow and clumsy, and more than once she bumps into the brown creature as it walks along—uninvited—beside her.

It mumbles an exclamation as if each new collision is a surprise. When she reaches her destination, an outcropping of jagged rock near the exit, she takes a deep breath and begins running, forcing the globe forward as fast as her unsteady feet allow. It strikes the rock with a force that first bounces her forward into its curved inner wall, and then, as it rebounds from the impact, rolls her about like a seed in a shell. By the time it comes to a stop, she is dizzy and sore, but her translucent prison remains intact, neither dented nor scratched.

The brown creature claps and hoots as Joy waits for the spinning world to settle. The impact on her second attempt is more violent than the first, but the results are the same; she is jarred and shaken, but the globe lives on. She whistles an angry tune, frustrated and bruised.

Vile, wretched, kish droppings!

Rubbing her head, she scowls at the brown creature as it attempts to echo her whistles. She is about to return to her feet, in slim hope of searching the remainder of the vale for a way out, when her captors return. She counts twelve; New Magister is not among them. The scion click sharp and fast, and the brown creature approaches as if by habit, allowing itself to be tethered once again. Taking the lead, its handlers move with it toward the eastern exit.

The remaining scion slide a long, slender pole through the center of the globe. Enough is exposed on either side that they are able to grip it with their front pincers, walking on their back four. In this fashion, they push Joy's prison up the sloping berm. She considers trying to break the pole, or walking in the opposite direction, but decides against it. Even if she were to run one of them over or spear a couple, others would soon take their place. Where would she be then? And so, marshalling her energy, she leans against the axle, letting it support her weight while her feet shuffle along.

As they approach the vale's eastern rim, Joy's antennae quiver with rising dread. Surely something awful awaits them. They crest the slope, the gate is opened, and the globe is rolled out onto flat ground where cracked land bakes in the sun. Joy's captors push on, arriving at a smooth road, wide and flat, running east to the anemic river and west to the parched horizon. They choose the eastern way. Near where the road crosses the water via a roughly formed bridge, a remarkable sight greets them, and Joy's feet would have stopped moving had the rolling globe allowed.

Oh my, she thinks.

From the river to the shallow lake, a menagerie of creatures forms a long, impatient line, smelly and loud. The road is filled with animals of every shape, size, and color, some passive, others resisting and bound. Scion scurry up and down the line to maintain order. There are ten-horned talihew, colossal yits, and a type of dow. But many of the animals are foreign. Some are kept in cages pulled by the tentacled, four-legged giants. Others fly in sad circles, tethered to one or more scion on the ground. A few stand free, obedient out of fear or some allegiance Joy can't fathom, while others are ridden by their captors. She sees animals in globes like her own, some pushed, some not. From hooting cremlins to their cousins the yellow hoppers, from multi-eyed heads to multi-headed bodies, Joy stares amazed at a wider variety of life than she had ever thought possible.

Her captors push the globe to the western tail of this menagerie, led by the brown creature and its keepers. They roll her into position at the end of the line, and there they wait, as if for a signal.

New Magister appears from a nearby hole. A half dozen scion hasten forward to greet him. Their antennae twitch and bend as they communicate, but they shelter their thoughts. When they are finished, New Magister gives a mighty whistle, a shrill, piercing call taken up and repeated down the line. In response, scion at the head of the assembly—and the animals they escort—begin to move east, stirring clouds of dust.

As Joy's handlers wait their turn, New Magister passes close by. He examines the brown creature carefully, picking a bit of debris from its ebony suit. Satisfied, he climbs on the creature's back, taking hold of the leash around its neck.

Has it ever seen such an array? he wonders to Joy. *And it, at the place of honor! He must go to the front now, but he will see it again when they arrive.* With that, he clicks like a command and the brown creature breaks into a jog, moving east toward the bridge.

+ + +

The wave of motion begun by New Magister's whistle travels from the front of the line to the rear. Soon, Joy is escorted forward as well, pushed along inside her globe. They bridge the river, but many of the creatures could have crossed without its assistance. The current is frail, and rust chokes the parched banks. Shortly after, the lake appears, oily and dark, desultory waves lapping far below the original shore. Six gray towers rise from the island, and three roads extend outward: theirs, one to the north, and another heading into the sun. If there is an eastern version, it is hidden by the towers.

Onward! order her handlers. *To Queen!*

Yes! To Queen!

And so, they begin crossing the lake. Many scion have gathered at the sides of the road to observe their passing. They chitter in apparent fascination to one another when they see her. As they bend their antennae her direction, she senses some of their thoughts.

What is it?

Yes. What?

It walks vumierre!

Yes. Like New Magister's steed.

Yes. But the eyes are scion.

No. They cannot be.

Yes! They are. And see the antennae.

No. It is too much.

Yes. Too much to take.

Yes. But see! It tries to hide.

Yes. It is defective.
No. It is a freak.
Yes. A freak. A deviant vumierre.

This continues until, by the time the procession reaches the island, both sides of the road are crowded with spectators, twin rivers of blue and black. Here, the way branches, circling the towers to the north and south, but the parade continues east, into the deep, melancholy shadows. It snakes between the looming towers, and from countless windows high above, bulbous eyes peer down at them, topped by waving antennae as echoing whistles and clicks fall like rain.

While the rest of the parade continues to the east, its cacophony and dust cloud moving out of the shadows and into the sunny distance, Joy's end of the line finally arrives at the island's stony heart, a wide, open space, surrounded by towering walls of gray and filled with jostling onlookers. And here she is made to stop.

Before them, attended on the ground by dozens of bristly scion in tight formation, two spectacular specimens—one Joy's size and silver, the other larger and gold like the sun—ride in separate, ornately woven baskets. Each is suspended by gossamer lines held by scion flying overhead, bronze, not blue, six for the silver creature, twelve for the gold, their wings droning. New Magister dismounts and lowers himself to the ground. His antennae arc downward and the light in his eyes grows dim. He tugs at the leash, and the brown creature follows suit, kneeling and bowing its head.

Joy's handlers usher her forward, rolling her into position before the largest of the two baskets and its golden passenger. New Magister's tone is obsequious.

The offering is nearly complete, oh Queen. He has saved the best for last.

The gold scion addressed as Queen peers down from her basket. Her antennae quiver at the sight of Joy, and in the smaller basket next to hers, the silver scion buzzes, high, short bursts in rapid succession.

Another vumierre! it thinks. *Or one like it!*

A.P. Malloy

Queen's reply is a shrill, peremptory whistle, and most scion in attendance hunker at the sound—but not the silver one. It ceases its buzzing, but its eyes scatter sunlight and it holds Queen's wrathful gaze.

Princess will still her thoughts, thinks the gold creature. *Or she will be removed to the perimeter.*

Princess will not! thinks the silver one. *She will stay and examine the vumierre. Two! In only moons!*

Queen whistles again. Even as the silver creature protests, the bronze flyers suspending her basket sweep their burden about face and move off, bearing it to the gallery's edge, fifty strides away. There they hover as the silver creature clicks easily read frustration and coddles angry but sheltered thoughts.

At Queen's terse command, Joy's handlers roll the globe closer, and the singular creature comes into clear view, gleaming as if ladled in melting gold.

Ozag's antennae! thinks Queen. *What is this, and where did New Magister find it?*

Queen will be astonished when she learns.

He will not presume to know her response. Nor will he dare waste her time!

New Magister hugs the ground.

Never, Queen, he thinks. *Never. New Magister did not find it. Old Magister did. And if he knows what it is, he refuses to divulge.*

Queen's clicking is rapid and harsh.

Does he? She peers at Joy, her fantastic, obsidian eyes distorted through the globe, at once terrible and impossible to ignore, each facet alive and sparkling. *A scion twisted to vumierre form,* she thinks.

So it would seem, thinks New Magister. *But how, and why? By whom? Or was it a natural breeding?*

Queen shrieks in reply. New Magister's antennae wither, and the brown creature grovels.

He will lose a leg if he dares express such a thought ever again! thinks Queen. *This is an evil spawn. No scion would participate willingly in its creation.*

In spite of her dire circumstance, Joy feels an unexpected flicker of pride at the insult, and she considers an angry retort. But Queen's eyes hold her pinned, almost cowering, and she loses the nerve. She drops her gaze to the ground, focuses on the intricate cracks running across its parched face, and tries to hide her mind, as if shameful secrets are exposed.

The creature does not communicate, thinks New Magister, still bowing, *but he believes it can.*

She is not pleased, thinks Queen, leaning forward. Her clicking is now slow and deliberate. *It will respond. What is it? How was it violated to this form?*

A subtle pain grows between Joy's eyes, and her legs become slack. She supports herself against the pole, her breaths short and shallow.

Why does it pretend to hide?

He does not know, thinks New Magister.

Queen's whistle blisters the ears.

She addresses the aberration, not New Magister! He will still his mind or have it removed. And the beast will respond. Explain its defects!

Joy's antennae begin to curl. Queen rises from six legs to four. Her beaky mouth opens and closes.

What is it? she demands. *Tell!*

If Old Magister had probed with a mind like fingers, Queen's squeezes like a fist. Joy fears she will soon lose this battle. She fights the compulsion to respond, but near her breaking point, as quickly as she had begun, Queen ceases the interrogation.

It can wait, she thinks, her tone weary. *Egg-laying has left her worn. Send for Old Magister!* A trio of scion breaks away from the circled attendants and scurries from the gallery. *New Magister,* she thinks, *will remain and answer her questions.*

It will be his delight.

Queen suspects not. Two vumierre appear so close together after such a long absence—and on the tail of the drought? He is a fool if he considers this serendipity. Was it washed up on the seashore like the brown one? Did it descend from the sky in the same fashion?

No Queen. Old Magister's loyalists found it on the open plains, traveling with young sharksha—two of them, his drones report, though they cannot be sure why.

Sharksha! thinks Queen. *The mystery deepens. He will answer more! But first...* She turns to the scion who attend Joy's cage. *The aberration disgusts. It will be removed to the far side of the gallery.*

+ + +

Joy's handlers buzz in low tones, their antennae brushing the ground. Keeping their eyes dim and averted from Queen, they push their prisoner briskly across the aggrieved land, coming to a stop at the perimeter, near the southernmost tower.

From inside the globe, Joy watches as Queen and New Magister continue waving antennae and gesturing. She is too far away to sense their thoughts, or they have begun sheltering them, and so she is left to imagine the worst. When, not long after, Old Magister is escorted into the gallery, faded and limping, she doubles her efforts, determined to learn what thoughts are shared. Focused thus, she doesn't notice the droning of wings until the smaller basket has drawn to within ten strides.

It wastes its time, comes a thought.

Startled, Joy turns to see the one called Princess, hovering in her basket, so close she can see black facets scattering sunlight and smell the dust stirred by a dozen bronze wings. At the far side of the gallery, Queen and her consort maintain their posturing, deep in thought, unaware of or unconcerned by Princess' relocation.

It will never discern sheltered Royal thoughts at this distance, thinks Princess. She buzzes a somber melody. *Is it truly vumierre? Or is it a mutant scion?*

Joy quells her temper, clamping a lid on angry thoughts. She concentrates on the meeting at the center of the gallery, certain her fate is being decided there. But a novel sensation calls her mind back to Princess' basket, and she realizes a moment later that something is tucked

behind the silver creature, covered by a woven shroud—
something alive and squirming.

Princess asked it a question! the silver creature
thinks, and one of Joy's handlers raps the globe with its
pincers to prompt a reply. But Joy has attention only for
the thing that wriggles beneath the shroud. It sends a
single, beseeching thought.

Please, it thinks. *Whoever you are...help us!*

Joy has never sensed a mind more frail or desperate, so small its thoughts seem to come from many
strides away. Her antennae bend forward.

Princess notices this.

So! she thinks. *It is true, as she has suspected.
The Oddity* does *sense.* She caresses the hidden creature,
running her pincers the length of its form but keeping it
shrouded. Its squirming stills, but its mind continues to
send the same feeble thought:

Please...help us.

*And so it has been repeating since the Oddity's ap-
pearance,* thinks Princess. *"Help us" this, and "Help us"
that. Until now, Princess has sensed it thinking, but no
clear ideas could she discern. Now, without explanation, a
mutant vumierre appears, and this one thought—a call for
help—becomes clear. How?*

Seeing she has betrayed her ability to understand, only pride prevents Joy from sharing her thoughts.
She meets Princess' gaze, despising her image reflected
in the facets before her. She clicks rapid and low, unhappy at the way their antennae bend in the same supple
fashion, disturbed at how their eyes mirror one another
in size and sparkle. She looks away.

But Princess refuses to be ignored.

*Does the mutant vumierre know why it seeks help?
Can it understand more of its thoughts?*

Joy senses the questions, but events across the
gallery take her focus. The conference is coming to an
end. Old Magister is escorted from the space under duress, while Queen's basket is borne higher. New Magister
whistles, and bristly scion gather around.

The Oddity has little time to live, thinks Princess. *But she can see that it is spared—if it helps her.*

Queen and her coterie turn and begin to approach them. Joy can read no specific thoughts, but even at this distance she senses menace and foreboding. Whatever the silver creature's motivation, she has no doubt her assessment is correct. And so, she decides.

Help how? she thinks. *What is under there?*

Buzzing softly, Princess pulls away the shroud. Beneath, black and red instead of green, and no larger than Joy herself, lies coiled and serpentine what must be the smallest derka in the world.

+ + + + + +

At the edge of the landfall, twenty-five thousand strides north of Albion, Lightning stares in amazement.

It's Ari, she thinks. *Ari has come for us.*

But the next moment, her nose reveals the truth. The proud bomba landing before them, safely out of pouncing distance, is not her friend Ari, but his brother, Ansel. Cliff growls, appreciating the bomba's size—as a meal and a potential threat—and he crouches, baring his teeth. Lightning steps between them.

Keep your peace! she thinks. *His name is Ansel.*

It has a name?

Yes. And he's a friend.

But as she thinks this, she can't help wondering: *Is he, though?* She recalls the bomba's perpetual distrust and his angry thoughts at their last encounter. She can't say what has brought him here, so far from the maison, but it seems unlikely to be friendship.

Ansel, she greets him, bowing low. *We are surprised and glad.* When he fails to reply in kind, she curses her foolishness. *Of course he can't understand me,* she thinks. *Joy isn't here.*

Instead, Ansel waves a rainbow wing and turns away, striding and flapping to the west. He looks back, hissing, and he waves once again, continuing to stride to the west, his feathers ruffling.

What is it doing? thinks Cliff.

He, thinks Lightning. But to herself, she thinks, *Just like his nester,* and she recalls Oracio and their rescue from the kish. *He wants us to follow him.* She adjusts her vest, chafing at its tightness and freeing a button for relief. *Stay behind me,* she thinks.

Wait. We're following a bomba?

Ansel squawks and points to the northern sky. The kezel at first see nothing, but a moment later, a speck of soaring emerald appears, so small it could have been a trick of the eye.

There's your answer, thinks Lightning.

Who cares? It can't see us.

It can see him, Cliff! C'mon...

Ansel wastes no time; once the kezel are following, he takes to the air, heading west along the landfall and away from their enemies. They strive to maintain his pace, but he is forced to circle back several times, muttering frustration at the delay. Two thousand strides later, he alights without fear at the brink of the landfall. Beneath him, a portion of the rocky lip has broken away, creating a tiny step and exposing to its right a small, black hole in the face of the cliff. He hops into the abyss, spreading broad wings to catch his fall before landing on the narrow, crumbling step.

Lightning creeps to the edge. She pokes her snout over the brink and looks down. Cliff joins her, his reluctance evident. The step is a kezel-length below, wide enough for only one at a time. The yawning land calls to them with a message of wind and vertigo. Ansel hops and flaps through the hole, disappearing into the dark. A moment later, a swarm of small, eyeless creatures scurries out, screeching by the hundreds. They use their eight purple legs to descend the wall, joining in a high, piercing trill Lightning needs no interpreter to understand. The creatures hasten from sight, in search of another place to conduct their business.

Whatever that is, she thinks, wrinkling her snout.

She has never seen so many rixli in one place.

Ansel's impatient cackle calls to her.

First or second? she thinks.

Neither, is Cliff's wholehearted reply.

Lightning curls her lip and takes a deep breath, removing her pack and lowering herself over the edge. The wind tugs at her camouflage, zipping along the face of the landfall as if trying to scrub it clean of this intruder. With a *shhrriip!* the grass mat tears free and goes sailing away, twirling like a plaything, and Lightning grows dizzy as she watches it fall. She gropes blindly, reaching with clawed feet to locate the step. When, after terrifying moments, she feels the reassurance of solid stone, she releases her hold on the ledge and Cliff lowers the pack to her. The opening to her right is small, but she stuffs the pack inside and manages to squeeze through. A dirty cave awaits, lit by the sun. Ansel stands at a safe distance. Together they wait for Cliff to muster his courage and make the descent. His uncooperative leg hampers the effort, but he soon crawls through the opening, his gray eyes full of doubt.

He wrinkles his nose.

What is that smell?

Lightning has been wondering the same thing. Whether the rixli or some other creatures, noisome beasts have made a home in this cave for many moons. The floor is littered and slick.

Ansel cocks his head side to side. He points at Cliff, squawking and muttering.

He won't hurt you, thinks Lightning, reverting to useless habit. Growling at herself, she instructs Cliff to remove himself to the far side of the cave.

Sit quiet, she thinks. *And no eye contact.*

Gladly, he replies, his ears pinned back. *Looking at him just makes me hungry.*

With one eye always on Cliff, Ansel uses a claw to draw a sharply curved line, a half ellipse, in the carpet of filth. Lightning stares at this, uncomprehending. Ansel fans his tail and shakes his head. Next to the half circle,

Book of Dreams

he then traces a long, thin figure, pointed at the top. The images are crude, but had they been the finest art, it might not have mattered. Ansel points to Lightning, himself, and back to the images, spreading his wing in a wave to the north. Another bomba would perhaps have recognized the maison and Eye Tower, would have understood Ansel's desire for them to return there with him. But images have always escaped Lightning, slipping through the fingers of her reckoning like awl eggs. She looks from one to the other for long moments.

I'm sorry, she thinks, though there is no point in doing so. *I don't understand.*

But then Ansel makes a sound she understands perfectly: the unmistakable cackling his father and all their kind had first made upon seeing Joy, high-pitched and serial. It had become their sign for her and would always linger in Lightning's mind. Now, he swings his head left to right as if looking for someone. Lightning intuits the question and points out the cave's opening, then to the lower land.

She's down there, she thinks. *We're rescuing her.*

At this, Ansel repeats his pantomime with emphasis, jabbing his wing at the images then waving to the north as if trying to put out a fire. When Lightning shakes her head, indicating herself and Cliff and pointing to the land below, he sticks out his tongue.

Lightning sighs, but Cliff is scornful.

This is ridiculous, he thinks. *What are you trying to accomplish? I thought you said they could think.*

It's not that simple. I don't suppose you can tell me what these scratches mean?

They don't mean anything. How could they? And why does it keep waving like that?

I don't know. Lightning's ears droop. *I should have paid closer attention when Ancian was teaching me about images. They mean something...*

Ansel stops his jabbing and waving and hisses like deflated hope. He scratches away the images and again makes the cackling sound that indicates Joy. Then he points his wing out the opening and down.

Yes, thinks Lightning, and she nods, whether or not it does any good, pointing to the lower land.

The bomba squawks, shifting his weight from one long leg to the other, and he makes a sound as if struggling to swallow an awl bone. He cranes his neck, fixing Lightning with sharp, flashing glances. Regardless which eye he uses, he clearly dislikes what he sees; his muttering echoes from the deep recesses of the cave. Then, without warning, he strides to the exit, slips through the hole, and disappears.

Well, that's that, thinks Cliff. *Our best chance at fresh meat is gone now.*

No, thinks Lightning. *He'll be back.*

But for a long time, he is not.

+ + +

In the beginning, the two kezel remain in silence, exploring their surroundings and keeping their thoughts to themselves. Lightning seeks other exits to the cave. There are several, but she wishes to explore none; their smells are unsettling. Cliff spends his energy calculating the time since their last meal. His complaints wear on Lightning until she allows them both enough virble to subdue their nagging stomachs.

I'm exhausted, thinks Cliff. He gulps his food in two quick swallows. *How long are we going to wait?*

Until he gets back.

So I can take a nap?

No. But you can take first watch.

Lightning curls in a tight ball on the least filthy portion of the floor, wrapping her spiked tail to the tip of her snout. Cliff grumbles but wastes no energy on debate. He takes a cautious sniff of the crevices at the rear of the cave, his nose worrying.

Have you thought any more about why their bites didn't work on you? he asks.

Lightning growls, desiring sleep, not discussion.

Book of Dreams

No, she thinks, and then: *yes. Armacan.* But this is untrue. Traveling on the river had allowed abundant time to reconstruct events. Based on all the evidence, she suspects another, more difficult answer; she suspects awl gland. At the moment, however, weariness makes lying seem the easiest plan.

Armawhat? Cliff wonders.

Ancian gave it to me. It makes kezel sleep.

What you put in Rock's food!

Yes. It's the only thing I can think of that I've done recently and you haven't.

You ate some too?

When we were back in the Sugarfoot caves. I was...I needed to sleep. Like now.

Do you have any more?

Lightning opens one eye and scowls.

It's just, thinks Cliff, *if that is the answer, I should probably eat some too. In case we have to fight again. Which we probably will.*

If you don't let me sleep, you won't have to worry about those blue things. I'll just bite you myself.

Cliff shelters his thoughts and takes a position near the exit. He has just settled himself when he hears reverberating wingbeats.

That bomba is coming back, he thinks.

Of course he is. Lightning opens her eyes with a curse and a heavy sigh. She rises to her feet, shouldering Cliff to the side as she peers out the sunlit hole. At first, Ansel is nowhere to be seen, but moments later, he surprises them by appearing from one of the fissures behind them. He soars up and past, perching on a ledge out of reach. He points to the fissure, then to the lower land, cackling. Cliff shakes his head, confused, but Lightning inhales, surprised and delighted.

Clever bomba! she thinks, and she turns to Cliff. *Come on. We're leaving.*

Cliff's shoulders sag.

But we just got here.

+ + +

The fissure itself is a natural feature, a jagged tear in the stone through which they pass easily enough. The tunnel it leads to is equally unremarkable; it could have been one of a hundred such in the accrete. But that soon changes, as the tunnel grows narrower and assumes the appearance of something deliberately bored rather than formed by nature—but not uniformly in maison style. Instead, the way is crooked and constricted, with odd walls that are both smooth and lumpy, as if the stone has been incompletely melted.

Ever seen anything like this? Cliff wonders.

Lightning has not. But she has smelled something like it. This is a way made by their enemies.

The tunnel grows almost immediately pitch-black, forcing Lightning to use one of her precious crystals. Ansel flies the first hundred strides, but after that, there is no room, and he must go on foot. He leads from a distance, often craning his neck to look behind, hissing and raising crewels if Lightning gets too close. The awful smell grows at first, and the small, gurgling creatures responsible for it retreat before them, their forms remaining hidden in the dark. After a time, the smell fades, gradually replaced by fresh air. Soon after, the tunnel begins to descend. It does so steeply, at such an angle that Lightning would not have gone on had Ansel not been leading the way. Behind her, Cliff slips and slides but somehow keeps his feet.

Do you smell that? he asks.

Lightning sniffs carefully. Dry, dead odors reach her from far below, mold and excrement. But there is also something familiar, not just the scent of the bomba leading them, but the unmistakable aroma created when many of his kind gather in one place.

There's been a brood here, she replies. *A long time ago though,* and she recalls Oracio's proud claim: *"Bombas circle the world."*

A what? Cliff wants to know, but he is busy concentrating on his footing and doesn't complain when he gets no answer.

Down they slither, the tunnel sometimes veering left and right but never fully leveling, and as his beleaguered muscles grow weary of braking the descent, Cliff senses concerns brewing in Lightning's mind.

You're afraid I'm going to fall on you.

It had occurred to me.

Bet I don't!

Why would I take that bet? If I win, I lose.

They continue downward, slip and stumble, for dozens and then scores of kezel-lengths. Lover of caves that she is, even Lightning grows anxious at the weight of the world pressing down on her. When at last they reach bottom, they drop out of the shaft to the stony ground below, into a vast, airy cavern, dry as bone. Ansel stands at the edge of shadow, hissing as he waves them on, his colors muted in the crystal light.

What is this place? Awe and suspicion fill Cliff's mind. He hunches his shoulders.

Lightning quickly takes in their surroundings. The difference between the imprecise, lumpy passage and this new space could hardly have been more radical. The cavern is part of a wide, symmetrical tunnel, supported by a lattice of stone arches set at perfect right angles to one another and whose massive legs meet to form stout columns. Each square section of the tunnel is roofed over in curving planes of stone that peak five kezel-lengths above. From one column to the next Lightning estimates a dozen strides. The space echoes with distant wind, and its smooth faces glow gold in the dim light. Bomba feathers of every color litter the floor.

Lightning's answer isn't immediate, but it is sure.

The way of things in the maison, she thinks. *Not possible, but real.*

The maison? thinks Cliff, and he looks about, his gaze uneasy. *The place you went to with...*

With Joy, yes. Lightning strides toward where Ansel waits, shifting impatiently from leg to leg. *You have a hard time with her name.*

But we're a long way from there. And why is every-thing so…so smooth? That doesn't seem natural.

Just keep your nose open—and your mind.

As before, when Ansel sees them following, he takes to the air, passing under an arch and disappearing into the dark. The kezel chase the echo of his wings, jog-ging in bubbles of faint crystal light. The floor, formed from the same gold stone as the arches and roofs and covered everywhere in patches of rust, is not flat, but curved to form a trough. This, combined with the scent of dead mold tells a clear story.

Water used to flow here, thinks Lightning. *A lot.*

Yes, thinks Cliff. *But moons ago.*

Let's not be here if it comes back, thinks Lightning, and she increases her pace.

Small creatures who call the tunnel home scurry, fly, or slink away from the beat of bomba wings and the unexpected appearance of kezel bearing light. As they proceed, the floor's gentle, downward slope becomes steeper. Soon, the echoing fall of water competes with wingbeats and wind. Not long after, sunlight grows; the air turns warm and damp.

A hundred strides later, the slope steepens with dangerous suddenness as it runs to the tunnel's end. There, the bomba stands guard, warning them away from the perilous drop and directing them to a stair that de-scends to the wide, bright opening below. Like those in the maison, the steps are unnaturally precise, though here they are made of stone, and not all remain intact. Cliff struggles to navigate them, unable to find the proper rhythm. When he trips and falters—more than once—Lightning is not surprised.

Nothing good can come out of a place like this, thinks Cliff, and he bares his teeth at the wind.

Well, we're about to, thinks Lightning. *Eyes up.*

A moment later, they reach the mouth of the tun-nel. The river above them pours out in a mighty cascade that arcs and falls like a wind-blown sheet of liquid light between them and the sun. It plummets into its bed with a roaring voice. They have reached the lower land.

Cliff stares dumbly, but Lightning waves him on.

No time for spectating, she thinks.

They step out into the light. Above them and to their left, another stair leads up to the eastern bank of the river, opposite that of their enemies. The climb is not long, but it is nearly vertical, and the kezel are panting at its completion. There, Ansel stands waiting. Lightning bows, but as usual, he refuses to respond in kind.

Through the contrivance of their devices and mastery over their giant servants, the blue creatures have nearly finished lowering the contents of the floating caravan. Most have moved off into the hazy distance, traveling in a neat file while their companions finish the task. The personality of the river they follow changes as it approaches the horizon. It becomes narrower, less robust, even swimmable perhaps.

Well, thinks Cliff. *We're down. Now what?*

Follow the river. Cross it as soon as possible.

And then?

But Lightning has no answer for this. Ansel squawks in dismay when she moves south, skirting the riverbank and using its thorny hedge as cover. He cackles to indicate Joy and cranes his neck, as if expecting to see her. Lightning points to the train of shimmering blue.

She's that way. Stay with us, please; help us.

Cliff barks a rude curse.

You keep thinking to it like it's going to understand. How's that going for you?

Lightning bites down on her temper.

You'll see, she thinks. *When we get Joy back, you'll see.* She waves to Ansel and continues south. The bomba hisses, scratching the ground. But in the end, he rises to flight, his muttering objection hard to miss.

+ + +

As Ansel circles overhead, the jabi kezel continue

south until they reach a place where cracks spider across the parched land. Though its bed widens, the river itself dwindles between banks of rust. As hundreds of strides pass into thousands, it continues to shrink. Soon, Lightning guesses, they will be able to cross without more than a brief—and in this heat, welcome—swim. Fatigue weighs heavily on the travelers, and Cliff soon lags far behind, his camouflage long ago crammed into Lightning's pack. The growing warmth dulls their senses, as every step brings them closer to the sun.

They encounter no enemies.

Just as Cliff is about to beg for a stop, Ansel calls out and lands at a distance, waving for Lightning. As she approaches, head bowed as always, she crests a gentle slope and sees dark shapes rising above the horizon, though what they are, she can't say. Each is as tall as the maison, dull gray, and formed like weathered stone. They rise from an island in the middle of a shallow lake, once fed by the river, though the two are now separated by a wide lane of arid rust.

When Cliff arrives at last, the bomba tenses as if ready to take flight. But judging from the kezel's haggard appearance, he needn't have worried. Cliff casts himself to the ground with a weary sigh, his tongue lolling.

So close, thinks Lightning.

As close as we're going to get for now, Cliff groans. *I can't fight if I can't stand. Not that it matters. We're going to be completely outnumbered.*

You've never seen a bomba fight.

Cliff scoffs at this, but Lightning pays him no mind. She has smelled something. A thrill runs from her nose to the tip of her tail, and her spikes flare.

I smell them, she thinks. *I smell the kezel.*

But if Joy is out there, her scent is hidden.

CHAPTER SEVEN
Shimmer

PRINCESS WHISTLES SOFTLY. Queen, New Magister, and their coterie of bristly scion are fifty strides away and getting closer. A dozen pair of droning wings joins many tickety-tacking pincers in troubling harmony.

If it wishes to live, it will still its mind and follow her lead, thinks Princess. *Regardless its doubt.*

Moments later, Queen and her escort arrive, her golden skin flashing but her eyes dim. Joy wonders what fate lurks behind their facets, but as the procession draws within thought range, Princess clicks sharply, preempting whatever Queen or New Magister might have been about to think.

She is vexed! This oddity has insulted her!

Joy's handlers take this as their cue for action, and they shake the globe side to side, nearly driving her to her knees. But Queen only buzzes impatience, motioning for the handlers to cease their shaking.

It is an aberration, she thinks. *Hideous and stupid beyond compare. How could it insult her?*

It refuses to respond! Princess replies.

Because it is unable, thinks Queen, *in spite of what New Magister believes. It is a genetic defect.*

Princess considers this.

Queen is surely correct, she thinks. *Nevertheless. She wishes it brought to her personal garden. There, it will be taught the proper way to behave.*

Queen's eyes brighten.

This is not approved, she thinks. *She believes the aberration beyond redemption. It repulses.*

Princess agrees. She thinks it horrible. But she desires it; teaching it manners will give her pleasure.

Queen clicks, her impatience growing.

Vumierre, she thinks, *are not for collecting. And yet...* Here she looks at New Magister and the black-clad creature he rides. *She must admit she is pleased to see them brought under Command. She will allow this concession, though she feels certain her time is wasted.*

Undoubtedly, thinks Princess.

+ + +

The bronze flyers strive upward, the drone of their wings filling the air, and they bear both baskets out of the gallery and toward the three southern towers. Joy is driven behind at a brisk pace, forced to move her feet or be rolled about. They are followed by the brown creature, New Magister clinging to its back and whistling orders. Soon, they reach a place where the way splits in three. Here, the party comes to a halt.

Princess will take care, New Magister thinks. *The mutant vumierre is more dangerous than it looks.*

And New Magister, thinks Princess, *will recall his place and keep his advice to himself.*

New Magister's antennae bend low, but his eyes flash. Then he turns his steed toward the southwestern tower and disappears inside. Queen's basket is borne into the tallest of the towers, the one facing due south. But Princess' basket is carried into the southeastern tower, and Joy and her captors follow close behind, enveloped in shadow. The darkness is not complete, however, for shafts of light enter through small, irregular windows, painting the space subtle hues of amber, and as her eyes adjust, details become clear.

The tower is rough and misshapen on the outside,

but when viewed from within, it is a wonder of precise repetition. The passage is wide enough to allow two of the baskets to pass—though Joy sees none but Princess'—and its ceiling is a full kezel-length above the bronze flyers. It follows an exact pattern, traveling straight for twenty strides, then branching to the left and right in identical, obtuse angles. Each passage is the same size and shape and continues on for another twenty strides before branching again in the same fashion. All together, they form a matrix of hexagons, often opening to rooms with six sides. At three of the intersections, ramps lead them to higher levels, but these are the same as the ones below: branches and angles, straight ways of twenty strides, one hexagon after another.

Joy is soon quite lost.

Any scion they meet hug the ground at the sight of Princess, antennae wilting and incessant clicking silenced. But after the basket has passed, they look up. The hungry curiosity in their surreptitious thoughts is easy to read, but not the details. The tone of most makes Joy glad for this.

At last, the bronze flyers bear their passengers down a broad tunnel that opens to the sun, followed by Joy in her globe. They stand in the center of the tower, three levels up, in what she assumes is Princess' personal garden, its roof and southern face cut away and exposed to the sun. Narrow bridges connect flanking towers from base to pinnacle, and lines of glittering scion cross from one tower to the next like streams of living water. The garden itself stretches for five hundred verdant strides, lush and filled with color. Plants of many varieties border a swift-running creek, filling the air with rich smells, and the ground is carpeted in spongy, green grass—none of the cracked, pale land found everywhere else.

Plenty of water here, thinks Joy.

Laboring scion, smaller than others of their kind, climb into the flora to pluck and prune, while others collect water from the creek, using their proboscises to spray low-lying plants whose blossoms unfurl in broad, waving flags. In the distance, docile beasts with long necks stride on legs like tripods. Closer to hand, yits of many colors and sizes perch among the foliage, calling with voices Joy hasn't heard since the accrete. She sees creatures related to dow floating on the stream. They dive without warning, reappearing many strides away with wriggling young awl in their mouths. Near the high, green wall running the perimeter, a small herd of talihew grazes, apparently unconcerned by their captivity.

But Joy is not so sanguine.

Pretty, she thinks, *but just another cage.*

At that moment, the derka lets out a raspy croak and stirs beneath its shroud. As if emerging from a broken spell, Princess turns to Joy's handlers.

She desires to question the Oddity—alone. To nearby scion tending plants she thinks, *They will leave their tasks and clear the garden.*

The gardeners hurry away as if chased by fire. But Joy's handlers hesitate, buzzing softly amongst themselves, debating the wisdom of leaving Princess with a known killer. Their reticence doesn't last long.

Now! thinks Princess, and she lets out a terrible, whistling shriek, rising to four legs. Joy catches her breath in surprise as Princess spreads two silver wings that had been hidden, folded at her back. These agitate in a fierce, scintillating blur, and for a moment, she hovers above the basket, reflecting the sun as if shooting darts of light. Her shriek drives the dow underwater, honking distress. This is all the handlers need. Dimming their eyes, they turn and scurry from the garden. Princess settles to six legs, wings tucked away, and when she thinks, her tone is almost bored, as if the outburst had never happened.

She desires to be set down, she thinks.

The bronze flyers don't need to be told twice. They lower the basket gently and land nearby, stilling the drone of their wings. Princess steps out, bearing the derka before her. Black barbs, tipped in red, run from its toothy snout to the tip of its improbably long, forked tail, and its head bobs at the end of a serpentine neck. Its eyes blink like polished garnets.

We are Derka, it thinks to Joy, its mind feeble, the thought barely lucid. *Help us!*

Princess approaches Joy's globe.

It makes the mind of this derka sensible, she thinks. *How is that possible, when, prior to the Oddity's arrival, no one, neither Princess nor her pluripotents, could understand what it thought?*

Pluri-who?

Answer!

I don't know how, Joy cringes. *It thinks; I sense.* And when she adds: *You promised my freedom,* Princess clicks an irritated tempo.

Its life, not its freedom. If not for her, it would remain New Magister's plaything. Perhaps it desires to be returned to him? It will explain how its presence triggers understanding of the derka! Until this moment, it communicated crudely, using its snapping jaws to make a few scion words—click! click! But now she understands clear thoughts and complete ideas. How?

Like I told you, thinks Joy. *I don't know how.*

Why does it beseech the Oddity for succor?

Help? I don't know.

It lies!

Ask it yourself, then!

But at this, the derka fixes Joy with an intense gaze and spreads its wings. The thought it sends is tightly focused, requiring tremendous effort from such a weary mind, and she knows it is meant to be secret.

Exchange information for freedom, it thinks.

Princess' antennae straighten suddenly.

The derka thought something to the Oddity, she discerns. *They conspire! What did it share?*

Joy shakes her head.

Let me out first.

Princess changes from clicks to a menacing buzz.

It is as foolish as it is ugly, she thinks. *The Circle will claim it, and all of Albion will witness its demise. Even*

A.P. Malloy

now Queen prepares the feast of tey Ramota. If it has learned no manners by then, its life is forfeit.

Joy has no guess what either the Circle or tey Ramota might be, but trusts they are both awful.

Then let me out, she thinks. *Or secrets stay secret.*

She needs not the Oddity's permission! Princess' tone is sneering. *She will force the information from it like squeezing juice from a lova.* Her antennae bend forward like divining rods. *Reveal!*

A sudden pressure, like a nut about to crack, squeezes at Joy's temples. She closes her mind, looking at the ground and thinking about dirt, but Princess stares as if aware of her greatest fear and most furtive desire. Still, hers is a mind younger and not so strong as Queen's or Old Magister's, and after several moments, she clicks a rapid staccato and turns away.

It is hateful and disgusting, she thinks. *Even if it were to share the derka's thoughts, it asks too much. Assuring the Oddity's freedom is beyond even Princess.*

Joy looks up from the ground. Her head is sore as if waking from a poor sleep.

Then there's no deal.

Princess whistles in anger; her antennae quiver. Then, as before, her rage passes, and she slouches, a posture Joy reads as sadness or fatigue.

She must know the truth, thinks Princess. *At any price. If the Oddity complies, she will make the attempt to procure its freedom—or die trying.*

Joy buzzes her approval.

Spoken like a kezel, she thinks.

A spark lights in Princess' eyes.

If it lies to her, it will die in the Circle.

Yes, yes, Joy snaps. *Whatever the Circle is.* She raps at the globe. *First, open this thing.*

A silent order from Princess brings one of the bronze creatures to life. It crosses the ten strides in a flash and a buzz, landing near the globe and unlatching its small door. It returns with the others as Joy steps out onto the verdant carpet, her bare feet delighted at its forgiving, spongy feel.

That's a good start, she thinks. *Now it's my turn.*

She focuses on the derka. Its head lolls slowly, and ruby lids sag—but it remains awake. She knows it can sense her, can feel its intense desire to share information, tenuous and enigmatic though the thoughts may seem. Its mind labors for long moments to stitch the ideas together, and Joy attends closely.

The derka, she thinks finally, *it says...*

Yes?

This doesn't make sense...

Continue!

Joy hesitates a moment more, unsure how the news will be received, for it means nothing to her. But in the end, she decides to relay it word-for-word.

"Warning, warning! Vumierre mischief!" She rubs her hands together, raspy and dry. *"No Circle, no Albion."* Recalling carefully, she adds, *"Flee to Far Colossus."* And finally, hoping she is expressing the foreign idea correctly, *"Ozag commands: no Circle."*

+ + +

Princess' soft whistle is her only sign of surprise.

It thinks all of this?

Yes.

Is there more?

Yes. But it's difficult.

Divulge!

Joy concentrates and does her best to translate, though the thought is complete gibberish to her.

"Estimate ninety-one percent casualties."

What is meant by this?

I have no idea.

Princess clicks harshly, and Joy feels her doubt.

I'm telling the truth.

Its life depends on it! It will be still now.

Princess looks down at the derka, and her mind wanders to faraway thoughts. She embraces the creature, silver antennae draping its body, and her eyes are dim. Joy waits, expecting the worst, serenaded by the tremulous call of yits. When Princess at last opens her mind, she isn't sure who is being addressed.

Is it in league with Ozag? When she fails to answer, Princess' antennae grow rigid, and there is fire in her eyes. *The Oddity will respond!* she thinks in an imperious tone. *Does it owe its skill to Ozag? Or is there some other will at work here?*

What is an ozag?

Princess clicks low but fast.

It dares to mock her suffering? Is this a trial? Is Ozag testing Princess?

I am very sorry, thinks Joy, her tone sincere. *But I don't understand.*

Lies! How else could it possess such an ability? Only Ozag communicates with the beasts. Unless the Oddity is the spawn of some vile experiment? Its disgusting appearance indicates as much.

Joy checks her irritation.

Believe what you want, she thinks, turning to walk away. *Sense the derka yourself.*

The silver creature buzzes in distress.

Princess, she begins, but then falters, as if struggling to form the necessary thought. *Princess,* she tries again, *Princess...apologizes...to the Oddity.* Her antennae wave. *It will accept!*

But Joy ignores this order disguised as contrition and walks toward the stream, desiring to wash away the grime and stink of captivity.

Princess sends a chasing thought.

It must understand. She has been worried for many moons. It will accept the apology.

No, it will not. Joy steps into the stream. Schools of harmless, slender awl scatter in streaks of green light when she submerges, scrubbing at her skin as the current washes debris from her hair.

It infuriates! thinks Princess, and her wings shred the air. In the blink of an eye, she crosses to the stream, landing near the bank as Joy surfaces. *Time is short! She will be expected back soon. It will tell her what she needs to know, so she may contrive a way to free it.*

Joy, thinks Joy.

Princess rubs her pincers together.

She does not understand.

My name is Joy.

Princess' eyes sparkle, and she pauses.

Her name is Shimmer, she thinks at last. *Few aside from her pluripotents know this.* She gestures at the bronze flyers. *The Oddity will die if it shares the name.* She gazes at the derka. *Stay awake!* she chastises, but the creature's eyes have closed. *Cursed fortune. What to do? Very well. She will tell the Oddity her story, and it will understand the exigence.*

Joy whistles a gloomy note, resigned to her fate.

Of course she will.

She steps out of the stream, shaking her mane and letting the sun dry her skin. Hugging the derka, Princess begins her tale.

+ + +

It claims to not know Ozag, she thinks. *This is likely an evil lie. Who does not know the undying Ozag, First Thinking Queen? Who has not heard of her Hold near Far Colossus, or how she freed the scion from vumierre enslavement? Ozag lives! Ozag rules!*

But most of all, Ozag controls the flood. When tey Ramota approaches, the scion of Albion gather at the Circle and send their plea to Ozag. Even from far Colossus she senses them and opens her Hold, sending the flood. The flood brings the awl; the flood grows the lova.

Or it did.

Princess' eyes grow dim.

The trouble started with the passing of Albion's longest reigning queen, Beata. Her death was mourned, but not unexpected. The reign then devolved to the best of her pluripotents, the princess Adira, who had transitioned from bronze to silver moons earlier. Of course the usual contest was held in the Circle for a new Magister with whom Adira would couple and create pluripotents of her own. For that is the way of it, does the Oddity not know?

The Oddity does not, thinks Joy.

A probable falsehood. How could it not know of scion bondage, and how the vumierre leader during that evil time called itself Magister? But through Ozag, scion have overthrown their slavers, so that now they claim the title of Magister—as well as that of Queen.

Um, congratulations, I guess?

Congratulations indeed! And the winner of this Magisterial Gage was a fearsome soldier who gained the name Viktor, but who has since fallen in rank and is now called Old Magister.

Too bad for him, thinks Joy. But Princess stiffens as if about to erupt, and Joy prudently bows her antennae. *Sorry. Please go on.*

She will! With or without its permission!

Princess places the derka in the basket and runs her forelimbs across her eyes, polishing their facets.

Not long after the Royal coupling, the new queen Adira sensed the approach of tey Ramota and ordered the Circle be prepared to call on Ozag. Does it still claim to be unaware of this? How is it part scion form and yet ignorant of basic truths? Tey Ramota churns the soil, and if water is present, it soaks to the depths of the Bacca, the flood plain, and thus reaches the lova pods buried far below the surface. The bounty of Ozag is that, when called on by an Albion queen, the Undying sends the flood just prior to tey Ramota. And thus, lova flourishes.

So all gathered, and Adira led them in the call.

Princess Shimmer buzzes a grim chord.

But this time, for the first in memory, no water came from the Mouth of Ozag. The tremors and fumes of tey Ramota shook the land and prepared the Bacca, but there was no water to spill over the banks of the Royal, that river which falls from the upper land where it is known as the Doorn. The lova did not come that cycle, and great was the suffering in Albion.

But Queen Adira was not idle. She vowed to take her case to Ozag herself, Compassionate and Awesome.

"But what of the Prohibition?" everyone wondered, for Ozag forbade any to approach her Hold.

"She will trigger the Undying's wrath," thought Viktor, and he tried to prevent Adira's departure.

But she saw the suffering of her hive and would not be dissuaded. She left off egg laying and took leave of Albion, bound for Far Colossus. With her went five pluripotents, leaving only Princess Benica, Shimmer's mother and Albion's current Queen. By some, Adira was seen as a hero, for who could stand in the presence of the Timeless and Masterful and not be overcome? Adira dared the Prohibition, they said, because she loved Albion.

But others called her a fool.

Meanwhile, Benica took over as Queen, and Viktor lost all Command, for he had made an attempt to seek out Adira and return her to Albion, but he had been rebuffed at Ozag's Hold and badly injured. When he came limping home, it was clear a new magister was required. Viktor's name was revealed, his support withdrawn, and his color faded. A Magisterial Gage was held, Albion's new magister chosen and secretly named, a coupling made, and new pluripotents created.

Princess was one of them.

She clicks a harsh cadence and flutters her wings, glancing back at the towers as if hearing something.

She must hasten the tale. So little time!

Stilling her anxious wings, she continues.

Princess had not long left her egg cell and had her first metamorphosis when the second tey Ramota came that was not preceded by a flood. She was too young to understand the significance, but it was clear to others that Adira had failed in her quest and Albion was being punished for her presumption at daring to approach the Hold. Benica tried to soothe scion fears, reminding them that Ozag, Brilliant and Unerring, had never abandoned them since leading them from slavery.

A.P. Malloy

But by the time Shimmer found her wings and became the next Princess, Albion had missed a third flood. The Royal began to wither. Awl became scarce, lova disappeared entirely, Queen Benica produced fewer eggs—and scion began to perish. That is when some began to speak of a deposition and having a new queen. And they would have, too, but something remarkable happened then: a vumierre, the very same brown-skinned one under New Magister's Command, fell from the sky, spat out by some vumierre devilry, a flying device that crashed into Cyclonia Bay.

These thoughts smolder in Princess's eyes. But Joy, who knows nothing of Cyclonia and has never seen a flood, struggles to follow the narrative. Vumierre? Surely they are the bombas' Rumidelchia, yes? And the kezels' precious Moondwellers? And yet, not that precious, she recalls, for Redteeth despise their memory. How could the same creatures be viewed so divergently? Hated by some and revered by others? But the tale continues; her questions must wait.

Return of the slavers, thinks Princess. *This is what was feared. And no one dared depose queen Benica at such a time. Unity was needed, preparation for war! But no other vumierre followed, and there has been no war. The brown creature has been brought under Command, and it has been taken as a sign of Ozag's favor. Perhaps she sent the vumierre to show she has forgiven Albion for its lack of faith and its pride. And yet, vumierre or not, the question remains: what of the next tey Ramota? Will Ozag send the flood? Will there be lova?*

Princess' antennae curl.

Queen Benica does all in her power to ensure that this Circle will succeed. Unlike past Circles, this will be no faint-hearted affair with simple games and harmless contests. There will battles to the death! Symbolic sacrifices of creatures that go on two legs! And Queen's determination is warranted, for if she fails to entice Ozag's favor a third time, she is apt to end in Shiver.

Which is what, please? Joy asks.

Dolt! Cipher! The removal of her head, of course.

Oh.

Yes! So Benica has worked harder than ever, sending soldiers to the limits of her realm, seeking offerings for the Circle, even to the exotic domains of the Arid Flats and the deadly riverside dwellings of the Nodal Ooms, who reach up from the ground and drag scion to a hideous, unimaginable end.

So that's their name, thinks Joy, and she rubs her ankles. *Nodal Ooms.*

Indeed. But these and other jeopardies do Benica's soldiers dare in order to make this the grandest Circle ever. The call has gone out to every Tender, Builder, Awler, Soldier, Farmer, and Drone from here to Cyclonia; the Circle will be filled to the rim. And there are many who believe Benica's hope will be realized, for New Magister has great Command, and his soldiers, like most of Albion, descend from Ozag's original army, bred to be impervious to the cold. And during their explorations, these found, far to the north, near the land of spiky sharksha, an abandoned vumierre wain. In it were...

But here, Princess' eyes change their hue, and she leans forward the slightest.

Can it guess what was found inside?

What is a wain?

Simpleton! Dullard! A large, wheeled device the vumierre powered by their evil magic. But scion put them to Ozag's use and they are now pulled by babelracks. But this wain was one of the vumierre originals, still powered by its magic and left derelict on the plains. Can it guess what was inside?

No.

Larval scion, scores of them. Dead.

Oh.

"Oh," indeed. New Magister's soldiers noted the sharksha markings nearby and discovered in the awful shadows of that land a type of sharksha that play-acted as if it were vumierre, standing on two legs and dressing itself vumierre-style. Even using their weapons!

A.P. Malloy

Joy keeps her thoughts sheltered, though the news is apparently expected to inspire a response.

Is it not preposterous? demands Princess. *Outrageous? Does it not understand the significance? Sharksha loyal to slavers? It could not be suffered. And so, New Magister mounted an assault and killed or captured all that could be found living in praise of the evil vumierre. Now, with such a bounty, many hope that Ozag will be pleased by Albion, and they look forward to the upcoming Circle, of which the vumierre-posing sharksha will be the pinnacle. If Ozag is to hear our plea, Queen Benica believes, it will be at this next Circle.*

But Princess is not so sure.

What about the derka? Joy asks.

Princess whistles like a steam vent.

The Oddity will not interrupt! She was getting to that part. When she was fully transformed, and as silver as any princess could wish, not long after the great raid on the misguided sharksha, this derka came flying to her as she stood by the Royal. It did not fear her, but click-clicked its jaws, clearly imitating scion speech. Some of what the Oddity has shared was clear, but the derka's grasp of the language was weak, and only part of the message did Princess understand.

"Warning! No Circle, no Albion! Vumierre!"

Over and over, it repeated this message.

This was a thing unheard of. Scion revere the Mighty Derka, who fertilize the Bacca as they fly over, but never were they known to use the scion language, and never to be so small and discolored.

Of course, she shared the discovery with Queen Benica and New Magister, but none could say how the message had come to be or how it should be interpreted. Some believed it meant there should be no Circle, that the vumierre slavers would return for their fallen comrade. Others said it meant Albion would cease to be if the Circle were not held. Queen Benica is in this last group. She would not hear of the Circle being cancelled, and the derka was consigned to the Royal Garden, where it continued its repeated message, croaking and flapping and sending thoughts that Princess could feel but not understand. A terrible dread filled each of her hearts, and every day, the derka sickened, slept longer, and would neither eat nor drink. Who knows why?

Joy recalls bizarre and unclear lessons from the maison. She assumes the tiny creature is an infant of its kind. What else could something so small be? According to Ari, nestling derkas killed and ate one another until the last was strong enough to fly. But this one hardly seems able to fend for itself. She runs fingers through her hair, coaxing snarls from the dripping locks. Thinking of food only makes her tense.

And thus, thinks Princess, *we have come to this moment, where the warning tone of the derka's thoughts grows more desperate, but it thinks less often and with less vigor—thinks but cannot be understood.*

Her eyes glitter.

Until now.

Until now, thinks Joy. *When will it wake?*

Perhaps not soon enough, if it remains true to past form. What is to be done? She is late for the feast, and the Oddity cannot accompany her.

Then what will happen?

All will attend the Circle, of course.

Which means what, exactly?

But Princess is lost in thought. She chitters a quiet, rapid pattern, repeating it for long moments, her mind unreadable. Finally, her eyes brighten.

She has decided. She will leave the derka with the Oddity. It will tell her what it has learned when she returns. If it attempts escape or harms the derka—

Please let me guess, thinks Joy, clicking sharply. *Killed in the Circle.*

Slowly and with great pain!

An idea occurs to Joy, inspired by this threat.

There was an...artifact, she thinks. *It could be helpful.* Then, unsure what response it will get, she adds: *Old Magister had it.*

A.P. Malloy

An artifact?

Black, shaped like this. Joy traces a rectangle. *It helps me think.*

Princess' whistle is sharp and dismissive.

It clearly needs the assistance. But there was no such artifact, or Queen would have claimed it from Old Magister when she had him at the Viewing.

Not if it's secret.

Princess pauses to consider this.

She will search, she thinks. *But it will keep its thoughts sheltered. Queen has spies everywhere.*

With that, she hands the derka and the shroud to Joy using great care. When she leaves the garden, borne away to the accompaniment of bronze wings, it lets out a single croak like a snore. Joy holds it at a distance, sniffing its pungent aroma and surprised at its frailty.

Time to start sharing, she thinks, but the derka remains unconscious and does not respond.

+ + + + + +

Behind a lowly ridge overlooking the shrunken lake and the island towers of Albion, two jabi kezel crouch in a rocky depression, debating their strategy. Below them and to the west, the river flows spindly and stagnant, flanked by sloping rust.

Cliff's nose twitches.

Kezel east and *west,* he thinks.

Yes, thinks Lightning. *They're being kept in two places from the smell of it. West of the river, by that path, and east, near that giant hole.*

That's going to make things harder.

Maybe.

Lightning peers over the ridge. Two thousand parched strides away, the six gray towers rise from the center of the lake, half its original size. Bits of metallic blue paddle small vessels across the water, but if the lake could once support passage by larger craft, it can no longer. Chalky roads lead from the island to the shore. It is the one heading east that interests Lightning the most. After spanning the lake, it runs to a wide, open space, and there it ends at an enormous excavation, hundreds of strides across, as if a perfect scoop has been taken out of the planet. What purpose it serves she can't guess, but many of their enemies gather near or in it, and more arrive at every moment, scurrying in by the dozens.

So, what's the plan? Cliff scratches at his ear as he peeks over the ridge.

Don't have one yet.

I say we watch what happens. Watch and wait, that's the winner. We have no idea what they're doing.

You're correct; we don't know their ways. That's why we need to act. We've waited long enough. For all we know, they're preparing a feast of kezel. Lightning curls her lip. *Surprise will be our friend.*

Cliff eyes the growing swarm of blue.

We're going to need more friends than that, he thinks, and his ears droop.

When Ansel returns, we'll know more.

Knowing more isn't going to help us against their bites. Unless you've got more of that armacan.

Lightning sighs.

I've been meaning to discuss that.

I knew it! The armacan doesn't work.

No. I mean, I don't know. It might. But I lied about the armacan, so I can't say.

You lied... Cliff tilts his head. *Why?*

Because I ate something else, and I didn't want you to know. Reaching into an inner pocket, Lightning takes out of the orange spheres.

You ate awl gland? Cliff's eyes widen. *That's...you could get into a lot of trouble for that.* He looks around as if expecting a reprimand.

Then we're both getting into trouble.

I'm not eating awl gland! Cliff steps back hastily.

Lightning curses.

You would rather be poisoned again?

How do you know it's awl gland that does it? May-

be you're just naturally immune.

Think about it, Cliff! Lightning scolds. *You said most of the kezel taken away were bit and dragged off. But not all of them, yes? Some kept fighting and were still awake when they got tied up.*

So?

So which ones were they? Do you remember?

I don't know. A few different ones. Submission, for sure, and your amotiwot Digger. Why?

Because! This gland is the only thing I've done different than you since we met in the accrete. I get bit twice and nothing happens? My api-kan ate awl gland, and he doesn't fall asleep?

Submission ate awl gland?

Stay focused, will you? Lots of kezel eat awl gland and don't tell you about it! Including my amotiwot and...well...others!

But that's... Cliff founders. *They could get into a lot of trouble for that.*

Lightning groans.

They're in trouble, Cliff! This is why I didn't tell you. You think like a wabi.

And you think like a liar. Cliff scowls. *My apoti told me all about awl gland.*

Fine! I'm not going to force you. But if you get bit, you might also get left behind.

Cliff watches, dread and fascination in his gaze, as Lightning tosses a gland into her mouth and bites down gently, inhaling and closing her eyes. She swallows the shell, her expression softening, her posture relaxed.

She releases a deep breath and shudders.

And that's why they eat awl glands, she thinks.

But when she offers Cliff one of his own, he continues to refuse.

As you wish, thinks Lightning. *It's probably for the best, anyway. You couldn't handle the effects.*

You can't shame me into changing my mind.

I wouldn't think of it.

Sensing victory, Cliff moves to a new subject.

So why do you think the bomba showed up? Was he always so helpful?

No. He didn't like me, actually.

Then what's changed? And why now?

When we find Joy, you can ask him yourself. At the moment, I'm more interested in that gathering place.

That hole? What do you suppose they're doing?

Nothing good. Lightning looks to the sky, and her ears angle forward. *Finally,* she thinks.

Flying low and fast, Ansel approaches from the west, wings blazing color. His landing raises twin swirls of dust that spiral away on the wind. As always, Lightning bows low, and, as always, Ansel ignores the gesture. Instead, he fixes her with a sharp glance from one bright, green eye. He cackles to indicate Joy, then points a wing at the island towers. Lightning's heart sinks. She had hoped to find Joy somewhere on the perimeter of this dreadful place, not its center. She bows again.

A little fuel, she thinks to Cliff. *Don't know when we'll have the chance to eat again.* She downs a chunk of the virble in her pack and tosses a portion to Cliff. He wastes minimal energy chewing.

It's about time, he thinks. *You never—* He blinks. His eyes cross. *Whoa. That's weird. I feel...*

Yes?

I feel...

He looks from Lightning to Ansel and back, stares at his own fingers for a bit, then blinks again.

I don't know, he thinks. *It's funny. I can't describe it.* His eyes grow narrow. *What did you do to me?*

Don't worry, thinks Lightning. *I won't tell anyone.*

You put awl gland in the virble! Cliff leaps to his feet as if to accost her, but his head spins, and he is forced to sit before he falls. *I feel... I feel...*

I bet you do, thinks Lightning. *But it passes.* She tugs at her boots. *Whatever the vermin are doing, it's on that island and around that giant pit. Hopefully that means the kezel west of the river will be easier to get to. With their help, we can free the others.*

Sure. Cliff's eyes drift in and out of focus. He rises on unsteady legs and releases a nervous stream of urine. As he does, he gazes about as if seeing the world for the first time. *Everything's so...sunny. Kinda pretty...*

Lightning slaps him across the snout.

Pull yourself together! You've got the tail. And she turns, striding west toward the depleted river. She is unable to read the meaning in Ansel's harsh squawk as he takes to the air—frustration or resignation, she suspects—and she wonders what they will find in the place he leads them to.

+ + +

The bomba circles overhead as they make their way to the river. Its banks are bare and pale except for occasional streaks of rust. Schools of young awl are among the few living things they see, but they cast cautious glances up and downstream before stepping into the river. The current is noticeable but not dangerous, and the awl are no bigger than their hands, scattering at first sight. An easy swim of fifty strides gets them to the opposite bank, wet but refreshed. Lightning is shaking water from her vest and pack when she senses the powerful aroma of kezel gathered nearby. Five hundred strides later, they arrive at a pit, deeper and wider than the river. They approach, slow and careful, staying downwind as Ansel alights at a distance.

I smell wabis, thinks Cliff. *And...* His tongue wags. *Do you smell that?*

I do.

That's a babelrack, that is.

Yes. Lightning points. *There!*

At the far side of the pit, mottled yellow and white, the giant octopod has been harnessed in place and stands with both tusked heads drooping as if asleep. Not even Cliff's prodigious hunger is foolish enough to think the two of them could kill such a beast, but he can't keep himself from drooling.

Stay here, thinks Lightning. *Keep your nose open and your mouth closed.*

She creeps to the edge of the pit, pausing for a last, quick smell before daring a glance into the space below. It is divided into three sections with kezel in each, all crested females, some with wabis on their backs and the ibiwa Snapper heavily pregnant. There also is Lightning's amotiwol Stone, as well as her oti-kans' fancies, Bliss and Yellow. Measure, part of the thrower brigade, stands alone, reading the wind, while Gully and Bridger, Lightning's apoli and amoli, lean against one another, shoulder to bony shoulder. And there! Fall, her apoliwol, a cousin who had actually been kind to her on occasion. Lightning whimpers at the sight. Their waste stands piled in heaps. Poor Old Buttons slouches, gray and dejected. The wabis Hurly and Burly wander aimlessly over ground parched in places, muddy with urine in others.

And all are naked, head to toe.

Lightning bites down on her emotions and searches for an opening. She finds one, on the pit's opposite side, near where the babelrack dozes, sealed by something she can't identify. She smells enemies near this opening, but their numbers are small. Withdrawing, she spits as if ridding herself of a bad taste.

We split up, she thinks after making her report. *Circle around opposite directions, heartbeat pace, so we meet them at the same time.*

My heart is beating pretty fast, thinks Cliff.

Lightning removes her mask and rubs her eyes.

We each take the ones closest to us—clean and quiet. I'll race you to the others.

Why doesn't the bomba just shoot 'em?

Lightning snarls.

I'm not going ask him to waste crewels on enemies we can handle ourselves. She returns her mask to its place. *Any more questions?*

Cliff has many, but he keeps these sheltered, and so the kezel part company, each beginning their trek in opposite directions. Ansel remains on the ground, watching and muttering.

Lightning is first to arrive at the southern edge of the pit, where, beneath the dozing babelrack, a broad tunnel has been carved into the rocky embankment. Twelve blue creatures stand, six on either side, at the opening to this tunnel. Lightning smells others below ground, at what she guesses is the entrance to the pit. Praying for the wind to remain favorable, she stalks in silence, staying low, her ears angled forward. Fifty strides away, her enemies cluster and bend antennae, chittering and buzzing, unaware of their new company.

Forty strides. Thirty.

She has just drawn within striking distance when Cliff appears from the west. She pauses, waiting as he gets into position. His liability considered, he demonstrates admirable stealth. It is the wind, not his leg, that betrays him, swirling for a moment and alerting his enemies. The blue things shriek and whistle. They scatter, eyes filled with fire.

Lightning leaps forward, cursing their luck as she reaches full speed in three bounding strides. Cliff's attack is no thing of beauty, but between their ravening jaws, the scion are ended before they can change color, the thirsty ground soaking up blue blood. Lightning dashes into the tunnel, sprinting another twenty strides before reaching an antechamber outside the pit's entrance. There in the gloom she finds the last of their enemies, more with her nose and ears than her eyes. Clicking in terror, they saw with their beaky mouths at a thick rope stretched taut from the floor to the ceiling where it holds aloft an enormous boulder, suspended before the entrance. This rope is all that prevents the boulder from falling to block their way.

Lightning charges, muzzle stained blue, and her enemies abandon their efforts, shrieking as they scuttle away. Two are dispatched before they complete their color change. But the third, dodging with the frantic genius of terror, eludes her jaws and scrambles toward the exit, just as Cliff bursts into the room. He is caught off guard and misses his first lunge—but doesn't miss the second.

Well, that wasn't nearly loud enough, thinks Lightning, her tone bitter. A strand of the rope snaps with a singing note. Cliff winces.

What do we do?

We can't both go in, thinks Lightning, and she concentrates, trying to catch her breath. *If it falls, someone has to be free.*

I'm not going in there by myself.

I wasn't going to waste energy suggesting it. Find something to hold up that rock!

A moment later, she is off, passing under the suspended stone and down the tunnel, leaving Cliff alone with wide eyes and a racing heart as another strand of the rope gives way.

+ + +

The passage Lightning travels is short, and she reaches the inner gate without incident. Except that it is not one gate, but three, each the same size, massive slabs of stone, tall as a bibija, three strides across, and half a stride thick. The smell of kezel comes from behind each of the barriers, but she can see no way to move them.

A thought confronts her from behind the gate to the left. It has a dazed quality, sleepy and confused.

Kezel? it thinks. *Are there kezel out there?*

Yes! We're coming for you!

Kezel! A second mind thinks from behind the right gate, equally amazed. *There are kezel outside!*

Who's there? thinks a mind from the middle gate. Soon, others join the conversation, each more anxious and bewildered than the one before.

How many of you are there? thinks one.

How did you get here? thinks another.

It's Lightning—from Crystal and Submission, she replies. *And Cliff is here too. The Clawpaw. We have a bomba outside.*

Their confusion is easy to sense.

Two jabis? No one else?

I thought Lightning was dead.

Did she say a bomba?

Lightning? a new mind thinks from behind the right gate, a mind she remembers well: it is Bliss, her oti-kan's fancy. *Little Spark? Rock's oli-su? You're alive?*

For the moment.

What's happening?

We're freeing you. Or we're trying. Lightning leans all her weight against the middle of the three gates, but it has no effect. *How do I move these things?*

They slide, thinks Bliss. *Side to side.*

That seems impossible to Lightning. Two bibijas working together may not have been enough to move the slab a single stride. She casts her gaze from top to bottom, growing desperate.

Slide how? I don't see it!

The babelrack, thinks Bliss. *Topside. When it moves, the gates move, one at a time.*

The babelrack?

Lightning has just begun absorbing this information when Cliff's wild thought reaches her.

We're about to have visitors!

+ + +

As he watches Lightning disappear into the tunnel and hears another snapping strand of the rope, Cliff casts about for something to prevent the rock from falling. His frantic search in the shadowy chamber reveals nothing, so he exits the tunnel, squinting at the sun as he climbs the bank, seeking but not finding.

Cresting the embankment, he spies the babelrack and immediately begins to drool. Its eyes, four on each massive head, are all but two closed. These peer from beneath sleepy lids, scouting for danger with the air of a creature who has long ago stopped expecting any.

Temptation winks at Cliff.

Favorable wind, it notes. *Element of surprise.*

Book of Dreams

But no adult babelrack, regardless how sleepy, is a rational target for a lone hunter. Cliff swats away vain fantasies, and, as looking only aggravates his stomach, he turns to the south, cursing the sun and the arid, briny wind. A small cloud of dust approaches, a thousand strides away. It doesn't move in haste, but it does move directly toward the pit.

We're about to have visitors! he thinks.

The warning call that accompanies this thought is inadvertent but loud enough to startle the babelrack, harnessed and snoring. A nostril-flaring revelation opens all eight eyes, wide and rolling. Beyond comprehension and worst fear, a kezel has escaped the confine! Had it not been drowsy and unprepared, the babelrack would have realized the true nature of the threat, but surprise makes Cliff a slavering giant, and for a moment, it loses both of its heads. It stomps and snorts and backs away with such force its bindings threaten to rupture. From inside the tunnel a victorious call.

Yes! Cliff! Do that again!

Do what again? You'd better get out here, there's a bunch of them. They're getting close!

Make the babelrack move! It opens the gates!

Cliff's tongue wags.

Opens the gates...?

He glances to the south. How long before he becomes visible to their enemies? Not daring to stand, he growls and clashes his teeth at the babelrack, scratching his claws across the ground. The poor creature likes none of this, and it backs farther away, the head closest to Cliff brandishing its tusks.

Yes! thinks Lightning. *And again!*

The line of blue grows close, its zig-zagging tracks driving a dust cloud to the sky. Their pace is not one of alarm—they don't appear to be responding to the skirmish—but it is implacable and motivated.

Cliff rushes at the babelrack.

Move, you big meathead!

+ + +

When the first gate slides open, dazed captives
stumble out of the pit bearing wabis on their backs and
smelling as foul as a kezel can. First comes Boots, then
Serenity, Tail, Yellow, and Curly. Their eyes dart side to
side, uncomprehending, and their passengers cling fear-
fully, trembling and baring tiny fangs.

Hurry! thinks Lightning. *Run to the light!*

The prisoners shuffle and stagger up the tunnel,
none of them running. They are still in sight when the
second gate opens. From behind this waddles Snapper,
the most pregnant kezel Lightning has ever seen, followed
limpingly by Old Buttons, escorted by the jabi Splay. Last
is Gully, fancy to the Brigadier Bone, bearing the wabis
Powder and Crust. These join their companions in what
seems to be a contest to see who can move the slowest.
Lightning senses Cliff's alarm and wonders what good
any of these will be in the upcoming fight.

But when the third gate opens, her hope rises.
Out lumber two massive bibijas, Bridger and Measure,
and three rangy ibiwas, including Bliss, her amotiwol
Stone, and the unfortunate Feather, who had been visiting from the Bristle range when the scion attacked.

All are hungry for blood.

Fight first, questions later, thinks Lightning.

Feather and Bliss have just stepped out of the pit
when the gate begins to close again—and quickly.

Hurry, thinks Lightning. *Go!*

And another strand of the rope snaps.

+ + +

Cliff hugs the ground and holds his breath, afraid
of exposing himself to his enemies. The tormented babelrack continues to froth and snort, stomping plumes of
dust. No longer able to back away, it resolves to charge
forward. But its tethers hold fast, allowing it to move no
farther in the direction of the one head than it had in the

other. Still, the damage is done. Its panic has caught the attention of the approaching scion. Their pace increases, their path straightens from a zig-zag, and their chittering and raspy strides become audible.

Here they come!

But Cliff's warning goes unanswered. He considers for a moment retreating into the tunnel—he reckons there is just enough time to reach the entrance before his enemies—but to what end? Being trapped in darkness seems to him much worse than a fight in the open—and no fight seems best of all. And so, he turns, limping his way to full speed as he retraces his steps around the western rim of the pit.

At the sight of him, half the column of blue peels away and follows, gaining on him slow but sure.

The other half proceeds into the tunnel.

Cliff rounds from west to north, enemies on his heels, when Ansel comes into view. The bomba cackles when he sees the chase, and he takes to the air.

Yes, thinks Cliff, panting. *Shoot 'em!*

But Ansel passes overhead, ignoring the kezel and his pursuers, now so close Cliff hears their buzzy, metallic breathing. He races on in disbelief as the bomba sails to the opposite side of the pit and dips out of sight.

+ + +

Eighteen clicking, bristly-legged scion file into the tunnel, the first of whom encounter an awful surprise in the dark. Five enraged adult kezel, joined by Lightning and led by Bridger, charge heedlessly forward, plowing into their line and bringing it to a sudden, bloody halt. Those scion at the rear of the line scramble from the tunnel with snapping jaws close behind.

Once in the sun, blue skin changes to match the pale ground. But privation hasn't cost the kezel their sense of smell, and rising trails of dust betray their quarry. One by one they are ended, until the lone survivor, zig-zagging east, rounds the pit in desperation, Lightning close enough to smell its fear.

When Cliff suddenly appears, chased by scion of his own, he alters course to avoid her—too late—slipping, stumbling, and colliding against Lightning, sweeping her from her feet as neatly as if he'd intended it. Her target takes this opportunity to join its companions, falling in line as its shrill, whistling terror tells them all they need to know. Veering to the south, they change colors and scurry away so that neither Lightning, dazed and struggling to stand, nor Cliff, for the moment breathless, are able to pursue.

But Ansel is.

One pass incinerates half the scion line, revealed by the dust it raises. A second finishes the job. Lightning is about to cheer his effort when a *crack!* and an echoing thud tells of the rope's demise. Billowing dust rolls from the mouth of the tunnel.

Next time, thinks Cliff, *I'll go and you can stay.*

Let's hope there isn't a next time. Lightning glances at him. *How do you feel?*

Like you care. Cliff's tongue lolls, and he puffs like a bellows. *You made me eat*—but he stops, looking sidelong as the other kezel approach. *I feel fine.*

Glad to hear it. Lightning points at his ear. *Because you got bit—twice.* She turns to the freed prisoners. Huddled in the sunlight, the haggard kezel, wabis and adults alike, stare at her through sunken eyes, some licking blue blood from their chops. Together they drag the bodies of their enemies into the tunnel and cover signs of combat with rusty soil.

As Cliff rubs his welting ear, Lightning looks up to where Ansel circles high above, and she reads the wind. She detects no enemies but guesses that won't last forever. Waving to the others, she turns due west.

Bridger hastens to join her.

Where are we going?

Away, thinks Lightning. *West first, then north.*

I'm not leaving without the ah-tahs.

I'm not asking you to. But we need to get these wa-

bis away before we do anything else.

To this, Bridger has no objection.

A sudden howl breaks the silence.

Scale! comes a desperate thought from the ibiwa Boots. She casts wild glances from side to side. *Where is Scale?* A lone wabi clings to her back where once there had been two; dazed, it offers no response. When a hasty survey reveals the grim truth, the band is allowed no time to mourn. Even Boots marches west, silent and sharing no thoughts, leaving behind the giant rock, both tombstone and ruin of the tiny life crushed beneath it.

+ + +

The escapees' pace grates on Lightning's nerves, and they are soon spread thin as the weakest fall behind, tongues wagging in the heat. They cast haunted glances all about, as if enemies linger behind each stand of thorn vines or dusty hill, and when Ansel circles, they wince at the sight. Cliff takes his usual position at the tail, encouraging stragglers and herding miscreant wabis. At another time, he would have been disregarded by both, but now, no one questions him.

What's been done to them? Lightning wonders to herself, but she knows better than to ask.

After a thousand strides, they angle north; another thousand returns them to the river, bending west to meet them. They wade into its shallows, drinking and bathing as they go, some of their gloom and fear washed downstream. They continue on like this until the river resumes its northern course. It is here that Lightning at last pauses, waiting for the others to gather close. They stare in naked hunger as Ansel settles out of reach.

Do you have any food? asks Bridger.

Only for fighters. If you're not pregnant or caring for wabis, you'll go back with me to rescue the others. I'll share what I have once we're away from the river. The rest will follow Cliff to the landfall and hunt on the way.

A solid plan, agrees the bibija Gully. *But you'll be*

A.P. Malloy

*going back without Splay. Someone's got to help Old But-
tons or she'll never make it.*

And what do we do when we reach this landfall?
thinks Yellow, who is Crag's fancy, and who, like Curly
and Tail, carries a pair of wabis on her back.

Cliff will show you, thinks Lightning. *There's a
tunnel you can use to get to the upper land.*

Is it a long way? asks Snapper. With her dis-
tended abdomen and waddling gait, she doesn't look sure
of traveling far.

We made it, thinks Lightning. *You can too.*

And if, thinks Bridger, *we don't re-join you after
one sleep, go on without us.* This command is received
uneasily, but Bridger, the most senior bibija, is adamant.
No debate! Get those wabis home!

With this, the company parts ways, the fighters
joined by Lightning in a team of six, the others led by
Serenity, whose wabi goes by the name of Wander, but
who hugs her ami-kan with no intention of wandering
anywhere. As the kezel bid a brave farewell, touching
noses and offering thoughts of safe travel, Serenity steps
forward, her tail held low and Wander gripping tight. Her
thoughts catch Lightning off guard.

Whatever else happens, she thinks, *however this
turns out, we're in your debt. I used to make awful jokes
about you—about you both. I'm ashamed now.*

Lightning grimaces, unsure how to respond.

Good luck, Cliff thinks to her.

*You're the one who needs luck. If these wabis don't
get some food in their bellies, you're in a lot of trouble.*

Cliff groans.

What about my *belly?*

He wades out of the river and heads north, Serenity at his side, eight weary ah-lahs and ten hungry wabis
straggling behind. As Lightning watches, a profound desire to offer one last thought fills her mind, something
meaningful and sincere—but she can't think what it
should be. Each idea that passes seems more feeble than
the last. And then it is too late. She watches until the pro-

cession is little more than a trail of dust.

At last, she turns to face the others.

Let's head downstream and step out on the east bank, she thinks. *We can eat there.* Five pairs of eyes brighten at this. *Then I'll share our secret weapon.*

Is it the entire Bristle range with throwers? thinks the unlucky Feather. *Because that would be helpful.*

No. But you won't have to worry about getting bit.

And she offers no further details, striding through the shallows of the southbound river. The others follow without question, and Ansel takes to the sky.

CHAPTER EIGHT
Circle

THE TINY DERKA lies draped across Joy's arms as she searches the garden for possible escape routes and waits for her passenger to wake. She walks the entire perimeter, losing count of how many different creatures and plants she sees, but as expected, aside from the entrance to the tower, which is guarded by six bristling scion, there is no other way out. She buzzes a melancholy tune as she returns to the stream and sits on a nearby stone, dangling her feet in the water. Torpor nearly claims her when the derka's ruby eyes flutter open.

Finally, thinks Joy. *I was getting worried.*

The creature yawns wide, snapping its toothy jaws, and it wriggles to be let free. Joy places it on the turf, glad to have it away from her. The stories she has heard make her nervous, and marvelous as its red-tipped scales are to look at, they have edges like tiny blades. A squirming derka is an unpleasant thing to hold.

We are Derka! it proclaims. *What is it? Food?*

It stretches its serpentine neck and snaps at Joy's fingers, and she, startled, slaps it briskly on its snout.

Dirty beast! she thinks. *I'm not your food.*

It looks like food...but not the color...not the eyes... not the brain stems....

Not any of it!

Some of it...walks like food...has the same body...

Too bad. Joy clenches her fists. *Bite and get hit!*

We are Derka...not hungry for food...hungry for Elixir...flee to Far Colossus...where Elixir is...

Sorry, thinks Joy. *But I'm stuck here.* She makes flapping motions with her arms. *You can go, though.*

No longer fly...weak...need Elixir...

Then we're both stuck.

Where is silver scion?

She will be back, thinks Joy. *You asked for help.*

The derka croaks.

Yes...have many messages...must deliver...no Circle...no Albion... flee...Ozag commands...no Circle...

Yes. I told her.

So why not fled? Vumierre mischief...ninety-one percent casualties!

What does that mean?

We are Derka...don't understand the message... were sent from Ozag's Hold near Far Colossus...deliver it because no one else could...able to fly then...no longer...were promised Elixir if...delivered...message... spent all our energy getting here...so tired...

It pauses, then gathers itself.

Trouble for scion...that's what...so thought the food who sent us.

Um...food sent you?

Yes...scion call "vumierre," derka call food...so delicious! But these food were different...allies...lived with We are Derka at Ozag's Hold...promised Elixir for delivering the message.

Its pause is longer this time.

Oh...so tired...who will get us sweet Elixir?

I don't have...elixir, thinks Joy, who has never sensed the word before. *But fleeing sounds good.* She clicks quietly. *We should work together.*

The derka's eyes blink, each independent of the other. Its nostrils flare.

It believes we are young...because we are small...no! Ancient! The oldest...hard to think...so tiring...

It spreads its wings, not feathered like a bomba's are, but

black skin stretched over a frame of slender bones. As the wings settle, the derka fixes Joy with an intent gaze, as if trying to burn a hole with its eyes. *Where...from? What type...creature? Part food, part not food...how?*

Joy whistles absently, trying to concentrate. If the derka is struggling to think, so is she struggling to understand. Its thoughts are full of gaps.

The land of bombas, she answers the first question. *And before that, kezel.* But the others are less easy. *I'm Joy, that's all.* And finally, *I don't know how.*

The derka opens and closes its mouth snap-snap as it ponders these replies, trying to wring lucid thoughts from its weary mind.

Ozag's Hold...Far Colossus... It croaks and flaps its wings, a loose, noisy affair, its claws digging into the turf. *Must stop the Circle...many scion will die...Ozag's Hold...* It yawns again and blinks its ruby eyes. Its head begins to sink at the end of its serpentine neck.

Must stop the Circle, repeats Joy, hoping to keep it awake. *OK. Good. How, though?*

Ozag's Hold... Its thoughts become soft and lose their focus. *Deliver the message...no Circle, no Albion... Far Colossus, that is where...Elixir...*

The derka's head lowers, and its eyes close. Just as Joy thinks it has fallen asleep, it stares at her with renewed intensity, sending one last, clear thought:

We are Derka! Flee Albion...flee the Circle... With this, its eyes close, its body falls slack, and its scales rise and fall as it begins to snore.

I already knew that, thinks Joy, and her antennae droop unhappily. So what now? The answer comes easily, for the derka's snoring is contagious. Joy flattens a tussock of the thick, wavy grass, making a pillow for herself, surprised at how tired she is.

Just for a while, she thinks, And soon after lying down, the song of yits and the distant call of strange beasts lull her to sleep.

+ + +

Book of Dreams

Joy wakes with a dull ache at the base of each antenna. The sensation disquiets her, not for the pain—she has suffered worse—but for the latent dread it brings, a presage of danger. Sitting up, she casts quick glances to all sides. The derka has curled its ropy, black tail around itself, holding it like a companion. Its snore is sibilant and regular; no trouble there. Nearby, the dows paddle upstream, honking foolishly. Whatever the threat, it doesn't come from them.

She clicks unevenly, rising to her feet. In the distance, droning wings announce the arrival of Princess. A moment later, her basket exits the tower, borne now by five bronze flyers, the sixth absent.

Shimmer is coming back, thinks Joy to the derka, and she nudges it. *You should wake up.*

But the tiny creature sleeps on.

As the party approaches, she attends with care. Are her captors the source of the anxious pain? That would make sense, but if so, why now? Why not when they first met? In the end, she determines that Princess, though despicable, is not the cause.

She knows what is, she thinks, buzzing in a certain tone. *She feels it too.*

The flyers approach until the basket is mere strides away. It is eased to the ground, and Princess sends an imperious thought.

It will escort her to the Circle.

Not without food first. Joy's clicking is abrupt. *And something to drink.*

Princess bristles at the impertinence, but she has anticipated the demand. On a sharp, clicking order, one of her pluripotents produces from the basket a strip of awl and a spongy green lova. Joy accepts these without thanks. The food eases her hunger, and the lova juice clears the last sleep from her mind, but they do nothing to soothe her nerves or her discomfort.

My head is aching, she thinks.

The Oddity senses tey Ramota. Princess' tone is dismissive. *All scion sense it. The pain will only worsen as the event grows closer.*

Wonderful, thinks Joy. *Then what will happen?*

Enough questions! It will come!

And so, Joy climbs into the basket, seated so that she and Princess are at opposite ends facing one another, while two pluripotents lift the sleeping derka and place it between them, snoring and oblivious.

Though it is more difficult without the sixth member of their team, the flyers lift their burden up and over the garden's northern wall, the pitch of their wings rising. There, they come to the main road, where they take a place at the end of a bristly cavalcade of blue, marching in tight formation. At its head, Queen floats in her regal basket, borne by a dozen bronze flyers droning in unison. The entire assembly moves east toward a bridge built up from the lakebed and standing high above the water. It travels toward the eastern shore for a thousand dusty strides, the stagnant lake visible on either side.

Was it successful? asks Princess.

I sensed the derka, thinks Joy. *If that's your question.* Her eyes grow dim. *But I missed parts,* she admits. *What about the...artifact?*

Princess glances from side to side, looking down at the marching scion and ahead to Queen's basket.

Now, she thinks, *while Queen is occupied. The Oddity shall be graced with Royal touch. Thus shall secrecy be guaranteed.* She leans toward Joy, eyes sparkling. *It shall extend its antennae.*

No, it shall not.

It wastes time! Princess chitters angrily. *Her vow has been given. It will trust or not, but it will gain nothing by delaying—and only Royal touch ensures privacy.*

Fine, thinks Joy. *But I don't trust.*

As the derka snores on, she does as instructed, her antennae tilting until they touch those of Princess, silvery and lithe. The sensation that burns at their tips passes in a moment, replaced by an intense but localized pressure centered between her eyes. She feels suddenly exposed, as if naked on the inside. Dozens of her own reflections play across Princess' facetted eyes. How repulsive she must appear to a scion! But this is not a one-way connection. Laid bare as she feels, Joy also gains a heightened awareness of the mind before her. The bronze flyers, the bristling guards, even Queen in her basket all disappear from her senses. Princess is her only concern, her consciousness coming into focus with sudden, disconcerting clarity. There are her emotions, and there is the complex stream of her thoughts. Surely with a little time and effort, she could discover where her secrets are hidden as well.

And it would die soon after, thinks Princess. *It will confine its attention! It has little time; Queen will not approve such an honor being shown a defect.*

Joy clicks a rapid staccato.

I don't feel honored.

Attend! Princess' wings stir the air for an angry moment. *It is as the Oddity reported: Old Magister was indeed in possession of a singular object. But there was no time to retrieve it from its hiding place. Her prime pluripotent is en route to do so now. And the Oddity? Has it learned anything of value?*

You judge the value. Joy recalls the brief conversation. *It says it's old.* She whistles a low note. *Doesn't seem possible though.*

But Princess waves this away.

Of what use is this information? What is the point, whether the derka is this age or any other! Is that all the Oddity has been good for?

Joy suppresses the urge to sever the connection.

It was sent here, she thinks. *To deliver this message.* She orders her thoughts. *Ozag's Hold, Far Colossus,* she thinks. *Those names came up.* She pauses to remember. *Also, stop the Circle.* What else was there? *Many scion will die.* She saves the most obvious for last. *Flee Albion.* She buzzes like a sigh. *But no news there.*

And that is all that was shared?

Um. It needs Elixir.

And what would that be? It will speak clearly!

That's all I know.
So it claims. But who sent the derka?
Food—vumierre, I think.
What? There are more vumierre in the world?
That's what it said.

Princess probes her mind for deception, but when she finds none, the silver creature clicks a solemn cadence and withdraws her antennae, breaking the connection. The outside world rushes back, its sights, sounds and smells crashing into Joy like being dropped into cold water. For her part, Princess reclines with a casual air as if nothing has happened, idly adjusting the derka's shroud and staring at the sun.

The procession has reached the lakeshore.

To the east, from a source she can't identify, Joy senses a huge gathering of scion hidden by a decline in the road a thousand strides ahead. Unlike the many different frequencies she encountered in New Magister's parade, she now senses a powerful, homogenous energy, many of the same type of minds, all focused on the same thing: the Circle.

Whatever that *might be,* she thinks.

The farther east they travel, the more intense the collective energy becomes. Every wingbeat increases the ache in her head and the dread it accompanies.

Why, thinks Princess, *does it camouflage?*
What?
It continues to attempt hiding, all the while wasting valuable energy. For what purpose? All scion can perceive it, does it not know?
Who says I'm hiding? Joy is surprised by profound self-consciousness, as if caught in a shameful act. *It's just what happens.*

Princess clicks her disapproval.

The Oddity is truly defective, she thinks. *If it were to think "unvelum," much energy would be saved.*

I... I don't... what? Joy falters. Is she being played with? Ridiculed?

Irritation glitters in Princess' eyes.

Concelar, she thinks, and without warning she disappears, her silver skin fading to the silken white of the basket as if both had been painted by the same brush. Only her shadow remains, sharp and still.

Fools and defects waste energy on camouflage. Only Royal skin can hide from scion eyes. Unless the Oddity has already made the attempt and is unable? Is its brain as deformed as its body?

Joy's buzzing is coarse, her thoughts surly.

My brain is fine.

Then it shall think "unvelum," Princess scolds, and she reappears, her eyes alight.

Joy deliberates. What harm can come from making the attempt? So, she thinks the strange word and concentrates on blue, imagining her skin as it was.

And so, it learns. Princess buzzes mild derision as Joy slowly reverts to her metallic sapphire.

If I want camouflage? she asks.

It will think "concelar," of course, Princess replies. *Pays it no attention?* As the entourage moves away from the lake and toward the hidden gathering, she gazes at the derka and bends her antennae. *It will not wake.*

No, thinks Joy. *Its mind is tired.*

Vexation! Princess whistles. *What is to be done? How can the Circle be stopped? Queen has already interpreted the derka's original message in her own way. She is determined to proceed with the Circle. And when Princess shared what the Oddity discovered earlier, Queen called it a liar. Only with Princess' persuasion was it allowed to keep its head.*

Thank you, I guess.

It should be grateful! If she were to share this new information, it would seem like more fabrication, and the Oddity would not be spared. Queen will see this Circle to its end; she believes her reign depends on it.

They draw near the invisible throng. The power of its thoughts presses down on Joy. It is not the cause of her headache but worsens it. A throbbing buzz grows, soon joined by a clicking and chittering that overwhelms the voice of the wind and the drone of bronze wings, rising up with the sound of a boiling ocean.

A hundred strides later, the Circle appears.

+ + +

At once, Joy hates and fears it.

In spite of its name, the space is not circular, but a series of six concentric hexagons forming an enormous, terraced bowl, carved into the rocky ground, symmetrical, wide, and deep. It teems with blue life, thousands of scion filling all but the bottommost part of the bowl. This center portion, a hundred strides in diameter, forms the only true circle in the place, but even this is comprised of a lattice of hexagonal trenches delved into the ground to form a labyrinth. Hidden beneath the smell of her enemies, Joy senses creatures from the earlier procession, though where they are now, she can't say. She smells old blood soaked into the stone.

The derka was correct, she thinks. *This place is horrible.* She tugs at locks of hair. *It should be stopped.*

Princess dismisses the idea.

The Circle cannot be stopped once begun. If Queen herself ordered it, no one would heed. And she will not.

The entourage approaches a place near the lip of the bowl where an entrance has been carved, guarded by an enormous, revolving gate. On their side stands a massive, two-headed creature. By its white and yellow carapace, giant tusks, and eight, knobby legs, Joy easily recognizes it from Lightning's description as a babelrack. But when it stomps and snorts, spittle flying, she is jolted by recognition and surprise.

Thinkers, she exclaims. *That's what babelracks are!* She struggles to shelter her emotions. *Not two separate creatures,* she realizes. *One with two heads!*

Acting on impulse, she leans over the basket's edge and, as they pass through the gate, she whistles to the babelracks, sending a tightly focused thought.

Thinkers! You sense me?

At this, the babelrack heads, though burdensomely harnessed, turn and look, trying to determine the source of this unexpected thought.

We traveled the river, thinks Joy hopefully. *Do you remember me?*

But the babelrack, recognizing hers as the mind in question, stomps and bellows, sending simple, confused thoughts from one head to the other. Joy knows at once it is not her Thinker from the river.

What does it do? Princess' tone is stern. *To whom does it send thoughts? It will sit before it upsets the basket—and it will have no secrets!*

Joy re-takes her seat. What had she hoped to gain? Disappointment at not rediscovering her traveling companions? Sadness to see another of their kind held captive? The creature continues exchanging slow, bewildered thoughts one head to the other as the basket passes through the entrance. It snorts and stomps as it is driven to turn the massive gate on its axis, sealing them in. Vertigo grips Joy as she looks down. Each of the six terraces contains more scion than she could count had she abundant time and inclination.

Only the circular labyrinth is unoccupied.

The procession stops at a wide balcony overlooking the uppermost and largest of the terraces. Baskets are lowered to the ground, and bristly guards take up positions in a neat ring. The pluripotents land in formation to the rear, settling their wings. At the sight of their Queen, every pair of antennae bends, and the throng joins in a piercing whistle that threatens to go on without end. Then Queen rises to four legs. Her wings flash—and the whistling stops at once, its last remnant blown away on the wind like a memory.

Thousands of eyes stare at the golden creature, and impossible as it seems for such a large gathering, they make not a sound. At first, Joy's aching head relishes the silence, but after long moments, her heart beats in her ears, and she yearns for a single click or buzz, so heavy is the sense of imminence.

At last, Queen returns to six legs.

She folds her wings.

On this cue, an immense cascade of water comes pouring into the labyrinth at the bottom of the bowl, released from hidden openings[i] along the outer wall. It courses to the center of the circle, weaving and splashing its way through the trenches and meeting in the center, a thunderous collision spuming high into the air. Soon, the trenches are filled with deep, sloshing water, until only the tops of the pillars they surround remain dry. Of these, Joy counts twelve.

At the center of the circle, atop the widest of these pillars, a lone blue creature appears, though Joy can't tell how it got there. From this distance, it appears tiny, but it holds everyone's attention. Even Queen stares, leaning forward, her eyes blazing. Whether by some magnifying effect of the bowl or the skill of its sender, a powerful thought rises up from the blue creature, and Joy recognizes its origin as the mind of New Magister. He stands on four legs as Queen had.

By order of Ozag, Magnificent and Eternal, he thinks, *the Circle is closed!*

At this moment, the derka wakes and stretches its red-tipped wings, freeing itself from the shroud. It croaks and shakes its oversized head, blinking ruby eyes. Taking in the scene, it whips its tail in agitation.

Doom! it thinks. *Ruin! The Circle must be stopped!*

But far below them, in the maze of watery trenches and on top of the pillars, the terrible spectacle has already begun.

+ + + + + +

Two thousand strides away, a band of six kezel approaches the scion gathering from the north, after having emptied Lightning's pack and vest of every last morsel. They hug the river for most of their trek, using the vines trimming its eastern bank as cover. Lightning and Bridger take the lead with Measure close behind. Her woli Bliss and Bliss' longtime companion Feather follow next. Bridger's woli Stone covers the tail, and as always, she stews in a truculent mood.

Above them, Ansel traces wide circles.

I have a pocketful of questions for you, thinks Bridger. *Last I heard, you went rogue and disappeared. Chased off from the Sugarfoot range for banditry!*

Among other things, adds Stone.

Lightning glances from Bridger back to Measure. She had forgotten how large the bibijas are—despite moons of malnourishment. And the ibiwas aren't much smaller. Still, she doesn't feel the automatic deference, bordering on fear, she once would have.

It's true, she thinks. *But I'm back.*

I guess you are. And I'm glad, don't mistake.

Me too, thinks Measure. *But I also heard Three-legs was the one who gave up your secret, and now he's your traveling partner. So, there's another fine question.*

Some Redteeth kezel call you a murderer, thinks Stone, and she grumbles.

Don't forget the bomba, thinks Bliss.

I have some questions about that myself, thinks Feather, and she drools as she peers up at Ansel.

If we get out of this alive, thinks Lightning, *I'll answer all your questions, I promise. But for now, do you know anything useful about these creatures? Anything we can use against them? And what do you know about the other kezel? The ah-tahs?*

Bridger shakes her head.

Not much. We lost Whiff in the fighting, and Flake took to the caves to protect their wabis. The rest of us were split up as soon as we got here. Last I saw of Pounce, he was being dragged away with the others.

She growls.

You know as much as I do about the blue filth.

Lightning considers this, and she shelters her thoughts, keeping a tight lid on memories of Stone's fancy and wabis dead in the Sugarfoot caves. There may come a time when that truth must be revealed, but it is certainly not now. Each stride increases her sense of gloom. How can they hope to save Joy from the midst of so many enemies? Even if they manage to free the ah-tahs, their foes won't need poison bites to subdue them. Acting in concert, force of numbers will suffice.

Then we can't fight 'em head-on, thinks Measure. *Sorry,* she adds. *I wasn't trying to pry. But your thoughts were... easy to read.*

I can keep a secret when I need to.

No one's doubting you, thinks Bridger. *But this is no time for secrets. We're in this together, life or death. And Measure's right; we can't fight 'em head on. That means strategy and teamwork. It also means honesty. So,* she concludes, picking her way through the vines, *you might as well tell me who this Joy is.*

Tell us all, thinks Bliss.

And what about that secret weapon? wonders Feather. *Seems like a good time to get into that.*

Unless you lied, thinks Stone.

Lightning sighs, but she knows they are correct. Although they must travel due south to reach their enemies, the river will soon bend west, taking their cover with it. Before that happens, she must know who she can count on and what the plan is.

She comes to a stop; the others do as well.

We don't have time for the whole story, she thinks, *but I'll say this: among the captives is a...an orphan I found and brought home. Not a kezel.*

The others murmur dark, unsheltered thoughts amongst themselves. Stone's teeth glisten.

Then Crag told the truth, she thinks. *"She had a blue thing with her," he said. Do you remember?* She looks at Bliss. *Three-legs told us the same thing.*

I remember.

You gave refuge to an enemy, thinks Stone.

I didn't know they were enemies at the time, thinks Lightning. *And anyway, she's not one of them. She's different; she can think.*

Skepticism and open disbelief greet this.

I know, thinks Lightning. *I felt the same way. But it's true. And she's different in other ways, too.*

And what if, thinks Stone, *they attacked us and burned the accrete because they were looking for this "different" creature you found? Maybe if you'd left it where it was and minded your own business...*

I don't have a reason for what I did, thinks Lightning, dismayed at the turn the conversation has taken. *All I could sense was it begging for help—so I helped. I didn't know this was going to be the result.*

Stone's upper lip peels back.

Would you have done any different if you had?

That's enough, thinks Bridger, the only one who can give the order and expect it to be followed, for she is Stone's ami-kan and not to be trifled with. *I'm not thrilled about this news myself, but I don't see how it's going save the ah-tahs turning on the one who freed us.*

The one who got us caught in the first place, Stone clarifies, her ears angling forward.

You don't know that, thinks Bridger.

The one who turned the Redtooth clan against us, thinks Feather. *Sugarfoot and Bristle.*

They didn't need much help, though, did they? thinks Bliss. Her ami-kan Measure agrees.

That much is certain. Anyway, whatever she did, she's trying to make up for it. Whether we like it or not, we can use her help. She turns to Lightning. *Unless your secret weapon is just your imagination.*

No. We've tested it; it works.

Then let's have it, thinks Feather, running her tongue over her teeth. *I've been poisoned for the last time.*

When I have your promise to help rescue Joy.

The other kezel stare at Lightning, some incredulous, some angry. Stone's tail twitches.

You're walking on thin ice, jabi.

I'm just being practical. Bridger said we're a team; well, Joy is on the team. You don't have to like it, but she's family, and I'm not leaving without her any more than I would leave without you. Lightning's heart races, but she holds her thoughts steady.

We could take it from you, thinks Stone.

You assume it's something I have with me, thinks Lightning, trembling at her own audacity. *Anyway, if you tried, you'd lose two useful allies—and maybe more.*

Quick as a flash, she rises and draws both cutter and thrower. Sunlight gleams off blade and barrel, and Stone quickly steps back, snarling. Bliss and Feather stand bipedal, but at the sight of the thrower, their crests flare and their ears pin back. Events seem doomed to turn ugly as Measure stands as well, but Bridger steps between them, raising clawed hands.

Down! she commands. *All of you! Down! A fine story we'll have to tell the wabis and the others! Too busy fighting to rescue their apis and fancies. Shame!*

The others shake their spiky heads and grumble, but they drop to four legs, chagrined though far from content. Lightning remains standing, weapons drawn, and she labors to settle her breathing.

Bridger turns to her.

So. You did steal weapons.

Yes. And I know how to use them.

The others appraise her posture and confident grip and take this as proof. Among them, only Measure has fired a thrower, but all have witnessed their power. They keep their distance as if fearing a contagion.

I don't doubt you, thinks Bridger. *None of us do. But you don't have the right.*

Maybe not. But I'm not giving them back until I have your promise to help Joy.

The adults exchange hidden thoughts as Lightning's fingers tighten around the cutter. She strives to shelter her thoughts, hoping her bluff will remain uncalled. Finally:

You have your promise, thinks Bridger. *We're all in—aren't we?* The others squirm and scowl, but one by one, they make their vow, last of all the ibiwa Stone, who finally relents under her ami-kan's unwavering gaze. A brief but distinct tingling in Lightning's mind confirms it:

the promises are sincere. No honorable kezel would dare break such a commitment. Exhaling heavily, she holsters the weapons and hands the belt to Measure, one of the clan's most experienced brigadiers.

Sorry, thinks Lightning. *But the thrower's sort of... broken. I don't know what happened. It used to work.*

Measure takes the weapon confidently and works at its levers and buttons.

Well. That's as jammed as it can be, she thinks. *You didn't get it wet, did you? Or dirty?*

Um. Maybe.

Yeah. Well. Not a thing I can do without proper tools. Measure straps the weapon belt around her thigh. *But a cutter is better than nothing.*

Agreed, thinks Bridger. *But please tell me this is not your secret defense.*

Lightning grimaces.

No, she thinks. *But you may not like what it is. And I know what Ancian and lots of other kezel say...* She fishes into her pocket, taking out and opening the dowskin pouch to reveal the last of the small, orange spheres, six in total.

Is this a joke? thinks Bridger.

You want us to eat awl gland? thinks Bliss.

But Stone steps forward, eyes wide, drawn like a dow to water. She snatches up one of the spheres.

This doesn't make up for anything, she thinks.

She pops the gland in her mouth and bites down with the easy grace of long practice, inhaling deep and swallowing. Her eyes close, and her scowl relaxes. Watching this, Bridger's ears droop in resignation.

I don't know what to say, she thinks. *I guess it's going to be that kind of rescue party.*

With that, she takes two of her own glands, for she is gigantic and worries that one will not be enough. She wrinkles her snout at the taste. Measure takes two as well, leaving only one. Bliss insists it be given to her friend Feather, and the Bristle doesn't disagree. The band falls still for a time, each gazing to different horizons, and while he effects are not so pronounced on the adults as they had been on Cliff—or Lightning, her first time—the haunted look in their eyes is replaced by a glimmer of hope, and even Stone takes a break from her grumbling.

Bridger glances up.

Here comes your bomba.

He's not mine, thinks Lightning. *His name is Ansel, and he's family too. Yes?*

Ansel it is, Bridger nods. *Probably going to wish we had a bunch more like him.*

The bomba lands at a safe distance, near the base of the vines. Lightning steps away from the band and approaches him, her head bowed. When she looks up, he cackles and points due south, away from the towers and at the hexagonal bowl.

Lightning's heart leaps; Joy has been moved.

She's at that gathering, she thinks to the others.

The ah-tahs, too, thinks Bliss. *By the smell.*

Bridger considers this.

Then it's time to leave the river, she thinks. *Once we're in sight of the gathering, your bomba—Ansel—can show us where this Joy is. Our noses will find the others. Then we can make a plan.*

Lightning nods, glad to have someone else lead.

Fan out, thinks Bridger, *but stay within clear thought. Don't engage unless attacked. In that case, kill quick, kill quiet, and kill all. We can't raise any alarms.*

She gives herself a shake.

Weaver, please, she thinks, but what she prays for, she keeps to herself.

+ + +

The band moves quickly across the exposed space, a flat, pale expanse, and small dust clouds blow away behind them. Seven hundred strides seem to take the time of seven thousand as they move unprotected under blue skies, but they meet no trouble. Soon, the smell of their enemies grows overwhelming, and an awful buzz ing and clicking fills the air. Not long after, the land rises in a sudden, stony dune running west to east. The gathering is on its other side.

Careful now, thinks Bridger. *Nice and easy.*

They peek over the dune. Neither the smell of her enemies nor their dreadful commotion prepare Lightning for what she sees. The giant bowl lies below them, six sided, carved into the ground and filled with a seething lake of metallic blue, tens of thousands of antennae waving like black reeds. She ducks back down, her guttering hope blown away in a moment.

No way, she thinks. *Too many.*

Ansel alights at a distance, peering over the dune and muttering at the sight. But Bridger is resolute.

Remember: it's not an assault. She raises her nose to the wind. *It's a rescue. Find our targets!*

The ah-tahs are to the east, thinks Measure.

I smell them too, Bliss adds hopefully. *Ten? More?*

They're not in that wretched hole, Stone agrees. *They're outside it. A couple hundred strides, maybe.* She looks at her ami-kan. *That's good, yes?*

But Bridger has no answer.

Lightning risks another look. The bowl contains a perfect circle at its bottom, around which their enemies gather. This circle is the focus of their attention. Inside it, thrashing in the water and atop the pillars, various foreign creatures grapple and bite, locked in mortal combat. The sounds of their terrible struggle rise even above the spectators' chittering clamor.

Ansel squawks and points. There, at the western rim of the bowl, escorted by a ring of bronze and two unique individuals, one gold and one silver, stands Joy. How she lost her camouflage is a mystery, and at this distance Lightning can tell nothing of her condition, but she appears unbound.

The jabi kezel berates herself for losing faith.

I'm here, she thinks, though she is too far away to be sensed. *I'm coming for you!* To Bridger she thinks: *She's near the western exit, at the top of the bowl.*

In that terraced area? The one set off from the others? Which one is she?

Four limbs. Standing on two.

Bliss and Feather mumble to one another.

Where are its other legs? thinks Stone. *What does it think it is? Kezel? Moondweller?*

Bridger's nose twitches.

Stranger and stranger, she thinks.

The others share less generous thoughts, but when ordered to attend, they quickly obey.

Hold this position, Bridger thinks to Lightning. *Bliss will stay with you. The rest of us are going to find the ah-tahs and let them in on our plan.*

Which is? asks Bliss.

For now, don't get caught.

With that, Bridger, Measure, Feather, and Stone move east along the northern face of the dune. Five hundred strides later, it falls away, and they disappear around its end, leaving Lightning, Bliss, and Ansel alone. The bomba hisses discontent, and Bliss casts anxious glances to the sky.

Ancian told me derkas won't usually attack an ibiwa, thinks Lightning. *Anyway, Ansel can see 'em coming from a long way off.*

Maybe, thinks Bliss, *but I'll feel better when we're under cover. Seeing a threat and avoiding it are not the same thing. And usually isn't never.*

She joins Lightning in peeking over the dune.

Of the creatures that had battled in the center circle, most are motionless heaps on top of the pillars or murky shapes floating in the water. Only two remain alive, a many-legged abomination smeared in blood, and something with damaged wings and a mouthful of teeth. The former chases the latter, who leaps from pillar to pillar, squealing. It attempts to scale the walls, but they are smooth and high, and its pursuer is close behind. The inevitable end must come soon. The abomination closes in, gathering itself for one final leap, but as it does, it slips on the blood of a fallen combatant, and it pitches into the water. At once, the pursuer becomes the pursued, as ominous ripples approach the fallen creature, struggling to paddle its way to the pillar. Frantic splashing terminates in a final shriek, as it is dragged beneath the surface by something Lightning never sees, its demise accompanied by a crescendo of lusty, avid buzzing.

Lightning turns away, sickened. Bliss curses.

I didn't think it was possible to hate these things any more than I already do. She looks at Lightning. *Don't worry. We're gonna get the ah-tahs—and your...whatever it is...she is, I mean.*

She scratches nervously at her ear.

The sooner the better, thinks Lightning, and she looks to the east. *Where are the others?*

Her answer arrives soon enough, as Bridger and the rest appear from around the edge of the dune, jogging toward them. Lightning senses they have located the others. She also detects a troubling concern.

What is it? she thinks. *What did you find?*

Sharing quick thoughts, Bridger relays what they have learned and their strategy.

Lightning nods.

I'm not crazy about Ansel and me being left alone, she thinks, *but I can see it's the only way. But there's something you're not telling me. What is it?*

Nothing unexpected, thinks Bridger—*considering the nature of these vermin. But the ah-tahs are in bad shape. Their minds have been... Some have been tortured, and all have been starved. I think they're going to be turned loose in that...* She scowls at the bowl.

My api? thinks Lightning. *And Thunder?*

Still alive, thinks Bridger. *But Submission is...*

He's not good, thinks Measure. *He won't be one of our fighters. He and the others like him can't be sent north alone, so Bliss is going to lead them.*

Lightning grits her teeth, trying to remain calm.

So, we lose her as a fighter too.

It can't be helped, thinks Bridger.

Bliss sighs, a heavy, doleful sound.

No sign of Rock or Crag?

No, thinks Bridger, growling. *And no Prowl or Shadow, either.*

Or Hail, thinks Measure when it becomes clear Bridger can't bring herself to add her own woti to the list.

She looks at Lightning.

Wait here and keep your bomba—keep Ansel—on the ground until we get back, understood?

Lightning nods, but her thoughts are elsewhere. Such hard news! Her poor oti-kans... But everyone there has suffered loss. What can they do except rescue those who still can be?

Understood, she thinks.

And with that, Bridger and company retrace their steps, leaving Lightning and Ansel alone. Soon, their companions slip out of sight behind the dune.

+ + +

The kezel move single file, with Bridger at the head and the others close behind. Stone takes the tail, her lip curled in a perpetual snarl.

Bruiser's woli! she thinks. *If we get back to the accrete, she'll be called to answer for what she did.*

Save it! thinks Bridger. *Stay low and stay close!*

Keeping bellies to the ground, they make their way around the last of the dune, leaving its cover for the downward trek to the eastern rim of the bowl. Here, the bank has been excavated, leading to a wide entrance carved into the bowl's stony base. Below them, their enemies scurry busily, handling a restive menagerie of beasts waiting to be escorted inside. Creatures of many shapes and colors are assembled under duress, some tethered, others hobbled or blindfolded, and all at intervals prodded and bitten for reasons only their captors know. The prisoners create a din and stench sensible from many strides away.

And among them are thirteen haggard kezel.

Farther to the east, another four hundred strides,

three of the largest creatures they have ever seen stand idle, roped to massive pillars of stone. On occasion, the quadrupeds raise enormous, tentacled heads to the sky and make terrible, ululating cries. They strain at their bindings, seeming sure to break the ropes if not the pillars themselves—but both hold fast.

Measure hands Bliss the cutter.

Good luck.

And off goes Rock's fancy, gripping the cutter between her teeth. She continues east along the rocky embankment until she is almost out of sight. The others move closer to the bowl where the menagerie is held. They take concealed positions, hugging the ground where rocky debris provides cover.

There they wait.

From inside the bowl, towering to their right, the cries of beasts in combat mingle with a whistling bloodlust that agitates the menagerie nearly as much as the would-be rescuers. The kezel squirm with pent emotions, nerves and muscles taut.

C'mon, Bliss, thinks Bridger, and she looks to the east with her snout wrinkled. *What's the delay?*

At last, a dreadful, trumpeting cry comes from the east, and all three of the monstrous beasts lumber to freedom, cut loose by Bliss. The effect is immediate. Leaving their prisoners, most of blue creatures scurry in pursuit, chittering angst.

In the end, only two dozen remain.

The kezel do not hesitate. They fall on their enemies, raising a furious cloud of dust. Poison bites have no effect, and those scion who learn this do not live to learn anything else. In thirty heartbeats, every last one has fallen to teeth or claws, none able to change colors or send warning. The poor creatures in the menagerie call out in terror and strain at their bindings, seeking to flee this new dread. But the kezel give no thought to their stomachs. Feather and Stone stand guard while the others hasten to the captive ah-tahs.

Oh, Pounce, thinks Bridger to her fancy.

Crunch, thinks Measure to hers. *Dear Crunchy.*

But this is no time for sentiment. How long before the menagerie will be expected in the bowl? How many of their enemies will come investigating when that doesn't happen? And how long will the awl glands last?

The rescuers hastily remove muzzles from each of the captives, trying not to dwell on their woeful condition. To an outsider unfamiliar with kezel, the rangy creatures may have appeared ferocious enough, but to Bridger and Measure, they are all lank skin and sunken eyes. They are hobbled, with bands around their necks anchoring them to a pillar nearby. Some of the least damaged—Thunder and his amotiwot Digger among them—greet the rescuers as if scared to believe what they are seeing. Others stare through vacant eyes, some shying away at their approach. Submission takes no notice, attempting in vain to lick at injuries on his flank, and the scruffy gigika Trapper, oldest of all the captives, makes Old Buttons look like a champion.

Well done, thinks Bone, head of the Brigade.

It will be once we're out of here, thinks Bridger, and she counts quickly. *Bone, Crunch, Pounce, Digger, and Blue. Five able to fight...*

Six, Thunder scowls.

Yeah, OK, fair enough. And... She hesitates, as if afraid of the answer she will get, then asks, *What about Prowl and Shadow?*

Bone bares his teeth.

Gigika Prowl didn't make it a single moon. Afraid Shadow didn't last much longer.

And...what about Hail?

But no one can say. Like many of them, he had been taken away for some foul treatment better left unimagined, but unlike them, he had not returned.

Bridger's ears droop, and she closes her eyes. Stilled thoughts are the best solace the others can offer, and this they do, waiting until she at last thinks:

The rest of you get ready to move out once Bliss gets here, as if each word were a heavy stone.

Bliss arrives soon after, running in from the east and panting. With the cutter flashing in the sun, she makes short work of the bindings, allowing the captives to stretch cramped limbs before splitting into two groups, those who will attempt Joy's rescue, and those, like the jabis Cranny and Pockets, who aren't fit to help.

I should stay too, thinks the enormous bibija Fang. But his leg is badly torn and poorly mended; his pace is scarcely faster than Trapper's.

Bliss will need your help, thinks Bridger. *Someone needs to watch over Submission. Bruiser! Hey there!*

For Submission, stupefied, has begun wandering away to the south. Bliss gently ushers him back in line with the others. She looks at Bridger.

I wouldn't mind sinking teeth into one of these animals before we go.

No time, thinks Bridger. *Go quick, and we'll see you at the river.* She takes the cutter, returning it to Measure and facing the others. *Ready? Here we go then.*

+ + +

The two groups part company, ten fighters moving back toward the dune, while Bliss and her single file of derelicts snake their way north, away from the bowl and its awful sounds. Bridger soon loses sight of them. She turns her attention to the remaining ah-tahs, filling them in as best as she can while they creep up the embankment. She is often interrupted.

Where are Rock and Crag? Thunder asks.

No idea. Ansel scouted top to bottom, and we're all he found. That's the bomba I was telling you about.

What about Curly? Digger wants to know.

On her way with the others. Hurly and Burly too. And yes, Bone and Blue, your fancies are among them.

But she skates over the condition the ah-lahs and wabis are in, chooses to omit the sad story of the wabi Sniff, one of the first to die in captivity, and doesn't mention the fate of poor little Scale.

A.P. Malloy

You understand you can't kill the bomba, yes? she thinks. *Or the blue thing named Joy?*

But we can kill the six-legged ones, yes? Thunder asks in a tone that says he intends to either way.

As many as you like.

Stone wipes blue blood from her crooked snout.

Kill 'em, but don't bother trying to eat 'em. There's nothing good there—might even be poison.

The embankment is steep and littered with loose stones, but they make their way steady and quiet and soon reach the top of the bowl and the dune to its north. The din of the congregation rides the wind, offending their ears like a sandstorm, and though they are out of sight, they feel exposed. They hurry around the dune, glad to have it between them and their enemies.

We're close, thinks Bridger. *When we get there, there'll be no time for chatting. How ever you feel about Submission's woli, save it for later. Those are orders. And again—don't eat the bomba!*

No chance of that, Stone growls, coming to a sudden stop. Bridger jogs up next to her, looking west along the line of the dune.

Lightning and Ansel are nowhere to be seen.

CHAPTER NINE
Thunder

INSIDE THE BOWL, every pair of sparkling, black eyes focuses on the grisly action playing out in the Circle— every pair but one. Joy can no longer bear to watch. The pain in her head, which has worsened as Princess promised it would, is intensified by the derka's distress. Black wings tipped in red struggle against the shroud, and its head rolls side to side as it croaks and rasps.

Flee the Circle! Ninety-one percent casualties!

But flee to where? thinks Joy.

The derka thrashes its forked tail.

Ozag's Hold! Far Colossus! It writhes and contorts, becoming entangled in its shroud. *Elixir...*

Joy wrangles her fear, trying to coax answers from the derka, but as before, its mind is slippery. She feels sure key details are eluding her, and its thoughts become recursive, repeating a miserable litany.

Ozag's Hold... Deliver message... Elixir... Far Colossus... Its wings fall slack. *All will die... Flee...*

Never has Joy agreed with any advice so enthusiastically, but still Princess remains motionless, her eyes cloudy with doubt.

In the Circle, carcasses of fallen combatants are pushed or pulled off the bloody columns by teams of scion, dumped into the water, turbulent with monsters. On the central column, New Magister reappears, and with him, the brown creature, its headgear and shiny black suit impossible to mistake. In one forelimb, New Magister holds a whip, and in the other, a flaming brand. At his appearance, the throng grows silent.

New Magister waves his torch. The brown creature bows. New Magister circles and snaps the whip. The creature twirls as if a puppet on a string. Summersaults and leaps. More bowing, followed by two backflips, a display of athleticism Joy had not expected. Each wave of the torch and flick of the whip reads like a command, and the creature obeys them all. The scion click and whistle their approval, forelimbs rasping.

More! they think in unison. *More!*

As if saving the best for last, New Magister casts away his torch and leaps on the creature's back, prodding him with the whip. Docile as always, the creature climbs from terrace to terrace, bearing his passenger up toward Queen. When they reach the uppermost terrace, surprise! New Magister lifts an opaque shield at the front of the creature's headgear, revealing his face. His brown skin glistens, and his breathing is heavy. Another prod brings him to his knees, bowing before Queen.

New Magister has great Command, she thinks. *The vumierre has learned much in short time.*

It serves Queen, thinks New Magister. *As do all.*

And she serves Ozag, Infinite and Vengeful. Queen raises her eyes to the assembly and casts forth a mighty thought. *She will hear the Circle's plea and present it to Ozag! But she guarantees nothing; she is conduit only. None have power to bend the will of the Undying.*

New Magister's eyes dim. His antennae bend.

He relinquishes the Circle to Queen.

At that, a dozen bronze flyers rise slowly from the ground, the gossamer lines draw tight, and Queen in her basket is borne aloft. Majestic and stately, the basket is carried down toward the center of the circle, passing a mere kezel-length over the heads of scion who dim their eyes and bow. When the basket reaches the centermost of the pillars it is lowered, allowing Queen to step out. As she does, the flyers depart with the basket, landing on the lowest terrace and bowing their antennae. Alone on the pillar, surrounded by a labyrinth of blood-stained water and thousands of eyes, Queen spreads her wings and takes to the air, hovering like a second sun, and for a moment, even Joy is mesmerized by the display.

What is the plea? thinks Queen, and as with New Magister, her thoughts are magnified. Joy can sense them as clearly as if she stands within arm's reach.

Water, replies a single scion mind, one of the thousands, far away and barely sensible. *Flood!*

Like a pebble starting a landslide, its mind is soon joined by many others.

Yes! Flood, they think. *Ozag shall send the flood!*

Soon, hundreds of minds, then a hundred times a hundred, all demanding the same thing, join in telepathic accord. The bowl seems to tremble from the power of so many tightly focused, unified thoughts.

Yes! Ozag shall send the flood!

The thought is channeled to Queen and amplified, by what means, Joy can't guess. Its force wilts her antennae, and she buzzes in a senseless fashion, hunkering as if about to be attacked.

Time to go, Princess!

The derka croaks its agreement.

For one moment more, Princess delays. Then:

Yes, she thinks. *While Queen and New Magister are occupied. Leave on foot! Attract no attention!*

And they step away, surreptitious and slow, their bronze escort bearing the derka and following on foot, the basket left behind. Joy's fear of being accosted appears unfounded. The assembly continues its singular demand even as they retreat toward the gate, and nearby scion, their attention utterly Queen's, stand rigid as if entranced. Their departure goes wholly unnoticed—or so it seems to Joy.

+ + +

When they reach the main entrance, they are forced to stop. Wingless, Joy is at the mercy of the gate-keepers, and the scion in charge of driving the babelrack have gone to join the Circle. The massive beast stands in its place, stomping and snorting and refusing to budge. Princess' most imperious whistle falls on its four swiveling ears like the buzz of a yit. It is are aware of the sound, but it inspires in it no compulsion.

They will carry the Oddity over! Princess orders.

Her pluripotents attempt to comply, but pincers are no good for grabbing supple flesh—not without its injury—and when Joy tries to grasp their bristly legs, her hands are bloodied. She feels sure their time is short, a certainty only heightened by the derka's agitation, and when Princess extrudes filament from her midsection, planning to weave a rope, it sems to take forever.

Joy's nerves jangle.

Step aside, she thinks suddenly. Moving forward, she addresses the babelrack as before. *Thinkers!* She buzzes and bows. *It is me! Remember?*

Four eyes on each of the two heads turn her way, stupefied as ever at the sense of this inexplicable thought. Their jowls shake, and spittle flies.

Mmm...who thinks? one of the heads demands, whether the male or the female, Joy can't say.

Mmm...how a Thinker? wonders the other. It scrapes its tusks against the stone, cascading sparks.

How a two-legged Hunter? thinks the first. *Mmm...*

Please! Open the gate. Joy looks behind her, expecting pursuit at any moment.

Big Hunter says open, thinks the one head.

Mmm...Big Hunter says close, thinks the other.

Yes, that is good. Joy fails to restrain a nervous clicking. *But I am friend.* Then, thinking of her encounter on the river, she adds: *Gore hunters! Stomp hunters!*

This inspires a great deal of head tossing and tusk scraping as the babelrack labors to understand. Its eyes roll this way and that. How to reconcile the sight of this strange creature with the thoughts it is sending?

And still the gate remains closed.

Big Hunter says open, thinks the first head.

Big Hunter has whips and fire, thinks the second.

What happens? exclaims Princess, becoming suddenly aware. *Are the clods thinking? Are actual thoughts coming from their disgusting heads?*

At sensing this, the babelrack doubles its clamor. It bucks against its harness.

Another thinker! Mmm...but not a Thinker. A Hunter! A Silver Hunter! A Silver Hunter thinks? Mmm...

This is too much. No matter how Joy cajoles and Princess commands, it swings its massive heads to and fro, bellowing back and forth as if by making noise it might solve the riddle. Terrified its ruckus will bring trouble, Joy turns to see her fear realized. New Magister, riding his black-suited steed, has approached to within a few strides, his whip curling idly.

Leaving so soon? he thinks.

Though many times his size, the babelrack falls silent at the sight of the large, blue scion and his whip, as if recalling bad memories.

Mmm...Big Hunter, the one head thinks like a murmur, and its eyes turn away.

She is feeling unwell, thinks Princess. *She will retire and wait for tey Ramota.*

He is sorry to learn this, thinks New Magister. *But he advises leave the vumierre. He will care for it.*

She thanks him for his concern. Princess' tone is eminently courteous, but her eyes ignite. *Nevertheless! She is master of this vumierre. She wishes it to entertain her while she recuperates.*

New Magister digs pincers into his steed's ebony flanks, prodding it to step closer.

Without Queen's permission? He deems that most unwise. As he has said, it has killed—murdered. And Joy senses him sheltering greedy thoughts.

He dares judge her wisdom? thinks Princess.

He merely advises.

She will act on her own advice!

Then, thinks New Magister, and his whip quivers as if wakened from a dream, *he insists!* Quick like a bomba striking for rixli, the whip coils and lashes, its end looping around Joy's neck and cinching tight.

Affront! Princess takes to the air, whistling sharp and loud. *Outrage and insult! He will desist!*

But New Magister leaps from his steed, and though Joy digs in her heels and pulls back on the whip with both hands, she feels herself being strangled. He reels her toward him, pincer by pincer, his strength surprising and his eyes filled with light.

He will feel her wrath, thinks Princess, *if he does not stop molesting her vumierre!* The threat goes unheeded, and when she commands her escort to assist, they spread their wings, only to have New Magister still them with a single command. They silence their droning and remain on the ground oblivious to Princess and the derka who is left writhing in the dust.

None may assail him while the Circle is closed, thinks New Magister. *He has Command!* He is so close now Joy can smell him. Shrieking, Princess takes to the air, seeking to drive him from his feet. But he is highly trained and burgeoning with confidence. He ducks and strikes, one middle limb opening a gash across Princess' tail section and knocking her to the ground.

Joy has no time for fear and only a split second thought: *Don't let him bite,* before being clenched by his pincers. But she isn't bitten. As New Magister's leering eyes draw close, as he aims to sink fangs into her neck, she hears his whistling exhalation, a piercing cry of surprise and pain. The brown creature, his docility vanished like a footprint in hard rain, has leapt on his back with a guttural exclamation. Twice New Magister's size and that or more his weight, he crushes his master beneath him, his face twisted in rage. New Magister's neck is broken in a moment, the light chased from his eyes and his antennae falling slack.

"Mala durn!" the brown creature shouts, and he flashes his small, white teeth, scowling fiercely. "Ob dolla

Book of Dreams

bon din badolla!"

Joy peels the whip from around her neck, a dark blue welt beginning to rise, as Princess regains her feet. Her injury fuels her anger, and as she retrieves the derka from where it lies, she flashes her wings like a threat.

The beast will open the gate or feel her pain!

But something in the sight of New Magister, broken and still, has changed the tone in the babelrack's minds, making her threat unnecessary.

It killed Big Hunter, the one thinks, looking at the black-suited creature. *Mmm...it is Big Hunter now.*

The other rolls its eyes and stomps agreement. Together, they echo the same question:

Mmm...what does Big Hunter want? What does Big Hunter order?

The brown creature senses none of this.

Open the gate, please! thinks Joy, pouring all her sentiment into the request. *That's what he wants!*

This is enough for the babelrack. Its muscles bulge as it digs into the arid soil and opens the revolving gate, allowing them to pass. Princess and her escort, the bronze flyers released from New Magister's spell, take the lead, the cutting rhythm of their wings like a song of liberation. Joy follows close behind, hurrying to keep the pace. Uninvited and disregarded, her rescuer does the same, but Joy comes to a sudden stop.

Free them! she calls to Princess.

The Oddity will hasten! This is no time for sentimental foolishness.

Free them, Joy insists. *Or I stay here.* She rubs her welting neck. *Understand the derka yourself.*

The sincerity of her tone brings Princess to a halt. On her command, the pluripotents hasten to unharness the stomping babelrack. It offers not a single thought as it is at last unbound, but the sight of it stampeding away to the northwest, chased by its own dust cloud and bellowing a two-part harmony, is all the gratitude Joy needs.

+ + +

A.P. Malloy

And then they hurry on.

Princess makes no comment on her injury, in spite of the blood that has risen to the surface and a stride that betrays a noticeable hitch. Two of her attendants bear the derka between them as she leads the party—including their black-clad, two-legged shadow—through a narrow doorway in the rock. This in turn leads downward to a wide passage scored on either side with regular openings. Through these, Joy spies the distant shore of the lake and recognizes they travel west, back toward the island.

But beneath the road, she realizes an instant later. *And inside the bridge.* The sounds of the Circle fade in the distance. *What is the plan?* she asks.

It claimed its artifact an aid to understanding, replies Princess. *If her prime was successful, it will have opportunity to demonstrate this—if false, its lying will come to a painful end. If true—and if this derka can prove its claims—she will learn what she needs to make her plan. Until then, it will remain still!*

Once across the lake, they do not return to Princess' tower, but continue on to Queen's, the largest and southernmost. It appears very similar, and they make their hexagonal way up through identical passages until they reach another garden, though this is larger and more ornate. Here, unattended baskets lie waiting on the ground, their ropes neatly coiled.

New Magister's demise will be noticed the moment Queen releases her hold on the Circle, thinks Princess. *It will follow quickly!* She flits upward, zip-zip, smoother in flight than on land. Soon, she is many kezel-lengths above the garden. *Is it daft?* she calls. *It will follow!*

Joy takes a seat in one of the baskets, thinking at last to offer thanks to the brown creature and gesturing for him to join. But he shakes his head, stepping away as if the basket were an awl and he a waddling dow.

Have it your way, thinks Joy, and her stomach drops as the flyers place the derka in the basket and lift her up and away. She grips one of the slender ropes forming the basket's outer rail, knuckles whitening.

The first levels they rise past appear no different than those in Princess' tower. But as they continue upward, that changes. Instead of passages and chambers, levels of amber, translucent cells are stacked one atop the other. Inside each, a single, wriggling life, no bigger than Joy's head, floats in amber fluid, six legs twitching as if the creatures are asleep and dreaming. Their wispy antennae wave lazily above bulging eyes, dim yet aware, for some turn to look at her.

Joy guesses they number in the thousands.

What is this place? she thinks, but Princess is too far away or chooses not to reply.

The garden is soon far beneath them, and still the flyers ascend until they have reached the uppermost level of the tower. Here, they lower the basket carefully to the floor, and their burden thus delivered, they settle their wings, waiting for instructions as their passenger disembarks. They are in a spacious chamber, partitioned into large, six-sided rooms and walled in translucent amber—except for the southern side, which is open to the sun. There, nothing stands between them and a deadly fall. Large portions of the chamber have no roof, and Joy has the sense that they have become unmoored and will float into the sky.

Princess lands near the eastern wall, motioning for her to join. Far below, the eastern road stretches like a finger, pointing to the giant bowl and the scion gathered there. She glimpses the sparkle of water within, and the sight offends her aching head.

Wasting water, she thinks. *What of your drought?*

Princess clicks harshly.

The Oddity knows nothing. That water comes from the Great Saline. It is unsuitable for anything but the Circle. It cannot satisfy thirst. Lova cannot be grown with it. Only water from Ozag does that.

Fine, thinks Joy, feeling anything but, and she tugs at tangled locks of her hair. *Why are we here?*

Has it not been explained? She waits on her prime

pluripotent! In the meantime, she must tend her injury and prepare for her departure.

That's our *departure, yes?*

Princess whistles sharply.

It will keep watch and inform her if the Circle opens. It will stay vigilant! She strides away with a limping tickety-tack, buzzing to herself as she disappears into one of the back chambers.

Despite her orders, Joy is soon disgusted by the eastern view. As the derka slips into a restive slumber, she turns from the Circle and looks south, seeking comfort in the sun. Below her, extending from the island, another road is built up out of the lakebed. Once across the water, it continues south, staying east of the river delta. Following its course, Joy gets a surprise like a slap to the face. In the hazy distance, where the land ought to meet the sky, the road ends abruptly at a sandy shore. From that point to the horizon, east to west, twinkling waves dance on a limitless body of water. She struggles to make sense of what she sees. The awl lakes near the maison were large, but their opposite shores were always visible when the weather was clear. This water...this water goes on forever, blue meeting blue, one whitecap chasing the next, with no hint of land in sight.

End of the world, she thinks.

At this moment, Princess returns, carrying a woven bundle whose contents Joy can only guess. Her injury no longer bleeds, but her thoughts are anxious, her steps labored as if the burden is heavy.

The Oddity was to keep watch! she thinks. *And as always, it is wrong. Scion crossed the Great Saline long ago. It is how they reached Albion, of course. Out beyond sight, in a place where the sun rides higher in the sky, the land begins again.* She drops her parcel and flies to the eastern wall, peering out. *The Circle will open soon,* she frets. *Where is her prime?*

She makes two more hurried trips to the back chamber, each time carrying another loaded parcel, her anxious clicks increasing.

What takes it so long? she demands to no one.

The next moment, droning wings and a gleam of bronze provide her answer. A lone pluripotent, itself carrying a burden, rises up from the depths of the tower. Joy gasps when she recognizes her sling, stained but intact, and when the pluripotent drops it to the floor, she snatches it up, feeling the surprising weight and regular shape of the artifact inside. She raises the talihew hide to her nose and inhales, hungry for its scent, and a vivid memory of Lightning flashes through her mind.

Retrieving this object carried great risk, thinks Princess. *What reward shall she have for her effort?*

It seems to Joy the risk and effort were borne by someone else, but she lets this pass and releases the artifact from its confines. The first thing she feels is its gratitude for the sun, effulgent and uncontested, close enough to touch. The second is an image of Princess, a map of her mind, detailed and precisely drawn. In the presence of the artifact, naked thoughts, previously hidden, are drawn from behind their shutters. Joy reads her fear and senses beneath it layers of other emotion—pain that hasn't had time to heal, anger with no target, doubt and indecision masked by pride.

The third thing she notices is the derka. Its eyes blinking independent of each other, it wakes suddenly and looks about as if assessing their situation. The artifact makes its thoughts sharp and strong, complete rather than elliptical.

We are Derka! It spreads its wings and croaks. *Why do they delay? We have delivered the message as we vowed, and yet they do not return us to Ozag's Hold for the Elixir we were promised! We have said "stop the Circle," but it continues anyway. Have they not understood? We have said "flee," and yet they remain!*

Joy needs no confirmation to know Princess can sense the thoughts as clearly as she.

Ozag's bristles! The Oddity spoke truly. But you, derka! What proof that you also are true?

Its death will be proof if it continues to lag. Flee!

A.P. Malloy

But food, thinks Princess. *And lova. She cannot undertake a journey without sustenance.*

No time! To Far Colossus! Let no one stop them!

What does it mean? thinks Joy.

It means she must change her plans, thinks Princess. *She had hoped to visit the Royal stores, but... No more! To the garden, then, and the Secret Way. The Oddity will load the basket and follow.* She drapes the derka over her arms, flying down and away.

+ + +

The parcels are indeed heavy, but Joy doesn't risk the time to look inside. She hauls them into the basket and climbs in. Even with the return of their sixth member, the flyers labor to keep the basket aloft. When they reach the garden, she can scarcely believe her eyes: the brown creature stands waiting for them—or more precisely, waiting for her. He has lowered his faceplate, but his head turns to follow her every move. As the basket is borne through the garden to its western wall, he jogs along behind, black and silent.

They see no other scion.

Does its vumierre insist on following? thinks Princess, flying in the lead.

It's not my anything, Joy is quick to reply.

It should be made to carry burdens so she can re-enter the basket. She is not meant to tax herself so.

Tell it that yourself.

But Princess has disappeared into a dark passage at the edge of the garden. It is cleverly hidden by densely berried shrubbery, sculpted into abstract shapes that loom in a menacing fashion. The basket barely has room to pass, but Princess leads them confidently, and they enter a dark, sloping tunnel. They travel this downward for hundreds of cramped, claustrophobic strides, until at last, the tunnel levels, and they arrive at a windowed passage that has a familiar appearance. But now they travel beneath the *west*bound bridge, crossing the lake on their

Book of Dreams

way—Joy hopes—to freedom. On the road overhead, she hears the distraught chittering of a group of scion heading east to the towers. They are in a great hurry, and their thoughts are agitated, as if they hasten to deliver bad news. She doesn't dare try sensing details, concerned rather with hiding her own mind.

Moments later, they reach the point at which the road slopes upward to meet the western lake shore, and they move out into the sunlight. They are alone; they have escaped undetected. But the derka now squirms so violently Princess can barely keep hold. It whips its tail and extends a long ruby tongue, hissing.

Doom! it thinks, and it makes an awful croaking as it looks to the northwest. *They were too slow!*

Joy turns to follow its gaze. High in the azure and far away, a dark speck appears, moving toward them. She hears something like distant, continuous thunder. The speck reflects the sun, twinkling in a merry way, but as it moves, it grows. It soon takes on a tubular shape, and as far away as it appears, it is rushing toward them at an impossible speed, growing larger with each heartbeat and trailing a line of white smoke to the horizon.

Flee! thinks the derka. *Wait for no one!* But Princess no longer needs the encouragement. She whistles at her pluripotents, urging them to haste.

West! she thinks. *To the river!* In spite of the basket's weight, the flyers double their effort, wings beating a furious, whining tempo. Their sudden burst of speed drives Joy off her feet, and the brown creature must break into a run to keep up.

The faint thunder grows to a roar, and Joy looks up in terror. The flying thing is nearly a hundred strides long and twenty in diameter, a gray behemoth, its nose pointed and smoke pouring from its fluted tail. It plunges from the heavens—how could anything that large remain airborne?—falling in a perfect arc with a horrific, deafening sound. Heat warps the air as it passes.

Joy covers her ears and bows her head, but the bronze flyers panic at the sight, and they drop the basket, fleeing in six different directions. Princess disregards them, flitting away to the west, the derka held tight as the basket falls to the ground and Joy's breath is dashed away. Shaken and bruised, she rises on unsteady legs and runs blindly, giving no thought to her companions or the contents of the basket, sure that the nightmare will crash down on her. Instead, it passes overhead with a booming roar that flattens her antennae and drives her face-first to the dusty soil. Clearing the towers, it strikes the heart of the Circle, and the appalling impact is so powerful Joy feels it with her entire body. Clouds of terrorized ground-dwelling yits take to the air.

The moment when tens of thousands of scion lives are extinguished in flames is like an unstoppable scream in Joy's mind, goading her to a type of madness. She staggers west to escape it, thinking *Concelar! Concelar!* running until her legs give out and she collapses into the thorny embrace of tangling vines.

+ + + + + +

For some of the kezel taken captive moons ago, loss of freedom was the thing that had eaten their sanity. A lifetime of roaming the wide accrete hadn't prepared them for extended bondage. These kezel had withered early in captivity—among them, Thunder's api-kan Submission. He had been kept in solitary confinement and bitten often, until his immunity to scion poison had been overwhelmed. The toxin had combined with despair and loneliness to tip his psyche over an invisible edge. Eventually, his mind ran free across the snowy foothills, disconnected from his imprisoned body.

Others, like the gigika Trapper, his woti Fang, and the ibiwa Melt, had been undone by routine torment. Their captors' methods were heinous but effective. Over time, fear of lash and bite—or the terrible pain of fire— drove the fight out of the bravest. Thus broken, they cowered and grimaced in a pitiable fashion, trailing after their captors like shadows.

Book of Dreams

But none of that for Thunder.

When the scion had accepted they were unable to subdue his spirit, they had made hunger his constant companion, testing the lengths he was willing to go to ease the gnawing in his guts. What they learned is that two starving kezel, in proximity with food for only one, will fight to a bloody end. Thrown into a pit with Bridger's jabi Hail, Thunder had been consumed by burning hunger, the bits of food tossed between them no more than a puddle. When Hail had challenged him, something had happened in his brain. His vision had gone red, and though he knew it was wrong, he had felt helpless to resist. He remembers the voice of his victim, but not his thoughts. Hail was dead soon after, the food eaten, and the fire quenched—for a time.

But Thunder's worst ignominy was yet to come. For feverish sleeps he had been forced to remain in the pit with the body of his murdered clanmate and a hunger that worsened by the moment. When death alone offered an alternative to his suffering, Thunder had done something he believes is unforgivable.

Never again, he had sworn, his belly filled but his heart sickened. *I'll die first.*

Even as he was being dragged with the others to the Circle, he had repeated this vow to himself. He had stood, eyes hollow, near the giant bowl, along with other kezel, secured at a safe distance from one another and the miserable creatures surrounding them. Hearing the loathsome sounds of the gathering had cemented his conviction. Death would claim him before he satisfied his enemies in such a fashion again.

Never, he had repeated.

But even then, hunger was stalking him.

So it is that when Bridger and the other ah-lahs arrive from the north like a mirage, Thunder is unable to say which is the cause of his relief, the hope of freedom, knowing he has avoided another test, or the knowledge that Bridger is unaware of his crime. Once freed, he trails after, shaking his head and quickening his pace, striving to clear his mind of such memories. As they skirt the bowl, Thunder peers through openings along its rim. Countless enemies gather within, focused on some violence below. He doesn't know what transpires there and doesn't wish to learn.

Remain undetected, he thinks to himself. *Win a quick fight if necessary and get out of this nightmare.*

But when they arrive at their rendezvous point to find neither Lightning nor her bomba, he sees his hope for an easy escape may have been premature.

She went toward the road, thinks Bridger, nose to the ground. *Toward where it meets the lake. The bomba too.* The others quickly confirm this. Lightning's scent is impossible to miss, and no hungry kezel overlooks the smell of a bomba. They peer down into the bowl; Joy is no longer there.

Your oli-mu, thinks Stone, *causes a lot of trouble.*

Others agree. Thoughts of simply turning their backs and heading north percolate among them.

She wouldn't have left without a good reason, thinks Thunder. *She wasn't chased, that much is clear.* He sighs. *Going after that blue thing of hers, I guess, wherever it went.*

And I suppose, Stone thinks with an ugly growl, *you want us to do the same?*

What else can we do? We can't just leave her.

Bridger grimaces.

No one's leaving anybody.

She examines the road. It runs level from bowl to island, open to the sky, but while doing so, it also serves as a roof for another passage below, lined with narrow windows. Lightning's trail leads toward this.

Well, she thinks. *I guess we send someone to follow, but no bibija's squeezing through those holes.*

I'll go, thinks Digger.

Me too, thinks the Bristle ibiwa Feather.

Four's the score, thinks Bridger. *Who else? Thunder, yes? And how about you, Stone?*

Not a chance.

Book of Dreams

OK. Blue?

Er...

C'mon, someone's gotta step up! Three's as un-lucky a number as there is.

Fine, thinks Blue. *But I'm in charge.*

And no one disagrees.

We'll stand watch, thinks Bridger. *And we'll wait as long as we can. We'll protect your tail if we have to, but we're not staying if we can't win. Understand? We've lost too many already.*

Blue gets droopy in the ears.

I've sensed more encouraging speeches.

But he gathers his party as his companions take their positions, and when they are ready, he leads Digger, Feather, and Thunder south to where Lightning's trail—and that of the bomba—meets the lake road. Once they've squeezed their way into the covered passage, Blue points to Thunder and Digger.

We three are going on. You, he orders Feather, *stay here and keep this exit open.*

How long do I wait?

Until we get back, of course, and Blue turns away. Thunder and Digger follow close behind, noses to the ground as they make their way toward the island. Lightning's scent is clear to them all, like a ribbon of light in a dark sky, leading them toward the towers.

The covered road runs five hundred strides, but the kezel have covered only half that distance when they detect a rumbling in the air outside. It grows quickly, soon overwhelming all other sounds. They gather at the road's northern side, peering out to locate the source. They don't wait long. An immense cylinder of shining gray arcs through the sky toward them, hurtling forward as it blows smoke from its fluted tail.

It's going to hit the road! thinks Digger, a wild look in his eyes. *We can't get trapped here!*

Back! thinks Blue. *Back to the exit! Run!*

He and Digger turn without hesitation and sprint back the way they came, where Feather remains standing

A.P. Malloy

guard. But Thunder does not follow. With all the speed he can muster from his haggard frame, he hastens on toward the island, prodded by fear and pulled by Lightning's scent. Twenty strides from the island, just as he thinks to himself: *I smell blood,* Thunder hears as well as feels a terrible impact behind him. A blinding flash of light is followed by a wave of searing heat, and he falls heavily to the ground. Only once he has regained his feet and stumbled the remaining distance to the island does he dare look back. The covered road now ends near the lakeshore, disappearing into a wall of red-black fire.

There will be no returning that way.

He can see nothing of the other kezel.

Gathering his wits, he wheels about, ready for a wave of enemies or some other catastrophe. But when nothing happens, he takes a deep breath and moves on, sniffing carefully and trying to slow his racing heart.

+ + +

He follows the trail to the lowest level of the southeastern tower and discovers the carnage of a recent fight. Numerous blue bodies lie scattered, torn apart in unmistakable kezel fashion. Others are scorched black, their stinking remains still smoldering.

Then it's true, he thinks. *You fight with a bomba.*

This gives him hope, difficult as it is to imagine. But as the trail leads him out of this tower and into the tallest of the six, facing due south, he sees a thin smear of kezel blood staining the amber floor. He quickens his pace, following Lightning's trail up three levels despite the rank stench of his enemies. He encounters more of them dead on either side of the passage and soon after arrives at a courtyard in the tower's heart.

He treads forward in silence, his nostrils flaring. The place appears to be abandoned, and yet he senses movement, like ripples on a lake brushed by wind—ripples that travel vertically, up and down the courtyard's lofty walls. They are not waves at all, he realizes, but discrete units of languid, amber motion, tiny animals, each housed in a hexagon no larger than his head, thousands upon thousands, stacked to the tower's sunny peak.

Tail biters, he curses. *What is this place?*

In spite of his haste and worry, he steps closer to the nearest wall, unable to resist learning more. Inside each cell, filled with amber fluid, floats a single creature, familiar and eerie, wriggling its six legs. Their antennae wave in a languorous fashion, their black eyes distorted and overlarge. Identical they appear, and yet no two twitch or wriggle the same way; no two beaky mouths open or close at the same time. For a moment, Thunder stares, mesmerized by dread fascination.

Then, snarling, he returns to the trail.

The way leads to a verdant space, hundreds of strides across, open to the sky, split by a placid creek, and filled with an array of strange plants and creatures. Many of the latter stampede in fear of the explosion and the scent of fire, attempting to flee their confines. He dodges some, scares away others, hurrying across the pliant turf. At the center of this garden, woven baskets rest on the ground. From each, long, silky ropes lay coiled. His oli-mu's trail weaves between these, moving back and forth in a deliberate fashion.

On the trail of that damn blue thing, he guesses, and he sees more of Lightning's blood. *I wonder if she'll think it was worth the effort.*

At a well-hidden opening to an underground passage, Lightning's trail is joined by that of others, one with an unforgettable scent, last smelled moons ago under the eaves of the accrete.

So, you found it, he thinks. *Or you found its trail. But who are these other ones?*

He leans in, sniffing and puzzling. Several are enemies, that much is clear, and the one smells like derka droppings. But the other...that is something new. Warm blooded it smells, and delicious, by its prints nearly as large as Thunder himself, and bipedal. All these passed this way at the same time, followed shortly after by Lightning and the bomba. Drops of crimson invite him in.

Thunder bows his head and enters.

Complete darkness envelopes him, and his nose twitches fretfully. After a brief, initial descent, the tunnel grows level, but it is narrow—and empty. The stale, motionless air was disturbed, not long ago, by those he follows, but outside of his quarry, no one has passed this way in a long time. Not a sound can he hear as he treads through the darkness, unless maybe it is some faint echo of the panic and destruction behind him.

Every step increases his anxiety.

Sure could use a breeze, he thinks.

No sooner has he done so than a faint scent wafts his way. He stops, the spikes rising along his neck. Though he can't see her, he knows Lightning is ahead of him in the dark. The bomba is with her. They are no more than fifty strides away, though if they have detected him, they make no sign. Of Lightning, other than the fact that she is bleeding, Thunder can determine nothing. Her mind is still as if sleeping, and her voice is silent. The bomba hisses and mutters to itself.

The jabi kezel finds he is unable to move, his legs gripped by an icy dread of what he will find if he continues on. The faint echo of the bomba's eerie murmurings threatens to unnerve him.

He wills himself to take one more step.

Lightning, he thinks. *It's Thunder. It's me.*

But no answer comes from out of the dark.

+ + +

Blue, Feather, and Digger come scrambling out of the tunnel, their eyes wide with panic, and they join the other kezel fleeing the madness. Bridger guards the tail, driving the others and helping those who stumble. For a moment only does she lose her focus and look up at the roaring terror. The heat from its fiery tail distorts the air, and as it plunges, growing at a surreal pace, irrelevant details carve themselves into her memory. Its fluted tail?

Bloody red. Its nose? Black as an unlit cave and pointed. Indecipherable markings span its length. Then she turns and sprints away, fascination overcome by fear as the roaring voice becomes deafening.

This is not a good end, she thinks.

But a moment later, the nightmare passes overhead and crashes into the terraced bowl behind her, plowing nose first into the giant assembly with a shockwave of sound and heat that sends her sprawling to the parched ground. Battered and scratched, she lurches to her feet, ears ringing. Feather rises nearby, stunned, her eyes rolling white. Together, they turn on shaken legs and hurry away. Only when they have reunited with the others do they dare look back.

From the Circle, a huge fireball rises to the sky on wings of orange and black. The bowl is awash in hungry, licking flames, and of the thousands of their enemies—and the flying terror itself—not a bit remains. The explosion has collapsed the eastern end of the lake road. Flames leap out of the gaping hole in the lakeshore like a torch, and the southern wind carries a stench of burned flesh and toxic fumes.

Bridger can stand no more.

Come on, she thinks. *The show's over.*

Despite their fatigue, the others need no encouragement. Mustering what haste they can, they move toward the river spindling in from the northwest.

Digger jogs up next to Bridger.

What about Thunder? he thinks. *And Lightning?*

Bridger growls, but she doesn't break stride.

They're a lot of trouble, she thinks. *That's what.*

Digger doesn't disagree, but he glances behind.

I'll go back, he thinks.

But Bridger shakes her head, trying without success to banish the ringing in her ears.

Once we get to the river and the others have safely crossed, we can both go.

They march with their thoughts sheltered until the river bends to meet them. Here, the kezel move north, wading in its shallows and gratefully drinking brackish water they would have refused in the accrete. A thousand strides later, they find their brethren, those too weak and addled to fight, waiting for them on the western bank, overseen by Bliss. Crossing is easy, even in their condition, and they treat it more as a bath than a swim, enjoying the cool water as long as possible before climbing the rusty bank to shake themselves dry.

What was that? Bliss asks, gesturing to the smoke that snakes its way skyward. Her tone is one of awe, and her ears are pinned back.

Justice is what it was, thinks Bridger. *But how and from where, who can say?*

She and Digger apprise the others of their intention to return in an attempt to locate Lightning and Thunder. Stone looks ready to object, but before she can, Measure calls out, pointing to the south.

Bomba! she thinks.

The others turn to look. A colorful figure traces circles low in the unbroken sky. Soon, they can see another creature beneath the bomba, this one walking toward them bipedal.

It's Thunder, thinks Blue.

And they hurry forward to meet him. He carries a pack over his shoulders and Lightning in his arms. She is breathing, but her eyes are closed, her body is limp, and her torn vest and copper spikes are stained with blood.

CHAPTER TEN
Wake

JOY'S LIDLESS EYES sparkle to life. The sky, blue and free of trouble, looks down on her like a memory of happier times. Where is she?

She sits up slowly.

Her sling is on her lap; the artifact rests inside.

Thorns, she thinks, idly plucking them from her hands. *How did that happen?* But yes, there had been a thorn bush, hadn't there? She had fallen into it. Had she moved? She doesn't recall it, and yet she is now sitting near a lethargic river. That is odd. Hadn't there been others? Other people? And why is she camouflaged?

Unvelum, she thinks, and she pulls the last of the thorns from her feet, rising on legs that are scratched and bruised. Her antennae quiver, and at their bases, a pressure bordering on pain reminds her all at once where she is and what has happened.

She turns to the southeast.

There, a thousand strides away, a thick ribbon of black smoke spirals from the far side of the island towers and blows away to the north, as if the structures themselves are on fire. But no, the last of the blaze remains confined to the Circle. The memories of that awful place and the overwhelming scream of death threaten to sicken her, and she looks away.

Princess is nowhere to be seen, but the odd brown

creature sits on a boulder nearby, the fallen basket and its parcels beside him. He has removed the globe from his head and uses a small metallic device to cut his hair, snip, snip, snip. It falls to the ground and tumbles away on the wind. He has just cut the final lock when he notices Joy. He places the tool in one of his pockets and rubs hands over his newly shorn head and face, rising to his feet, the corners of his mouth curling up.

"Glar dee bonna mo bonna," he says, and he bobs his head. Pointing at the parcels as if expecting commendation, he adds, "Mung garoba, ali poo."

Joy's buzzing reply is guarded; she is unsure how to respond to the gibberish. Though her nose gives no reason to hope, she opens each of the three woven packages, hoping to find awl or lova. They are filled instead with perfectly clear, round spheres, each larger than a dow's egg and splitting the sunlight into tiny rainbows, pretty, but inedible. Disgusted, she seals the parcels and ponders her next move.

North, she thinks. *Lightning is there—somewhere.* For a moment, she wonders about Princess, but she banishes this thought. *No longer my problem,* she thinks. And she shoulders her sling, looking at the brown creature and wondering how to explain her plan, or if she should bother trying. At that moment, his eyes widen.

"Ah ha!" he exclaims, and he points.

To the southwest, two distant figures—bipeds—run toward them, kicking up a trail of dust. They move briskly, covering hundreds of strides without slowing.

"Vizzum, kona walla konaboom," says the brown creature, and his voice is quiet, almost reverent. "Habada ebbazeen da moristand."

When the newcomers draw to within fifty strides, they ease from their sprint to a steady jog. They are built like Joy's companion, though their color is alabaster, and they are naked but for the bulky packs they carry over their shoulders. One has a dangling appendage similar to the brown creature's, which leads Joy to assume it is a male of its kind. It has a clean face and bulging muscles to go along with the short, red hair on his head. The other is more gracile, and it runs trailing a mane of golden hair while a pair of tanned orbs heave at its chest. It has no dangler, and absent any other evidence, Joy concludes it must be a female. Both creatures' movements are easy and athletic. Besides the impact of their feet striking the ground, their approach is silent, and despite their pace, they don't appear to breathe. Quite unlike the brown one, neither perspires a single drop.

Unnerved by the sudden appearance of these newcomers, Joy thinks to herself, *concelar,* and soon becomes invisible, her skin shifting to match the pale, parched ground beneath her.

The bipeds slow to a walk, and when close enough to touch the brown creature, they stop. To Joy's amazement, they both drop to one knee, bowing their heads, vocalizing in his same crude fashion.

"Ryzle gern," they say in unison. "Ryzle opoleek."

"Ryzle gern gern," replies the brown creature. "Amaleek." He gestures for them to rise. This they do, adding to Joy's surprise by wrapping their arms around him and squeezing him as they gabble and flash their undersized teeth. When they break their embrace, the brown creature turns to where he expects to see her, startled when he does not. He glances left and right.

"Uma faha," he says to the others, waving vaguely in Joy's direction. "Opa dia vosa. Vosa pom alladat."

The alabaster creatures join him in his search.

"Toba loo," says the female, pointing directly at Joy. Her counterpart turns to look with disquieting certainty, and Joy is discouraged to realize they can both see her. The brown creature waves as if urging her to come out of hiding. She weighs options for escape, but before she can commit, a foreign mind reaches out to her.

Can you sense me? it wonders.

The red-haired male is thinking to her.

Joy holds her thoughts sheltered, unwilling to reveal herself in spite of the evident futility in camouflage. She labors to suppress a nervous buzz.

Yes sir, it senses you, a second mind thinks, this one belonging to the female. *It senses both of us.* She extends a hand in Joy's direction and curls the corners of her mouth. *It's OK. You don't have to hide.* Her blue eyes twinkle. *We're friends of Captain Monroe.*

Joy steps away, concentrating on stealth, but the alabaster creatures follow her progress with discerning gazes, as if she were clicking her loudest.

C'mon, little critter, the male thinks. *Cap'n wants to see you, and the clock is ticking.*

Joy seeks for signs of deception in the minds of the newcomers, but they are strange to her; she is unsure of what she is sensing. The minds are much different than the brown one's—than any mind she has encountered—but different isn't the same as better, and she continues to sidle away.

I'm Ensign Morales, the female thinks, and she points to her companion. *This is Lieutenant K.* She bares her teeth in the fashion of the brown creature, in what Joy has come to understand as a posture of good will rather than the threat she had assumed at first. In spite of this, she decides the time has come to leave. She turns and sprints away. With a shout and a cloud of dust, the male named Lieutenant is after her, faster than she had anticipated. When he catches her, he restrains her with a grip that is breathtaking and irresistible.

I said, he thinks, *Cap'n wants to see you.*

He lifts Joy like a bomba feather, setting her down before the brown creature. The moment he releases her, she is off again. This time, it's the female named Ensign who catches her. But instead of being surprised, Joy is ready. When the golden-haired thing is about to grab her, she wheels and strikes it with a kick to its knee. Shocking pain is the result, and she is sure she has broken her foot. She collapses to the ground, whistling in distress.

The ensign, unharmed, kneels by her side.

I wasn't going to hurt you, she thinks.

Joy attempts to scramble away, but even had her foot been willing, the one called Lieutenant is not. He has taken hold of her with terrifying strength, his smell disagreeable and difficult to classify.

Stop squirming and let her look at that foot, he thinks. *We're not your enemies.*

"Blatter dilly wun wun," adds the creature named Captain. "Wun inna grobble ink—mink ink."

Minkink your own self, thinks Joy. *Ugly thing!* She shrieks and flails but can't break free. At last, as if afraid she will do herself more harm by struggling, the brown creature motions. His companions release their hold, stepping away and watching her, keen expressions on their faces. Joy rises with care, testing her foot. It's not broken, she is happy to note, but is very sore.

I have hard bones, thinks the ensign.

So, no more kicking, capisce? adds the lieutenant. *Cap'n says you're to go free. But he'd consider it a favor if you'd become visible for a while.*

Joy clicks rapid and low.

Too bad for him.

Please, thinks the ensign. *We may be able to help each other.* Joy is unsure if the tone she reads is one of sincerity, but it seems less abrasive than that of the lieutenant. In any case, seeing no point in trying to hide, she makes herself visible, not to please these strangers, but to conserve her energy.

I'm following the river, she thinks, turning to limp away. *Do what you want.*

When his companions translate this idea, the captain bobs his head and hoots.

"Relook motata maha," he says. "Re-relook."

He retrieves the globe and places it on his head, easier now that his mane has been shorn. He picks up one of Shimmer's parcels and raises his faceplate, baring his teeth as he strides after Joy. Lieutenant K and the ensign take his example, each carrying a parcel with little sign of effort. They are soon walking beside Joy as she coaxes her sore foot toward the river.

+ + +

A.P. Malloy

Joy can't see a way to avoid the newcomers—or make them go away—so she does her best to ignore them. For their part, the strangers continue conversing in their vocal nonsense, the one named Captain making most of the noise. Once, he points at Joy's hands and feet, as if they are objects of great interest. At another time, he rests his hand on the lieutenant's shoulder, and the alabaster creature reciprocates by baring his teeth. Later, when Captain pokes the ensign with one finger, she returns the gesture, curling her mouth.

"Eeble arva folado," she says. "Inna serta lee."

"Waptagrompt!" the lieutenant agrees.

He turns to face Joy.

Do you have a name? he asks. *Cap'n tells us you're the reason he's free.*

That's not exactly true, thinks Joy. *He saved me first.* Then she adds, *And he followed me.*

A looming wall of thorny vines appears, and here, the riverbank becomes especially shallow. Joy aims for this, seeking the cool water.

Either way, thinks the ensign, *If we're going to thank you, we should at least know what to call you.*

My name is Joy.

As she wades in the river, the pain in her foot gradually subsides, but the tension at the base of her antennae only gets worse. To keep her mind from the discomfort, she decides to ask some of the many questions raised by the newcomers' appearance.

So, what are you? she wonders. *Where are you from?* Taking a guess, she adds, *West of the wedge?*

Before answering, the two males exchange indecipherable sounds in low voices. When finished, Lieutenant K turns to the ensign, sharing a thought so focused Joy can sense its presence, but neither its mood nor meaning. A moment later, the ensign faces her.

Before we can answer, she thinks, *what do you call this place, this world?*

That's a strange question, thinks Joy, surprised. *Aranae, of course. Why?*

Book of Dreams

Aranae, thinks the ensign, pursing her lips. *Interesting. You wouldn't happen to know anything about the etymology of that name, would you?*

The what?

Never mind. It's not important. We, she thinks, flashing her teeth, *are not from Aranae.*

Joy tugs at her curls, confused. Then she leaps to the obvious answer. Any kezel would know it.

You're from the moons! she thinks. But she is disappointed. *No? The sun then?* She considers this a jest, but the ensign responds in a somber tone.

Much farther away than that, she thinks.

Joy resists the urge to stare, wondering if she is being lied to or ridiculed. But neither seem to be the case. The creatures appear the picture of sobriety. And yet, she can't see past the implausibility of their claim.

Nothing's farther than that, she thinks.

At this, the alabaster creatures make low chuckling sounds and glance with bared teeth at one another. When Lieutenant K translates Joy's thoughts into garbled speech, the captain bursts into similar sounds of his own. Joy doesn't need to probe minds to know she is the butt of some joke. She concludes there must be other places of which she is unaware. Clicking annoyance, she grows stern to cover her shame.

Then how? she wonders. *You don't have wings.*

No, thinks the ensign. *But we have a flying ship.*

A flying what now?

A vessel, large enough to carry all three of us.

A vessel? Joy buzzes. *You're saying it flies?*

Wherever we want to go, thinks the ensign, and she renews her grip on the parcel, attempting to balance the load. *It brought us here.*

Yes? thinks Joy. *Where is it now?*

Crashed, Lieutenant K replies, pointing west. *Into the bay back there. Hit by a pulse mine someone deployed, if you want to be precise. That's how Cap'n was taken. We were inside but disabled. Only woke up when Cap'n signaled us, and that took time, 'cuz his flight suit needed to re-charge in the sun. Otherwise, we would've rescued him ourselves—you can bet on that.*

Joy buzzes morosely. What a bunch of nonsense! Not an understandable idea to be found.

Why are you here? she asks.

Exploring, thinks the ensign. *We like to see new places.* But a dissonance between her tone and her words makes Joy suspect she is being lied to.

What about that one? she points at the brown creature. *What's wrong with him?*

His name is Captain Monroe, the lieutenant corrects. *And there's nothing wrong with him.*

Why can't he sense?

The captain is sapiens, thinks the ensign. *He can't understand your thoughts any more than you can understand his speech. But the lieutenant and I are able to understand both; we're sentiri.*

Sentiri run very fast, thinks Joy, whistling softly. *And they're quite strong.*

The ensign shakes her head.

Some are, she thinks. *But we were designed differently than most.*

Lieutenant K's eyes narrow, and he frowns.

Maybe a little less chatter, he thinks.

Sorry, sir, thinks the ensign. She shelters her thoughts, and for a time, the group travels each in their own heads. As Joy is about to ask another question, Lieutenant K comes to a quick stop, holding up one hand. All three bipeds drop low to the ground. Joy leaves the river and follows their example.

Unidentified life form, the lieutenant gestures to the north. *Other side of this hill.*

The ensign nods in agreement.

Are you expecting someone? she asks Joy.

Images of Lightning leap to Joy's mind, and she doesn't wait to respond. Moving with what care desperate hope allows, she climbs the riverbank, hugging the ground and peering over its crest, antennae bent forward and black eyes sparkling. The others are quick to join her.

Book of Dreams

+ + +

They find no Lightning.

Instead, fifty strides away, Princess stands joined by her pluripotents. She holds the derka and stares southeast, watching the column of smoke coil to the sky. Her pluripotents become aware of the newcomers and form a defensive ring, wings droning like a threat. When Princess turns to look, the light is dim in her eyes.

The Oddity returns, she thinks just as the other bipeds come into sight. *It brings more of its vumierre!* Menace lades her tuneless whistle. *Have they come to destroy Princess as the other scion? But they will not catch her so easily.* Her wings flash in the sun. *She will be Queen soon!* And as she thinks this, Joy notes touches of gilding on her legs and antennae, streaks of gold that hadn't been there before.

Congratulations. Good for you, thinks Joy, meaning neither. *But I'm going north.*

Princess settles her wings.

She cares not. It will leave her to mourn the dead and take its beasts with—but they will place her belongings on the ground before they go, unless they are thieves as well as slavers.

Lieutenant K and the ensign lower their parcels.

Are you sensing this? the lieutenant asks.

I am, the ensign nods.

In spite of herself, Princess clicks surprise.

So! The beasts are not stupid after all.

The brown one is, thinks Joy, but she realizes this is the wrong way to express the idea. *Not stupid so much,* she amends. *Just can't sense thoughts.* Not sure if it will mean anything, she adds, *He is sapiens; Captain.*

Princess cares not for the Oddity's introductions. A pretense of courtesy will not remove its guilt, nor that of its repellent vumierre. If she discovers they are the cause of this heinous crime—retribution!

Is this creature a threat? wonders the lieutenant.

More of an irritation, thinks Joy.

A.P. Malloy

Worthless Oddity! Princess clicks a harsh rhythm, and her eyes blaze light. *Foul-figured herald of doom! It will take its beasts and depart!* She whistles, shrill and loud. *Can it not see with its deformed eyes? Does its mind malfunction? The Circle is destroyed! Ended in fire! She is to be queen of a wasteland...*

I am very sorry, thinks Joy. *I wanted freedom, yes,* she admits. *I didn't want that.* Her antenna droop.

Sorry! thinks Princess. *Queen Benica is turned to ash. Royals and Soldiers and Builders destroyed. What does its sorrow do for them? Tenders and Gardeners and Awlers burned! Can it bring them back? And the derka! No longer sleeping but dead! And Princess with no chance to thank it for saving her life.* Sparks kindle in her eyes. *She will have revenge on whoever did this!*

The derka is indeed no longer breathing. Its eyes are closed and its tongue protrudes, pale and dry. This saddens Joy, and she looks away. She has had enough of death and wishes to move on. But Lieutenant K turns to the captain and gestures at the distant smoke. The brown creature mumbles in reply, motioning to the north. His finger traces the arc taken by the flying terror.

Nodding, the lieutenant turns to face Princess.

May I interrupt? he thinks. *If you're talking about the rocket that caused that explosion, we didn't have anything to do with it. But we're just as interested in who sent it as you are.*

Are they "just as interested?" Princess sneers. *She very much doubts that. Did the disgusting thing just lose all its kind in flames? Does it know that many thousands of young will starve because their Tenders are brought to ruin? Revolting vumierre!*

We are sad to learn this, thinks the ensign. *There's no way we can understand your loss. But you have to believe us: we would never do anything like this, and we have no idea who did. But we might be able to help you find out. Captain Monroe says whatever it was came from the north. We have business that way. If we travel together, we have a better chance of getting what we want.*

Book of Dreams

Shimmer's whistle is sharp as a blade.

What Princess wants is revenge!

I have no problem with that, thinks Lieutenant K. The ensign nods.

Neither do I.

Joy shelters her thoughts on the subject.

It's up to you, Princess, thinks the lieutenant.

It will address her no further! But while her tone is sour, she pauses as if considering. *Tey Ramota comes soon,* she thinks. *If the vumierre are indeed not stupid, they will wait to travel north. Their worthless lives are lost if they approach landfall during the upheaval.* She hands the derka to her prime, who holds it while the other pluripotents begin wrapping it carefully from snout to tail in clean, silken strands.

If you don't mind me asking, thinks Lieutenant K, *what's this "tey Ramota?"* But Princess does seem to mind, ignoring him and his question.

The ensign steps forward.

Please, if we're going to help each other, we need to share information. But her effort gets the same result. As she and the lieutenant return to vocalizing with the captain, Joy approaches Princess, antennae lowered.

I am truly sorry, she thinks. *About all of it.* She proceeds carefully. *And I thank you,* she adds. *You saved my life.* Princess clicks sharply, but she doesn't interrupt. Joy points at the captain. *His too.*

Of what value is that? Princess erupts. *She would gladly trade her Queen's life for that of the stupid one—or the Oddity! If she discovers it lies, if it and its vumierre are to blame, great will be her pleasure in ending their lives. She could have bitten them thrice by now!*

Joy moves from sympathetic to annoyed.

What is tey Ramota? she demands.

And why should we wait to travel north? interjects Lieutenant K. *Our business is urgent.*

Princess' buzzing is harsh. Caged anger prowls within the facets of her eyes.

She will tell it why, oh spawn of slavers. The Royal

River comes from the north now, but not far from here, it will move to the east. Her tone is ominous. *North of there, the land becomes unsafe. During tey Ramota, schisms will rend the stone beneath their disgusting feet, and fissures of fire and toxic gas will open with no warning.* Her wings spread, newly edged in flashing gold. *Flightless fools trapped near the landfall during tey Ramota will be crushed by falling rock or plunge into the abyss.*

Of course! thinks the ensign. *Earth motion!*

Lieutenant K furrows his brow.

Carmela?

Sir. It's Latin—or related. tey Ra: as in ter-ra. Earth. Mota: motion. She's describing an earthquake, sir.

The lieutenant bows his head and sighs. When he explains this news to the captain, the brown creature looks as unhappy as his companions. He frowns and shakes his head, mumbling words only they can understand. Lieutenant K glances at the ensign.

An earthquake, he thinks. *That's fantastic. Want to tell me how she knows this? And in Latin?*

Seismic activity isn't surprising under these conditions, sir. And sensing it in advance provides an adaptive advantage we've seen in numerous species. Even the language connection is logical, considering what we know about...what we know.

Once again, Joy senses the creatures are working to shelter their thoughts, withholding information.

Lieutenant K scowls.

All the more reason to have a guide. He looks once again at Princess. *Will you join us?*

But the question has just left his mind when Princess clicks in alarm and takes to the air, bearing the derka and tracing a line of silver to the north. She is followed at once by her pluripotents, working together to carry the woven parcels. They soon vanish from sight.

Sir! thinks the ensign. *Multiple life signs.* Her eyes widen, and she wheels about. *They're all around us!*

"Nebbir gop!" says the captain. "Bee tee bee!"

A moment later, eight ragged but fierce adult kezel

appear, stalking from behind low hills and stands of thorny vines. In moments they have encircled the bipeds in a barricade of muscle and teeth.

+ + +

Joy hasn't seen a bibija kezel up close since her encounter with Crag. She has forgotten how enormous they are, and how menacing. The circle closes, slow but sure. The bipeds brace for combat.

We're not looking for trouble, thinks Lieutenant K, holding up his hand. *Can you understand me? Don't come any closer or we will defend ourselves!*

At a distance of ten strides, the kezel stop. Fleeting thoughts of surprise and disbelief bounce from one mind to another.

Moondwellers, they think in tones of awe.

Joy steps forward. Recalling what she has been taught, she lowers her gaze.

My name is Joy, she thinks. Unsure how the news will be received, she adds, *I know Lightning Sugarfoot.*

At the sense of her thoughts, the kezels' ears pin back, and they growl and grumble. But before they can respond to her introduction, a colorful figure soars into view, powerful wings driving it in tight circles overhead.

Joy whistles, amazed at what she sees.

Ansel!

The bomba squawks, swooping by low and fast. She glimpses one bright, green eye and feels a gust of wind on her face. He dips his wings like a signal but offers no thoughts before rising again.

At this, one of the largest kezel, a black ah-lah, rises to two legs and steps forward, breaking the circle. She approaches holding both massive, clawed hands up and open, palms facing out. Her spiky coat, which must once have been beautiful, hangs loose on her frame, but she is three meters tall when standing and towers over the bipeds. To Joy's surprise, when she has stepped close enough to touch, she drops to the ground in a deep bow, her tail brushing the dust.

Moondwellers, she thinks, keeping her gaze cast downward. *I thought you were part of a story.*

*Umm...*thinks Lieutenant K. *No. I mean, maybe. I don't know. First time we've been called that. But we're real, if that's what you mean.*

And not looking for trouble, adds the ensign.

You'll find none from us, the kezel thinks, rising from her bow, *if what the stories say are true.* She looks at Joy. *My name's Bridger. I thought Lightning was delusional, but I see I was wrong.*

Where is she, please? Joy buzzes at the sound of that name. *She is OK, yes?*

Bridger tilts her head in the direction of the bipeds, her eyes mere slits and her tone somber.

Vouch for these, she thinks, *and you can see for yourself. I'm sorry,* she looks squarely at the bipeds. *But Moondwellers or not, we can't trust strangers.*

I just met them, thinks Joy. *I can't...vouch anything.* She clicks anxiously. *Where is my ami-kan?*

The kezel mutter amongst themselves, repeating her words with varying degrees of amazement and scorn.

Its "ami-kan..."

Bridger hushes them with a wave.

Our scouts saw you with some six-leggers. Why?

They freed me—us, thinks Joy.

And they know this land, thinks the lieutenant. *We hoped they would guide us.*

And yet they left you.

You scared them away, thinks Joy.

My only regret, Bridger bares her teeth, *is that I didn't get to do more than that.*

Please, thinks Joy. *Take me to Lightning.*

Bridger drops to four legs.

OK, she thinks. *But stay inside the ring.*

And if we don't? asks the lieutenant.

Then I won't be able to guarantee your safety—no matter how many legs you walk on.

+ + +

Bridger retakes her position with the other kezel. They move north in unison, the circle holding form while Joy and the others are forced to maintain pace inside.

What's your relationship to these creatures? the ensign asks as they walk.

Kezel is their name, thinks Joy. *My ami-kan is one.*

Your... The word is unknown to the ensign, but the image it creates in her mind is of a nurturing character. *You were raised by them?*

Just one, thinks Joy. *Others tried...eating me.*

Why am I not surprised? The lieutenant glares. *And what about that one? The flying one?*

He is a bomba, thinks Joy. *He's from the maison.*

A friend then? thinks the ensign.

Most of them were, thinks Joy. *But not this one.*

Well, thinks the lieutenant. *This just gets better.*

He mumbles something to the captain, who responds in kind, motioning to the north. The ensign interjects, offering gibberish of her own, and the males nod. When the two alabaster creatures communicate with one another, they shelter their thoughts carefully.

Keeping secrets is rude, thinks Joy, inspiring Ensign Morales to quickly change the subject.

What did the bowing symbolize, do you think? And what do you suppose a Moondweller is?

I don't know, really, thinks Joy. *Bombas called them Rumidelchia.* She rubs her hands together and watches Ansel as he circles overhead. *Scion, vumierre.*

Bowing is better than open hostility, thinks Lieutenant K. *And I've been called worse. But until we know more, we need to be ready for anything.*

That may be good advice for you, too, the ensign adds, looking at Joy. She curls her lips upward. *If we're forced to attempt an escape, you're welcome to join us.*

Not without my ami-kan.

The unlikely band travels north for another two thousand strides, until the river bends away to the right, just as Princess had said. Though she searches the sky and the dusty plains, Joy can see no sign of her.

Hiding downwind, she guesses.

Ensign Morales points to the north.

Life signs, she thinks. *Other side of that hedge.*

Be prepared, thinks Lieutenant K, and he mumbles to the captain. *May need to make a move.*

Joy isn't sure what kind of move the creature has in mind. Unless they have many friends as strong and fast as they are, the naked things have no hope of breaking through this ring. In any case, she senses no deception, and their escorts seem unconcerned by whatever lies on the other side of the thorn bank.

Bridger is the first to reach the hedge, a dense stand of dark vines rising to twice her height. One after another, they brave the thorns and disappear inside. The kezel disperse, some to the west, others east toward the river. Dozens of prickly strides later, only Bridger ahead of them and a large ah-tah behind remain to escort them. A clearing approaches. As they draw near, Joy's antennae tingle and her heart races.

She can smell Lightning.

+ + +

Joy leaves the bipeds, hurrying forward and passing by Bridger as she enters the clearing. Three kezel stand near the far side, two adults and a jabi male. Ansel perches in the thorns far out of reach. Lightning lies on her side, eyes closed, tended by one of the adults. Her vest has been removed, and Joy's heart sinks at the injuries marring her coppery coat. She is terrified to approach, afraid of what she will discover.

You three wait with Pounce, thinks Bridger to the bipeds. When this is translated, the captain complies without a word, taking a seat and gesturing for his companions to do the same. The bibija Pounce takes a position nearby, watching them with more than routine diligence. Fascination smolders in his dark eyes, his nose twitches, and his ears lean forward.

Bridger looks at Joy.

Come on. No point in standing here.

With the bibija at her side and dread in her heart, Joy crosses to the far side of the clearing. The others make room for them to pass, but she has eyes only for Lightning. Her spiky pelt is bandaged, haunch and shoulder, with wraps taken from her own pack. Dried blood mats most of one leg and welts on her snout and elsewhere tell of repeated encounters with biting scion. She breathes but is otherwise motionless. Joy rests her hand carefully on Lightning's spiky neck. She feels strong and solid as ever, but cold, far too cold.

Ami-kan, she thinks. *I'm here; it's Joy.*

But Lightning does not respond.

What happened? Joy asks.

Bridger defers to the jabi male, cream-spiked with sunken, brown eyes. He stares at Joy in a most disconcerting fashion.

Thunder tracked her to the island, thinks Bridger. *She was that way when he got there.*

Joy clicks in surprise.

You're her twin oti, she thinks. *You found me first.* Her eyes glitter at the memories stirred by his sight. *You tried eating me,* she thinks. *Or having some sport.*

Thunder winces.

Relax. No one's gonna eat you.

The ibiwa by his side senses Joy's thoughts and shakes her tawny head in disbelief.

How is this possible? she asks Bridger.

How would I know? Bridger growls. *Isn't the first surprise we've had. Something tells me it won't be the last.* She points at the three bipeds. *Do me a favor, Bliss, and join Pounce. I don't trust our new guests.*

The tawny ah-lah does as told, her gaze torn between Joy and the bipeds. Bridger turns to Joy.

At first, we thought it was loss of blood, but those injuries aren't as bad as they look. More likely all those bites were too much for the awl gland...you can see what that poison did to Submission.

The bibija she indicates stares into the blue, and Joy notices for the first time that his mind is hidden from her. The effect reminds her of the one called captain, thick and slow, but induced, not natural.

But I don't understand. Joy's antennae brush against Lightning's flank. *What about awl glands?*

When Bridger explains Lightning's secret, a faint hope raises its head for a moment.

Would more gland help?

Maybe, thinks Bridger, *but we don't have any.* And so that hope is quickly dashed.

How about some food?

We tried. Waved fresh awl under her nose, dipped her in the river, shouted, pinched her ears...

What do we do?

Bridger looks up at Ansel, muttering to himself, his head cocking side to side.

Lightning claimed that bomba can think—claimed they all can. Is it true?

Joy whistles a low note.

It's true.

And you can communicate with it—him?

Yes. If he chooses.

Bridger flexes her claws.

What would Ancian say? Bombas thinking!

She wouldn't believe it 'til she sensed it, thinks Thunder. *But he was the last one to see her conscious; maybe he knows something.*

Joy looks up at Ansel, perched out of thought range—a deliberate move, she guesses. She remembers their last encounter in the maison.

He doesn't like kezel, she thinks.

Yes, thinks Bridger. *I got that. But if we move away, maybe he'll come down. I have some questions for those Moondwellers who just walked out of a story.*

And she and Thunder withdraw, escorting Submission, his eyes blank, to where Bliss and Pounce stand guard over the bipeds.

Book of Dreams

+ + +

Joy rises to her feet. She bows in bomba fashion, waving for Ansel to join her. He spreads his wings, a glorious span of color, but he declines her request. She can hear him, even at this distance, hissing to himself, partaking in some internal debate. At last, squawking resignation, he leaps from the hedge, catching air and landing nearby. Joy bows again. The bomba stares with one green eye then the other, ruffling his feathers. He does not return the gesture.

Can you understand me? he thinks.

Yes, Joy's antennae quiver. *I'm glad you're here.* She buzzes for emphasis. *And surprised.*

I am the second, Ansel replies. *But not the first. From the beginning, I recognized you as the bane of my existence, the ruiner of all I hold dear. You summoned me down here; what do you want from me?*

I... Joy stammers. *What happened to her?*

Ansel squawks derision.

The fool kezel was gored and trampled by stampeding beasts escaping the fire. And she was bitten numerous times. Too many crewels I wasted on this one.

Joy restrains her sudden anger.

Bombas are very wise, she thinks. *Can you wake her?* She clicks softly, adding, *I'll be indebted forever.*

But this is the wrong thing to think.

Foolish companion to a fool! Ansel fans his tail. *You are already in my debt—for life! But I know of no way to reverse this condition. Awl gland may work, but we are thousands of wing strokes from any of that.* He cranes his neck and cackles in a humorless tone. *I saved the kezel's life, but I cannot wake her to enjoy it.*

Please, thinks Joy. *She is my nester.*

Ansel shifts his weight from one leg to the other, and when he responds, his tone is less harsh.

I have sworn on the memory of my brother Ari and at the direct request of my own nesters, Ilda and Oracio, to find and help you both if I can. They, beyond all wisdom,

A.P. Malloy

found some...companionship with you. He hisses. *I have flown all the way to the salty shores of Mighty Faros only to keep that promise, so it should be clear: if I could wake this kezel I would, but I cannot.*

The glitter fades from Joy's eyes, and her antennae droop. Then, picking up on one of Ansel's thoughts, she looks up.

The memory of Ari?

Ansel squawks, a grievous sound.

Yes! he thinks. *Know this as you suffer: I suffer as well, for my brother Ari, kindest and best of the bombas, died saving you from the white scourge you wakened.* Ansel scratches at the pale, parched ground. *I will do all I can for you. I will even consider flying on a wearisome and dangerous quest for awl gland—but I will despise every last moment of it.* And he rises to the air in a cloud of dust, retaking his perch.

Joy stares without seeing, her thoughts chasing one another. Ari is dead? Because of her? And what will become of Lightning? Will she wake only to be a shell like her api-kan, vapid and helpless?

Panic rises in Joy's chest, but Bridger and Thunder are returning, followed listlessly by Submission, so she takes a deep breath, trying to shelter her emotions.

What did you learn? asks Bridger.

Nothing good, Joy buzzes. *And you?*

I don't think the Moondwellers are a threat. But they ask a lot of questions: "Know anything about Destiny? Heard about the colonists? Any idea where the compounds are?" Bridger snarls. *What do those words even mean? And when they answer instead of asking, they don't tell the whole story, that's for sure. Either way, they're itching to leave—and I'm itching to let 'em. But they were hoping to say goodbye to you before they go.*

Joy rests her head on Lightning's cold flank.

They can come here.

Bridger motions, and the bipeds step forward, escorted by Bliss and Pounce. The one called Captain leads the way, his black suit sleek in the low-riding sun. He has

234

lifted his faceplate and his brow is furrowed, but as always, his mind is thick like tar. From his companions, Joy senses sympathy, but also an urgent desire to move on. They kneel close by; the brown creature mumbles more of his usual nonsense.

Cap'n wishes we could help, translates the lieutenant, *but kezel is a critter we don't know anything about. We're all sorry. Real sorry.*

Joy looks up, her antennae rising.

You could get glands, she thinks. *You have a...vessel.* But here the corners of the ensign's mouth curve downward, and she thinks in kind but regretful tones:

I'm afraid our ship won't be flying any time soon.

Lieutenant K nods.

Look, he extends his hand to the captain who gives him one of the small, metallic objects attached to his suit, the size of an awl egg, but flat. *Keep this. It will tell us where you are. If we can come back to help, we will.*

Joy accepts the object but takes little comfort.

The captain rises to two legs and bows.

"Ernderna fola," he says. "Omnot om illa won."

His companions rise and bow as well.

Cap'n believes he owes you his life, thinks the lieutenant. *He won't forget it. Neither will we.*

The ensign extends her hand, fingers up and palm facing out. Joy senses she is meant to copy the action. This she does, until their palms meet. Though different in size and color, the forms match well, a fact the kezel note with murmurs and grumbling.

Maybe we'll meet again, thinks the ensign.

And the bipeds turn away, moving west. Not long after, they disappear into the vines, the sound of their departure soon hidden by the wind. Moments later, a new kezel enters the clearing, a bibija male with red spikes. He shares a sheltered thought with Bridger, who nods and turns to the others.

The hunt is back, she thinks. *But don't get excited. Looks like we're rationing.*

On her orders, the other kezel leave the clearing,

A.P. Malloy

presumably in the direction of whatever food has been found. Bridger looks from Lightning to Joy.

You can join us, she thinks, *if our food agrees with you. Looks like some young awl and a couple creatures we don't have names for.*

Joy buzzes disconsolately; food means nothing.

Thank you, she replies. *But I'm not hungry.*

Bridger wrinkles her snout.

We'll be back, she thinks. *Call if there's a need.*

+ + +

Joy runs her hand across Lightning's cold spikes as Bridger moves off to join the others. Soon, they are left alone in the clearing, overseen by Ansel.

Awl glands! she thinks. *I will find them.*

As she weighs the options for fulfilling such a promise, her thoughts are suddenly interrupted.

Stupid Oddity, a mind thinks, heavy with scorn. *Awl gland is not the answer for this malaise.*

Joy leaps to her feet and turns to the north. She sees nothing, but only one mind could be responsible.

Show yourself!

Did it mean what it thought? Princess replies, and of course, she ignores Joy's order. *About a life of debt for the waking of this horrid sharksha?*

Joy's eyes sparkle.

Get in the line, she thinks, her tone bitter. *I owe my ami-kan.* She clicks harshly. *I owe the bombas.*

Slicing wings draw a line of arcing sound, and Princess' thoughts now come from due south.

The ugly beast has been bitten many times. Even so, Princess can help. Indeed! She is the only one who can.

Then do it! Please!

Upon a promise, only, thinks Princess, *whose breaking will mean death. For the waking of this animal, the Oddity must vow to assist in her quest for revenge.*

And now the wings zip zip! And the thoughts come from the west. Joy wheels around.

You help my ami-kan, she thinks, *and I will promise.* But another thought occurs to her. *The other one too,* she adds. *Submission. The black one.*

The Oddity aggravates! thinks Princess. *She will help this other sharksha, but its commitment will be the same as the Oddity's: help slay the murderer of scion.*

I can't promise that, thinks Joy. *He may refuse it!*

Princess cares not. If the Oddity does indeed value honor, it will obtain this promise from the other beast in return for its healing. Nothing else satisfies.

Joy's antennae twitch.

Fine! I'll do it, she thinks. *Just help her, please!*

Very well. The Oddity will step away.

Joy moves from Lightning's side.

If you hurt her, she thinks, *I will kill you.*

Zip zip! No reply.

Princess remains invisible, but she must now be standing beside Lightning, for on each of the angry, red welts an amber substance appears, spread on the bites as if under its own power. At once, the inflammation eases and the burning color cools and fades. Her eyes remain closed, but Lightning takes a deep, shuddering breath, releasing a long-pent sigh. Her tail quivers.

This is the limit of her treatment, thinks Princess, zip zip! her thoughts now coming from the east. *She makes no promises about these other injuries. They may keep the disgusting sharksha asleep in spite of her efforts. Who can say? But the promise will bind in any case! And if it does wake, the other beast will be brought and the second commitment sealed as well.*

Low, weary buzzing fills Joy's ears.

Now she is off to lay the heroic derka in its final resting place. But poor Princess gets no rest!

And zip zip! she is gone.

Joy steps forward, her antennae bent toward Lightning. She has already grown warmer. Turning, Joy sends a thought of gratitude, but the only reply she receives is the fading sound of wings.

+ + +

When the kezel return from their meal, paltry by everyone's standards, they exclaim in surprise at Lightning's improved condition. But when Joy explains the situation and the price to be paid for Submission's treatment, they fall to arguing among themselves about the plan's wisdom. At last, Bridger waves the others to silence, growling as she looks at Joy.

First things first. Let's see if this...treatment works as promised. If Lightning wakes up—and seems normal— we'll decide about Submission. Until then, change the watch and find a place to rest. From what the supposed Moondwellers told us, there's no point in moving north until that quake has passed. She grumbles, plucking a thorn from her toe. *Wake me if there's any change.*

She and the other kezel move off to stand watch or sleep until only Thunder remains.

How are you going to get my api-kan to make a promise in his condition?

I don't know how.

Thunder looks at Lightning, and when he next shares a thought, his mind is clear and his tone decisive.

I'll do it. I'll make the promise for Bruiser if he doesn't—or can't. But only if she wakes up.

Joy's eyes brighten.

When, she thinks. *Not if.*

Thunder curls his upper lip.

That sounds like something Lightning would say.

And he turns away, seeking a place to sleep.

Joy watches him disappear into the vines. Alone except for occasional, disdainful glances from the bomba, she lies close to Lightning, feeling new warmth growing slowly inside her. She vows to stay awake, but the moment she rests her head on Lightning's flank, the spark grows dim in her eyes and she is asleep.

Soon after, she falls into dreams.

Tucked in her sling, the artifact begins to glow.

Book of Dreams

+ + +

In Lightning's mind, blackness gives way to a dream that begins as a pinhole of light and a whisper.

The sound grows, becoming the din of the Circle. The light becomes an image, and the image becomes clear: Joy and a bizarre escort, including a bipedal creature wearing a skin of black and a half dozen enemies, one of them silver. They leave the Circle and cross a lake stricken by drought toward an island.

Lightning follows, Ansel close behind.

She dreams of invisible pincers and many bites.

Blue blood splashes the walls and floor.

Crewels ignite and spread like flaming acid.

The dream shifts, and she envisions amber cell upon amber cell, hexagons filled with tiny wriggling creatures. She sees a verdant, open space, bathed in sun and filled with exotic plants and foreign animals. She dreams of hooves and horns and a desperate attempt to flee a ball of fire, an unintended blow from an unseen source, massive and terrified, and then pain, the taste of her own blood, and cold darkness.

But then, sounds change again, and darkness turns to warmth and sunny gold. All around her, Lightning senses murmuring thoughts. She can't tell whose they are, but their tones are familiar and comforting, stirring powerful memories.

In her dream, she thinks to herself:

Those are kezel minds. Bibija kezel! And that's Thunder! Her snout wrinkles. *But how can that be?*

Fatigue gives way at last to irresistible curiosity, and though it takes an effort like lifting heavy stones, Lightning opens her eyes.

Joy, black on blue, sleeps in peace at her side.

Please don't be a dream, thinks Lightning, and she buries her snout in raven hair.

A.P. Malloy

CHAPTER ELEVEN
Submission

CLIFF AND COMPANY—nine beleaguered ah-lahs and ten wabis of various sizes—hug the river's western bank for half of their northern trek to the landfall. When the heat becomes too oppressive, they wade in its shallows, snatching up some of the unsuspecting finger-length awl that dart there in shimmering schools.

The river eventually bows to the east, then back to the west, and at this point, the kezel cross, wabis clinging tightly. From there, they take a more direct route. The meandering river and its viney fringe provide better cover but also rougher terrain, and since no band of adult kezel fears a derka, they make their straight-line way under the naked sun, their only goal haste.

Cliff recognizes from the beginning he is not in charge. Serenity and Gully, the two massive bibijas, lead by tandem, both burdened by wabis and the latter working with her woili Splay to escort Old Buttons across the thirsty land. The ancient kezel would have been the slowest among them if it weren't for Snapper, so pregnant her belly threatens to brush the ground. When anyone has a question, they direct it to one of the bibijas as if Cliff was invisible. The pair lumber along in game fashion, sending thoughts of encouragement and scolding those who don't keep pace. As the strides add up, only their unflagging spirits keep the weakest of them from succumbing to heat or fatigue.

They encounter no scion.

Is that good? Serenity asks Cliff. *Or suspicious?*

Um, well, he thinks, surprised to be asked. *We saw lots of 'em on the way downstream. Maybe they're all back there,* and he nods in the direction of Albion.

Let's hope, thinks Gully. *Pick it up; we're close!*

The appearance of the flying terror, falling from the northern sky and trailed by smoke, brings the group to a full stop, awestruck. As it passes, its deafening voice drives them to the ground, their eyes rolling and their ears pinned. It crashes far to the south with an immediate flash of light and a thunderclap that arrives moments later, driving yits to the sky. They stare in disbelief at the massive fireball rising from their enemies' stronghold, thinking of the ah-tahs and imagining the worst. Some argue they should go back. But the bibijas quickly put an end to that. They grit their teeth, rounding up terrified wabis and driving the band north.

At the face of the landfall, where the river drops from its bed in a roaring cascade, they rest for a time. While the others exchange worried guesses about the nature of the flying thing and sniff char on the wind, Serenity and Gully discuss with Cliff details of the subterranean path to the upper land. From their sheltered position on the bank, they examine the yawning mouth behind the waterfall and the stairs leading to it. They detect no motion from the device used to raise and lower objects, and they smell no babelracks. The four-legged monsters have also been relocated; their dreadful cry would have been audible over wind or fall.

The tunnel is easy, but it's terrible strange, thinks Cliff. *Climbing out will be the hard part—and the high stair at the end is the worst.*

One thing at a time, thinks Serenity.

Where's the crystal Lightning gave us? asks Gully.

+ + +

The tunnel is as unnerving as Cliff remembers, and what's worse, it now slopes upward. Heavy breathing soon echoes through a space dark but for the lone crystal, the two halves of which are carried by the bibijas. The company shares nervous complaints, displeased by the unnatural symmetry of the columns and arches.

After many strides of this, a low voice calls to them, a song of fresh air, drawing them to the sloping shaft and the promise of the upper land. They gather around its opening and peer up.

You sure we're going to fit? asks Serenity.

Fitting is the easy part, thinks Cliff.

What's the hard part? Gully wants to know.

Slippery and steep. Should probably go strongest climbers first. And Old Buttons might need a push.

They do, and she does.

Cliff waits long, anxious moments as the others make their slow way up. He fears one of the clinging wabis will fall, and that his will be the blame if he fails to catch it, but none do, and when his turn comes, he climbs until his muscles burn. When finally in the cave, he must rest and catch his breath, mustering his courage as much as his stamina as he peers out at the precarious ledge. But Old Buttons navigates it; what excuse does he have? At last, strong, clawed hands help lift him from the dreadful stair, and he is returned to the sunshine of the plains. He rolls away from the edge and lies in the yellow grass, content to stare at the sky.

When the first tremor strikes, he sits up.

The second brings him to unsteady feet.

The land is moving.

Amid a low, sustained rumbling, a third shock bends the ground beneath him. Cliff leaps away, his spikes on end. Around him, the ah-lahs scramble to gather their wabis, stumbling over terrain suddenly grown treacherous. The land trembles like shaken water. A resounding *crack!* fills the air as a jagged chasm tears open behind them, widening until a massive sliver of the upper land simply disappears, sliding away to the barren plains below. A cloud of ruined stone mushrooms to the sky in a crushing roar.

Away from the edge! thinks Serenity.

Run! thinks Gully.

But Cliff needs no persuasion. He staggers away as quickly as three legs and the lurching ground allow. Behind him, explosions punctuate the groan of rock grinding against rock. He doesn't know what causes them, but they are followed by an acrid smell that rides the wind to burn his lungs and wring tears from his eyes. On he stumbles, pausing once to retrieve a fallen wabi. How long does it last? Too long! Only when they can no longer feel the ground tremble beneath them do they collapse into the grass, breathless and numb. The toxic reek endures, and to the south, an occasional crack and boom speaks of aftershocks and falling stone.

No one's living through that, thinks Cliff, though he is careful to keep the thought sheltered.

Have you ever felt such a quake? asks Serenity.

Gully bares her teeth.

Never, she thinks. *But it's a perfect fit for this damnable place!* She looks south, squinting against the sun. *Was it caused by that thing from the sky, do you think? Hardly seems like a coincidence.*

But Serenity has no answer.

I know what you're thinking, she addresses the others. *You can forget it. We're not going back! Either one of those nasty things could happen again.* She wrinkles her snout. *I don't like it either, but we're sticking to the plan: we wait one sleep. If they don't show, we cross the river and go north. Wabis are our concern.*

No one disagrees, but anxious thoughts cloud their minds as the bibijas assign responsibilities. Those with the most energy are sent hunting, though their ears droop and they cast worried glances to the south. The others go about digging holes and attempting to deflect the many questions asked by curious wabis for whom recent events have been novel and fascinating.

You're on sentry, Three-legs, thinks Serenity.

A.P. Malloy

She means Cliff, Gully corrects. *Don't mess up.*

Cliff straightens his posture and marches the perimeter, eyes wide and nose twitching. But after a long time of this, encountering nothing remarkable (a lone derka prudently flies on), he grows weary and bored. He decides to steal some rest until called back—assuming the hunters succeed—and he makes his way to the south, climbing a rock finger protruding from the ground.

From this vantage, the hazy plains are visible far below. Small fires burn there, scattered as far as he can see, appearing fueled by the ground itself. Smoky clouds of yellow and gray smudge the air. Cliff traces the course of the withered river, straining for a sign of Lightning or the others, but the distance is too great or the air too polluted. He sighs heavily, trying not to dwell on all the ways his kindred might have met their end.

And after we sleep? he wonders. *Are we really going to march on without them?* His modest allowance of courage, recently grown larger, objects to the thought. *Lightning's gonna be real mad,* he thinks, *if something bad happens to that blue thing because I didn't go back to help. Thunder would do it. Submission too.*

But Submission is missing or dead.

And who knows where Thunder is? he thinks.

His heart falters as he imagines a return to the lower land. How would he get there? Had the tunnel been destroyed? What would he say to the ah-lahs? Would they attempt to prevent him? And what would he eat? Already his stomach growls, and he turns to the north, wishing the hunters would come into view with a large kill. All he sees are digging kezel and wabis running through the grass—wabis who will be fed before him.

He returns his gaze to the south, and his vision swims. He rubs his weary eyes, attempting to bring them into focus, but it does no good. One of the smudges continues to move, not to the sky, but obliquely, as if approaching from a great distance. Where the narrow line of the river bows hard to the west, the smudge coalesces then stretches thin, becoming a single, snaking file of in-

Book of Dreams

dividual dots, each nearly too small to identify. A moment later, the dots disappear into the smoke and shadow. A moment is all Cliff needs. Stumbling from his rocky perch and nearly falling, he calls out in a wild, yelping cry.

I see them! he thinks. *They're alive!*

+ + + + + +

Throughout her long life, filled with adventures, Lightning takes particular pleasure in hearing retold the story of how Bridger leads the remaining kezel from the riven, smoldering domain of scion to the yellow plains of the upper land. As her part in the tale is reserved to being carried while recuperating—most of the while asleep— she enjoys learning about the arduous journey because it fills in missing memories like an itch well-scratched. And though the tale itself is short and simple, it never fails to please. It reminds her of a sublime feeling, a peace beyond pain and fear. Many kezel had been rescued, and she had found her Joy, healthy and whole.

She loves hearing how Bridger, with Ansel's help, finds an alternate route when fallen boulders block the subterranean passage. She enjoys descriptions of perilous climbing and noxious gasses whispering from cracks in the ground. To her, the devastation of tey Ramota is someone else's problem; she can appreciate its value as entertainment. The journey may have been dangerous labor for others, but her memories are of riding on strong backs, her aching legs finally given a chance to rest. Surrounded by family, her sleep is one of familiar smells and swift healing, while her brief occasions of consciousness are graced with sparkling black eyes, a bomba overhead, and kezel all around.

Of all stories, this is one of her favorites.

The tale is not without surprise, but she never recalls feeling threatened. Even the presence of the silver and gold one, the one called Princess, can't dampen the tone of her memories. When she is joined by others of her kind, refugees fleeing the wasted Albion, all Lightning recalls is Joy thinking, *They will behave themselves,* before she falls asleep again, blissful and content.

The scion keep their promise and their distance, throughout the journey from lower to upper lands never closer than a hundred strides. They form a protective ring around their leader, who in turn refuses to converse with anyone from the kezel clan other than Joy. Her pluripotents have retrieved her basket, and she is thus spared the ignominy of having to walk or fly. Others carry her loaded parcels on their backs.

Lightning's memory of events clarifies not long after reaching the upper land. By the time the two bands reunite, the worst effects of the bites have worn off, and her mind clears like sun from behind the clouds. Her injured leg and torn shoulder make hers a slow, limping gait, but Snapper, Trapper, and Old Buttons are slower still, so no one complains—Joy least of all. She skips alongside, buzzing and clicking. Kezel family and friends embrace without shame, many having given up hope of meeting again, and if they notice gaunt frames, sunken eyes, or patchy coats, they shelter these thoughts. Wabis bark and howl as the mood strikes.

You did good, thinks Lightning to Cliff.

I was just about to come back and rescue you, he thinks. *By myself, if I had to.*

I don't doubt it.

You, too, he thinks to Joy.

At which she clicks a steady tempo.

I didn't need rescue, she replies. *But I thank you.*

As the others continue their greetings and commiseration, Thunder and Submission draw near. Lightning grimaces at the sight of her oti-mu's haggard frame, once so splendid, but worse yet is her api-kan, stupefied by long exposure to scion poison. He remains unresponsive in spite of Princess' treatment, following Thunder like a mindless wabi, and though he looks at Lightning, he does not see her. She leans in and touches her nose to Thunder's, savoring his smell.

I owe you, she thinks.

Book of Dreams

The brash jabi of past moons would surely have responded with insult or sharp humor—and would not have accepted the gesture—but the Thunder before her is a different creature. He sighs.

We're even, he thinks. Then, seeing Lightning's concerned glance, he adds, *Don't worry. Your new friend said it might take a while; he was poisoned...a lot.*

She's not my friend, thinks Lightning, and she rests her head against Submission's shoulder, offering thoughts of courage. He shows no sign of noticing.

With their chief disabled, the clan selects Bridger as their leader, and her first orders are for food and sleep. These are gladly obeyed. Another hunting team heads out, and when all have returned, they share a meal of hoppers and awl that, meager as it is, seems in the spirit of reunion to be a grand feast.

To her surprise, one kezel after another approaches Lightning to offer thoughts of gratitude. Wabis clamor for her attention, and she and Cliff are given first taste at the meal. Joy they avoid, staring from a distance as she nibbles her awl. Not every kezel feels so big-hearted. Some, like Stone, remain bitter that so much death and suffering should have resulted—to their way of thinking—from one jabi's rash decision. These, however, keep their thoughts to themselves, and their unhappiness fails to darken Lightning's mood.

After the meal, as kezel take turns on watch, the troop rests in preparation for the long march ahead. Fancies and wabis pack into holes that are cramped and smelly, but none recall greater comfort.

Before going underground, Lightning searches for Ansel, finding him seated high on a jutting stone.

I want to thank him, she thinks. *Come with me?*

But Joy's antennae melt.

He won't like it.

Why? What is it? What's wrong?

Joy's eyes grow dim as she shares the tale of Ari, without whose assistance neither would be alive. When she is done, they sit for many heartbeats, considering private thoughts. Lightning listens to the shrill gossip of ground-dwelling yits and the distant call of a babelrack, but her mind is in the maison, and her feet tread the snowy expanse of the upper plateau. Ari's voice is clear in her imagination, his bright eyes and rainbow plumage as vivid in her memory as his perpetual good humor.

Grief bows her head.

He found my food, Joy recalls. *When I was hungry.*

Yes, thinks Lightning. *And when you...fell asleep, he and I walked many strides together. He was a terrible hunter, but he always kept my spirits up.*

Joy whistles a melancholy tune.

Remember? she thinks. *He joked about Uda.*

Lightning does. She recalls the awkward way he dealt with hatchlings underfoot, his skill with rixli, and the sound of his cackle. The happy memories remind her of all the young bombas who had lost their nester, as well as the chicks who would never be—because of her. Sadness leaches into her bones, and she realizes for the first time since arriving at the upper land that she is exhausted. Taking Joy's advice, she leaves Ansel to himself, and they retreat to their hole. Thunder, Cliff, and Submission are already crammed inside, snoring. With little room to move, Lightning curls next to Joy and falls into deep, dreamless sleep.

+ + +

She is the last to wake, roused by the noise of the troop preparing for departure. Joy sits outside the hole, gleaming sapphire as she stares at the sun.

You look much better, she thinks.

I feel better, thinks Lightning, a moment later adding: *As long as I don't think about Ari.*

Joy clicks a slow staccato.

Bridger's looking for you.

The two make their way to the far side of the camp, where several of the adults hold conference. Seeing Lightning and Joy approach, they still their thoughts. The mood of the group is difficult to determine, but the bibija Pounce warms to their arrival when Lightning bows before handing him his lost glove and telling him of the role it played in their rescue.

You were really smart to drop it, she thinks.

And you, Pounce thinks, *were smart to find it.*

Are you fit to travel? Bridger wonders.

I could eat an entire talihew, thinks Lightning, not exaggerating by much. *But otherwise, yes.*

Then tell us about these scion.

The other bibijas grumble and curl their lips.

Lightning defers to Joy.

They follow their Princess, she thinks, and her eyes glitter. *They are no threat.*

They should be more concerned about us being a threat to them! thinks Stone. *What's to prevent us from jumping them now? We're ready!*

Honor, thinks Lightning, *If I might say.*

I notice Bruiser isn't healed yet.

He will be.

Either way, Bridger interrupts. *We're counting on the two of you to keep the peace—and them to keep their distance. I want regular reports, and if things go bad...*

They won't, thinks Joy. *She needs me—us.*

Stone and others growl in obvious doubt.

I guess we'll see, thinks Bridger. *Gather the wabis and get ready to move.* She looks at Lightning and Joy. *Better tell your Princess.*

+ + +

The unlikely company follows the river until they reach the moored floaters. Using them to cross the water is a story unto itself, and some of even the bravest kezel nearly refuse to make the attempt. But observing the scion example—and using Lightning's rope—all are eventually on the eastern bank, some wet, but none the worse for their experience.

From there, the company heads north. The coarse

terrain is at first unpredictable and full of thorns, hampering every prickly step. Then, once these are finally cleared, there is the threat of nodal ooms. The clutching tendrils are kept at bay only by the heavy tread of kezel feet. Wabis—and Joy—are forced to be riders, and scion must stay closer than anyone prefers, or surely some would have been pulled beneath the surface. But had the land been perfectly free of obstacles, their pace would have remained sluggish. Wabis, pregnancy, injuries, and moons of abuse ensure it.

Circling overhead, Ansel squawks impatience.

Not making it before the next moon, thinks Cliff.

Orange, Thunder guesses. *Or Mother Green.*

But storms are no concern to Lightning. She limps along in a game spirit, tail higher than most, and she and Joy pass the time sharing details of their experiences while separated. As they do, the tip of a square, black corner peeks out of Joy's sling. Lightning's eyes grow narrow, and she wrinkles her snout.

I told you to leave that.

Joy rubs her hands together.

I know, she thinks. *But there's no worry.* She buzzes a simple tune. *It doesn't do anything.*

Yeah, let's hope.

Their strides add up to the thousands as the troop moves slow but resolute across the plains. At long last, the air grows chill, and as the land begins to climb, patches of crusty snow become visible. Every kezel, even wabis unfamiliar with the accrete, feels drawn north, hastened by the wind at their backs. The change displeases the scion, who buzz gloomily to one another as their antennae lay flat. But the kezel find new energy, and they march on, noses twitching. Thunder's guess was correct: Oti-kan the Orange nips at their heels, the first crystalline flakes appearing like early guests to a party.

There's a smell I've missed, thinks Cliff.

Pick up the pace! thinks Bridger. *I'm not spending another sleep in a dirty hole.*

But Big Brother disagrees, and soon, even Bridger

recognizes the need to take cover. Everyone able to do so sets to digging, their tongues awag.

Lightning, thinks Thunder suddenly, and he takes a break from his labor, pointing to Submission. Their api-kan's eyes have snapped into focus, and he stands with his head tilted at an attentive angle. He stares at the whitening ground as if seeing an old acquaintance whose name he struggles to recall.

Snow, he thinks to no one in particular.

He looks up and sees Lightning.

Crystal, he exclaims but then shakes his head. *No. It's Lightning!* He leans forward, touching her nose with his. *You've gotten big! You look like your ami-kan.* He turns to see Thunder, and he rises to two legs, pulling them close and engulfing them both in a colossal embrace. *It's been so long. How many moons?*

Lightning relishes his scent.

Too many, she replies.

But you're back, thinks Submission. *And I'm back!* He takes a deep breath. *I feel like I've been in the clouds.* He steps away, looking at them both. *I like being on the ground better.*

Lightning indicates Joy and Cliff. Submission's ears pin back at the sight. He spies the kezel band spread out around them—and their scion counterparts to the west. Peering up, he sees a flash of color circling in the falling snow, and his brow furrows.

It looks like I missed a lot, he thinks.

You did, thinks Thunder.

I'll tell you all about it while we dig, Lightning promises. *It's a long story.*

CHAPTER TWELVE
Tale

IN THE FUTURE, there will be twenty-two children gath-ered around an outdoor fire and listening to a story read by a man with curly, black hair. His name will be Jere-miah. When he closes the book he is reading, one of the youngest girls will ask:

"Then what happened?"

"Yes," one of the boys will be quick to say. "You can't just end it there. Did they get home, or what?"

"Who says I'm ending it?" the storyteller will want to know. He will have a bearded face and eyes that wrin-kle at their corners when he smiles.

"Well, did they get home or not?" the boy will de-mand. "That's what I want to know."

"And what about the scion?" another girl will ask. "And why did Ari have to die?"

"Yes," her friend will chime in, tying and then un-tying her shoe, never satisfied with the results. "That wasn't very nice, killing a good bomba like that. Why'd that have to happen anyway?"

"You know," the storyteller will say as he runs hands through his hair. "It wasn't me who did it."

"Did Ozag?" one of the older boys will ask.

"Pretty sure Ozag's not real," one of the older girls will say. "It's just a story, you know."

"Is not," her younger brother will say, and he will

look to the storyteller. "It's real, isn't it, Jeremiah?"

"As real as the ground I'm sitting on."

"Sounds made up to me," the older girl will say. "Why have I never seen any of those nodal ooms?"

"Would you like to?"

"No thanks! They sound disgusting."

"I kinda like 'em," the older boy will say.

"You would," a curly-headed girl will exclaim. She will fidget with her neighbor, putting her arm around the boy one moment and poking him the next.

"My mom's going to the mainland," the oldest boy will say. "She'll take video. That'll prove it's true." He will look at Jeremiah for confirmation, but the storyteller will merely shrug his shoulders and hold his hands palms up, as if the answer is floating in the sky. He will smile at a group of adults, three men and a woman, who will have climbed the hill to join their party.

"Bedtime," the woman will say, to which the younger children will respond with groans and protests. Some will leap rebelliously to their feet and begin an unruly game of tag. But the older children will wave to Jeremiah and make their way down the hill without complaint, followed at last by most of the others.

"Joining us tomorrow?" one of the men will ask.

"To the mainland?" Jeremiah will reply. "No, I think I'll stay here and help with the preparations. Our visitors will be here any day."

"Will you read us the rest of the story when we wake up?" the shoe-tying girl will ask.

"As soon as I am able. But only if you—if all of you—do as you're told and get ready for bed. We all have lots to do in the days to come."

"Promise?"

Jeremiah's eyes will wrinkle at the corners, and he will shake the girl's hand with appropriate solemnity.

"I promise."

"About Lightning? And Thunder?"

"Of course."

"And Joy? And Cliff? And the crabby princess?"

"And the vumi—whatchacallems," the smallest boy will add. "And the bombas, too? You'll remember?"

Jeremiah will hold up the storybook.

"I don't have to remember," he will say. "I just have to read. Now! I'll see you all tomorrow. So much to do! So much to look forward to! Sleep deep, sleep well."

And they will.

The adventure continues in

Volume Three of The Moonstorm Series

available at moonstormseries.com

www.ingramcontent.com/pod-product-compliance
Lightning Source LLC
Chambersburg PA
CBHW021957170626
46808CB00001B/198